2012

Timeline Apocalypse

a novel of the end of the world by

Bob Nailor

ISBN
0-9824777-0-8 (10 digit)
978-0-9824777-0-0 (13 digit)

Library of Congress Catalog Number: 2010935294

First Edition

Printed in the United States of America
Published by 23 House Publishing
SAN 299-8084
www.23house.com

The paper used in this book meets the minimum requirements of the American National Standard for Permanence of Paper for Printed Library Materials, ANSI/NISO Z39.48-1992.
Binding materials have been chosen for durability.

Dedicated to my loving wife, Violet

Table of Contents

Chapter 1 :
The Call

Mayan Date: 8 Chuen 14 Mac ~ 12.19.19.17.11

"O Mighty Sun God, K'inich Ahau, we honor you at this last of time. May this offering of flowing blood, sacred of the royal line, guide you on your path across the sky. May your light shine upon this house and its residents. Give us your happiness and allow our enemies and those who incur your wrath to drown in your light. We have seen the shadow strangers and stand ready to accept, if they are friends or do battle, if enemies, as you desire."

Prayer of Chac Tun B'alam
Ruler of L'akam Ha

Metro City: 1:04p.m., Wednesday, December 12, 2012

I entered my apartment and locked the door behind me. The television, still on from earlier in the morning, blared the news of all the impending disasters. A volcano exploding on some distant island in the Pacific, forcing natives to be evacuated. Another earthquake had shaken most of the Andean

1

mountains. A huge solar flare that would cause major outages was due in about a week; there had been two smaller ones that offered some very spectacular light shows. Three planes had been hijacked and were currently circling London, Paris and Los Angeles. An epidemic of huge proportions, reminiscent of the Biblical plagues, was ravaging Egypt. The stock market was dropping. Doom and gloom was the hot topic. Like always, I let the television become background noise.

I shook my head disgustedly. My involvement level with all this end-of-world hullabaloo had become pretty low. Everyone seemed to be on the bandwagon. Besides, I had issues of my own and I felt most of these catastrophes could easily be explained. The stock market dropped back in 2008. It took some time but it rallied back up and once again had stabilized in the mid-1100s by the end of 2010. It wasn't the full recovery everyone had hoped for, but it was a stable one. The volcano exploding wasn't anything new; it had blown back in late 2009, a mere three years ago and was therefore, in what I like to call, a still relatively volatile status. Peru and Chile have had quakes since the beginning of time so this wasn't anything strange for them. As far as planes go, of late, it seemed to be the "hijack of the week" with different dissidents claiming it as their coup. This time it was animal activists and the newly formed al Kadaun People's Republic. So this week's radical groups had their bragging rights until the next hijack. The solar flares weren't anything to fret since we'd been having a lot of them of late. If the 'big' one actually did happen in about a week, it would be what I call a fortuitous moment for the Fates. The Egyptian plague thing seemed new but why the sudden panic? Simple. Toss it into the fray. It was just part of the hoopla about the world ending in a couple of weeks; December 21, 2012. I still vividly remember the frenzy at the turn of the century with the 2000 scare. Some people went hysterical fearing the end of the world strictly because a simple electronic device couldn't deal with a four-digit year. People really needed to get a grip on reality.

I ambled into the kitchen and stood there staring at the cupboard contents, mulling over the possibilities for lunch. The can of chicken rice soup looked like an easy fix but a bowl of chili with rice sounded a little tastier. Of course, that meant more work. I grimaced, closed the cupboard doors and moved to the refrigerator. I opened the frig and took inventory: leftover fried chicken, some gamey tuna salad, a chunk of cheese with growing culture, three boxes of take-out, two beers and a partial bottle of cheap wine. Reheating a meal was faster than fixing one. I grabbed a beer and the top take-out box. *Lunch surprise,* I thought while lifting the lid of the container. I stared at the contents; it was still a minor mystery. Chinese. There was fried rice, broccoli, a dark sauce and chicken. I didn't see any seeds so that eliminated Sesame Chicken.

I thought back. Saturday night, Don and Elaine had set me up with a blind date; I think her name was Sheila. She'd ordered something with chicken. I shrugged my shoulders. Whatever it was, I popped it into the microwave, pushed some numbers, pressed 'Start' and then twisted the cap off the beer bottle. A refreshing slug of beer gushed down my throat; it was crisp, cold and satisfying. The TV in the living room caught my attention so I ambled into the room. Flopping into the recliner I almost spilled the beer.

"...and now live from Mexico."

The screen blinked from the news anchor, Jim Mc-something-or-other to an image of a young woman standing near a pile of stones.

"This is Lucia Camal and I'm standing near the Temple of Inscriptions here at the Palenque ruins. We are watching the

latest development of a new cult, which I'm told has quickly grown to very large proportions. Part way up you can see a scuffle as the followers of this cult are trying to hold back the authorities. We've been able to ascertain that at the very top, a self-proclaimed high priest of the Mayan religion is preparing for the first of many supposed sacrifices to K'inich Ahau. This is in conjunction with the Mayan calendar coming to an end next week."

The camera panned up to the figure near the top.

"He has a goat, which I was informed he will be sacrificing to the sun god."

A man, dressed in a dark body suit with a white skeleton printed on it and a skeleton mask strutted about the top of the temple, his robe of bold blue, black and white feathers flowed in the wind. He held a dark object that glittered in the sun. It was a knife - an obsidian knife. He raised the knife above his head using both hands, and then plunged the black blade into the animal with a single swoop. There was some movement then his hands came up, clasping a bloody mass. Blood oozed down his arms.

"Oh my god, he ripped the animal's heart out–"

The screen blacked out and reverted to a caught off-guard news anchor flipping a pen into the air while his feet rested on the desk. He grabbed at the pen, fumbled it and watched it roll to the edge of the desk and fall off. In his hasty attempt to sit up, Jim Mc-something-or-other nearly fell out of the chair.

"What? Uh, yes, folks, we'll have more information after this word from our sponsors."

Jim Mc-something-or-other slapped on an insincere smile for the camera while straightening some papers on the anchor desk. The commercial cut in.

The phone rang, startling me from the hypnotic view of the screen. I sat back in my chair, reached over and grabbed the receiver.

"Hargrove Detective Agency," I snapped before realizing I wasn't at the office.

"Mr. Hargrove?" A timid voice asked. "Ah... er... are you Detective Barry Hargrove?"

"Yes," I replied and frowned. "Can I help you?" In the kitchen I heard the microwave chirp. It had finished and was waiting for me to remove the food.

"Hello. My name is Dr. Alvarez Martinez," he said. "I am in... If you could... Would you be willing to accept a case, Mr. Hargrove? I realize this is very short notice."

There was a pause. A case? He had definitely piqued my interest. I mean, after all, it was work. Things had been a little slow at the office, so anything would be a start. Of course, I was curious as to why he was calling me at home. Then I realized I'd put the office phone on call forwarding.

"Sure," I said nonchalantly. "Exactly what are the details of the case?"

"Perhaps we could discuss this at my office," Martinez said. "Is there any particular time which would be convenient for you? Later today? Maybe tomorrow?"

"Any time after nine tomorrow will work." I replied. "Of course, I could stop by this afternoon if that's better." I still had no idea what was happening or where I was going but it sure sounded like I'd be taking the case. That was a good thing. The sooner I started, the sooner I collected some much-needed money.

"Nine thirty tomorrow would be fine," he said and proceeded to give me the address. "Oh, wait. I have a meeting

5

at nine forty-five. Hmm?" There was a pause. "You said this afternoon? Could you be here by two thirty? I realize that it would be tight but–"

"See you then, Dr. Martinez," I replied cutting him off while scribbling his name and address on the newspaper in front of me.

"Fine. Fine," he said absently. "See you then."

"G'bye." I slammed the phone into its cradle.

I glanced at my watch. 1:20 p.m. I didn't have much time. I grabbed my coat and keys and left the microwave chirping: a hot dog from a street vendor was a better bet than that mystery container of salmonella in the microwave.

Chapter 2:
The Cult

Mayan Date: 8 Chuen 14 Mac ~ 12.19.19.17.11

"Father Sun, I implore your aid with the
Shadow people. I offer my blood to honor you.
Help me to understand a true meaning."

Prayer of Chac Tun B'alam
Ruler of L'akam Ha

Palenque Ruins: 12:20p.m., Wednesday, Dec. 12, 2012

The cult mob cheered and rallied around the man in the feathered robe. He stood there, hand held high, blood oozing down his arm from the goat heart. The feathers fluttered lightly in the gentle breeze and his golden headdress glistened in the bright sunlight. He tossed the heart to the mob and they burst into screams, stretching, reaching to grab the bloody mass.

A gunshot echoed across the grounds. Hysteria and melee swept the group and they fled down the steps, which were dangerously steep and severe. The park guards, suddenly assailed by the downward surging crowd above them, were pressed backwards. The guards treaded carefully so as not to fall while the mob streamed down in a hurried descent.

A scream arose above the bedlam, and a brightly dressed human rolled, bouncing downward to knock two guards off balance. The three tumbled down the steps until one, a guard, finally broke free of the other two and turned around to brace his legs on one of the steps and stop gravity's pull.

The other two bodies continued on their way down and Lucia watched them silently. She knew, without even getting close, that they were dead. Emil, the cameraman, followed their path, filming the gruesome death scene.

"I know those sons of bitches cut my feed," Lucia yelled. "But I'm not finished here. There is a story, a big-assed story, that will put me on top. I'm not about to lose it. Emil! Maribel! Follow me. Where'd the asshole with the knife disappear? Come on folks, somebody dressed up like Big Bird's shadow shouldn't be that hard to locate. Find me those feathers."

Lucia stretched on her tiptoes and attempted to locate her man in the mob. The group continued to escape down the stairs of the Temple of Inscriptions. A few clusters of tourists wandered about the grounds. She looked to the Palace, no feathered person there.

"This is one hell of a story, Lucia," Emil huffed. "I can't wait to get this in the editing room." He lowered the camera. "Just remember, I'm your cameraman when the big guys come calling. I know how to make you look good." Emil glanced over at Lucia and she motioned for him to continue rolling the camera.

"On me," Lucia demanded, and then continued for the camera, "As you can see over my shoulder, some mayhem has broken out here at the Temple of Inscriptions at the Palenque ruins. An unknown person who has declared himself a high priest of the Mayans just performed a live sacrifice to the sun god, K'inich Ahau. The police and the followers of this so-called priest were in a furor when a lone gunshot rang out. At that time, again over my shoulder, in the background, the mob and police all started down the steps. One person slipped, knocking down what I believe to be two officers. One of the officers was able to stabilize himself, but it appears that the other officer and the person who tripped continued to roll to their death at the foot of the pyramid. I will be interviewing the priest, some of the members of this new sect and, of course, the police. This is Lucia Camal coming to you live from the Temple of Inscriptions, Palenque, Mexico." She smiled.

"And that's a wrap," Emil said. "How in the hell are you going to find the priest?"

"I won't," Lucia said with a sly grin. "He will find me. Trust me, Emil, that guy didn't go up there to commit a sacrifice and then decide to slip into anonymity. He will be hunting me so he can strut his stuff to the world. Extraverts, like this guy, always want to talk about themselves."

"I still think he's a quack," Emil said. "I'd be real careful if I was you, Lucia. Remember, that dude ripped the goat's heart out with his bare hand. Tell me, is that really a talent you're looking for in the dream man of your life?"

Lucia laughed and waved her hand to dismiss his comment. "I'm not wanting to date him, just interview him, okay? Besides, he actually *cut* the heart out."

Emil put down the camera and started to wrap up wires in preparation of heading back to the station. "Cut... ripped... who cares? Bottom line is that the heart is no longer on the inside," he mumbled, and then noticed Lucia was scowling at him. "Fine. Just be careful, okay?"

She handed him the microphone so he could pack it away. "No problem, Emil. I'll watch my step." She wrinkled her nose at him. "And my heart."

"Miss Camal?" a man called out as he approached.

"Yes?" she replied while doing a snap evaluation of him: a

9

solid six foot tall, maybe six two, Mayan, muscular, brown eyes, black, wavy hair, very attractive and a smile. It was the smile that pulled her in. She didn't care who he was; he had her under his spell. Then she noticed the red on his one sleeve. Blood? She pulled back.

"Please don't be alarmed," he said, putting down the bag he carried.

Lucia cocked an eye at the black feather that fluttered at the puckered cord drawn opening. He gently stuffed it into the hole and tightened the leather strap holding it closed.

"I saw your station's van pull up while I climbed the steps," he said. "I take it you got the notification of my event and that is why you are here." He glanced about and sighed deeply. "Actually, I was hoping for more coverage but one takes what one can get. Would you like more information?"

"Hey, Emil," Lucia said. "Hold up a minute. Not so fast with cleanup." She turned back to the stranger. "Exactly what was your event here all about?"

"As I am quite sure you are aware, the Mayan calendar is coming to an end," he said.

"Wait a minute," Lucia said, leaned over and grabbed the microphone from Emil's hands. She shoved a cord into the end while Emil plugged the other end of the cord into a camera beside him. "Let's start this over. Who are you? What is your name?"

He smiled warmly at her then bowed. "My apologies," he said. "I should have introduced myself when I first approached. My name is..." He hesitated, smiled and held up a one finger. "Let me start over. I call myself Ah Pukuh now. I took my name from the Mayan gods. Ah Pukuh is the Lord of the Dead and ruler of the lowest level, vilest of the nine levels of the Mayan underworld."

"My, isn't that impressive. Could I get you back into your piñata costume by any chance?" Lucia asked and pointed to the bag leaning against the man's leg.

Ah Pukuh's brow furrowed. "This is not a costume, Miss Camal. This is my ceremonial garb for the moment when I and my god, K'inich Ahau, commune together and I am able to assist him on his journey across the sky." He held one hand up and slowly waved it in an arc to designate the sun's movement. "Perhaps you and your colleagues consider this just a prank to cash in on the fast approaching moment, but trust me, this is neither a joke nor is it bullshit mysticism. The lines of time are coming into conjunction. The vibrations of renewal flow toward us. Even the heavens are joining in the celebration."

Lucia held the microphone outstretched before her, glad to have the extra distance between them. She pulled her hand back quickly.

"So this is connected with the Mayan calendar and its end of time?"

Ah Pukuh rolled his eyes. "That is the misconstrued concept. Time is not ending. Only this existence of time is ending. Time will renew itself. Think of it as more like the regeneration of the end to a beginning, so to speak."

"Fine," Lucia said. She motioned to Emil in an attempt to have him zoom in on the duffel bag with the feathered robe. "If you won't put on the robe, would you at least pull it out so my viewers can see it?"

It was then she noticed the necklace the man was wearing. A leather tong held it securely around his neck. The black obsidian, finely chipped knife glittered in the bright sunlight. The handle, in the shape of a parrot's head, was made of jade with inlaid turquoise. Lucia rolled her eyes at Emil hoping he would zoom in on the knife necklace; she was sure it was the same one he'd used for the sacrifice.

The tall man looked around at the mob and police in the distance. One could barely hear the distant howler monkeys for all the commotion of the group. The jungle birds, for the most part, were silent.

"I really don't think I should be doing that," he said and motioned with his thumb to the group behind him. "I don't need the police over here right now."

"Actually, sir," Lucia said, "I do believe one of the policemen is headed this way."

Ah Pukuh glanced behind him and grabbed his duffel bag. He casually swung it over his shoulder.

"Miss Camal," he said excusing himself with a disarming smile. "Let me assure you the pleasure was all mine. I will be getting in contact with you later."

He ambled away toward the van and the parked cars in the distance beyond. The officer quickly approached.

"You guys are with a television station, right?" the officer asked while coming closer. "Did you get all this on tape? Any chance of us taking a look to see who the guy was at the top?"

Emil rolled his eyes and put the camera down into its case. He started playing with the cords, stalling for time.

"We were doing a small segment on the ruins," Lucia said then looked to her cameraman. "Ah, Emil, did you happen to pan up on the pyramid during that mess? Did you get any of the action?"

Emil looked up with absolute innocence in his eyes. "Yeah, I tried a close-up but really couldn't see anything. It could have been a guy. Maybe it was a woman." He snapped the box shut. "What were they doing up there? At first I thought it was some sort of park exhibition." He shrugged his shoulders and grimaced at the officer. "I'm guessing it wasn't?"

The young policeman shook his head. "Nah. Just some idiot demonstrating. Sorry to bother you folks. If you see anything on the tape you feel could help us, I'd really appreciate the support."

Emil cast a knowing eye to Lucia then glanced back to the

officer. "Any idea who shot the gun?"

The officer stood there silently for a few seconds then looked back at the pyramid and shook his head. "I'm not sure, probably either Gomez or Alvarez; they're the ones who get to carry firearms." He took a deep breath. "Guess I can go clean up the dead goat now; I'm low man on the rosters." He tipped his hat, turned and walked back toward the crowd still milling about at the Temple of Inscriptions.

Emil looked up at Lucia. "That was easier than usual," he said. "He must be really new."

She laughed. "There will be repercussions, Emil, honey." She watched the young officer heading to the Temple of Inscriptions. "Not only for us, but also for him." She smiled and pointed a finger at the retreating officer. "That I can assure you. Let's get the equipment packed and back to the station before some veteran officer shows up." She snapped her cell phone out. "Angela? Hey, get me all the information you can on K'inich Ahau. Also see what you can find out about Ah Pukuh - you figure out the spellings. While you're at it, grab some Mayan calendar data, too. I've got a hot one this time." There was a pause. "Oh, you saw part of it? Well, I got a lot more since. Just you wait and see... Momma is coming home with the bacon."

Chapter 3:
The Theft

Mayan Date: 8 Chuen 14 Mac ~ 12.19.19.17.11

*"Father Sun, I have offered my blood and now beseech
your help with the shadow strangers."*

Prayer of Chac Tun B'alam
Ruler of L'akam Ha

Metro City: 2:12p.m., Wednesday, December 12, 2012

I briskly hiked the couple of blocks from the subway to the
address I was given. The wind, snow and cold air blew against
my back. I hunkered down into my coat, shoved my hands
deeper into the pockets and trudged down the street. I looked
up at the grand building: a museum. I nodded my head in
satisfaction. Dr. Martinez had never really told me exactly
what he wanted. *Finally, a break; a decent job*, I thought. I
popped a mint in my mouth and started sucking on it, hoping it
would calm my stomach and kill the sewer scent in my mouth.
The coney I'd consumed was excellent but I shouldn't have
doubled-loaded the onion. Once again I wasn't thinking ahead.

14

Museum: 2:47p.m., Wednesday, December 12, 2012

I followed Dr. Martinez through the museum into the Mesoamerican Arts Exhibit. In his office he'd been informative, yet very cryptic. All I knew for sure was there had been a theft of an item, and the item was quite valuable. I quietly snickered trying to think of any item on display in a museum that was worthless. He had alluded to Mayan history, a calendar and something about an upcoming timeline or deadline. I now questioned if it was a part of the 2012 frenzy. Dr. Martinez had fidgeted all the time while we were in his office. Here, now, in the hallways, his mannerisms had completely changed and he was very calm.

For the most part, this area of the museum appeared empty but as we turned and entered a large room, we came upon a small group of school children with their teacher who ambled about the exhibits. They were about as quiet as a passel of nine-year-old kids can be when in a group environment. Dr. Martinez nodded to the young woman in charge.

"Good afternoon," he said then smiled at the children. "Are you finding the exhibits interesting?" His eyes twinkled as he watched the children's responses.

They nodded excitedly and raised their voices in acknowledgment. The teacher immediately shushed them and thanked him.

"Have fun and be sure to come back again," he said and then turned to me. "Shall we continue?"

"Lead on," I said and politely nodded to the teacher.

She was approximately thirty years old and possibly single, since there were no rings on her finger. My nod was more than polite.

"Mr. Hargrove," Martinez whispered. "In just a few more steps, we'll enter into the antiquities section of the Mesoamerican exhibits. You'll be able see what I've been

15

talking about." He produced a key and opened a door to another dimly lighted section of the museum. "We quickly secured this section so we would have the proper time to assess and address the situation."

I frowned. "Please, call me Detective Hargrove, or just Detective; mister sounds so formal." Actually I hated when people referred to me as mister. I had struggled to get my license just as he had for his doctorate. Suddenly it hit me. "*Situation?*" I thought and was now confused. "*Wasn't this a theft?*" I kept my mouth shut.

"Here it is," he said stopping in front of three displays. "What do you think? I figured I'd show you the crime scene before going up to Security to view the tapes."

The pieces were striking: a crystal skull, a small, finely beaded satchel and a baton inset with colored gems. I was clueless about what was wrong.

"Can you believe the audacity of some people?" he asked while waving his hands wildly in front of him to encompass the three displays. Suddenly he was once again the nervous Nelly I'd first met up in his office. "Did they think we wouldn't realize it was a fake when we saw it? Just look at it."

A fake? I continued to look at the three displays; one of them was a fake. The crystal skull appeared quite authentic but I wasn't trained in ancient Mexican art. Maybe it was plastic? The beadwork on the satchel was very detailed and almost perfect – maybe it was machine made? The baton was covered with colored stones and turquoise. It appeared very real. All three items were contained inside glass domes and it was quite obvious they were sealed and probably electronically protected. I'd already seen other items in the museum in similar domes.

"Any idea of how it was stolen?" I asked, stalling for time and a possible hint to which item Dr. Martinez was referring.

"We are guessing it was done during the monthly

cleaning," he replied. "If you touch or push them, nothing really happens; but, if you lift the dome, an alarm will go off. They are electro-magnetically locked." He lifted the dome. "The alarms only get turned off when the domes are being cleaned."

"Is it a silent alarm?" I asked, again stalling for time and not hearing anything when he lifted the dome from the crystal skull then replaced it.

"Yes, a silent alarm. As you can see, the security on these displays are of the utmost complexity and sophistication. We knew children would probably push and tap on the domes." He rolled his eyes and tapped the dome covering the crystal skull. "I mean, have you ever watched a child at the aquarium? They are going to tap on the glass no matter how large the sign you put up telling them not to do so."

"Very ingenious," I replied and stared at the crystal skull. It was stunning, shining under the bright lights, glistening and gleaming. I bent over to get a closer view and see it head-on. "How can you tell it is fake?" The eye sockets glittered at me and I felt as if it was looking directly into my soul and could read my thoughts. The hairs on the back of my neck hackled. My mind raced; the answer was in front of me. I couldn't see it, but I was close.

"The skull is real, Detective Hargrove." The words were spoken snidely and it stung, yet he stood there wringing his hands nervously. "It is the Scepter of Time that is the fake." He pointed to the baton. "The dullness of the rubies and sapphires was the first clue, but anyone with the most elementary knowledge of turquoise would see the flaws in that reproduction."

He reached over and removed the dome. Again, nothing happened. I gave him a questioning look as he placed the dome on the floor.

"We're economical, too. We've closed this exhibit and

17

secured the room. We have an alarm on the doors so we're not going to waste a lot of time and money on individual pieces," he said and removed the scepter from its display pedestal. "See how the jewels are cloudy? This isn't even quality, cheap cut glass." He ran his finger over a piece of turquoise. "This is nothing more than shellacked clay mixed to appear like turquoise and jade. A very poor imitation. In fact, a jewel" - he slurred the word - "fell off and the cleaner was very distraught at the thought of losing his job."

"Fell off?" I repeated. "Cleaner? You let the custodial staff touch these?"

"Of course not!" he screamed. "Whatever possessed you to think we'd let one of the custodial staff clean or touch these on purpose?" Dr. Martinez asked shaking his head. "As to the staff having access and touching the items, our custodial staff consists of seven bonded and well-trained personnel." He frowned at me. "Do you actually think we just hire anyone who wanders in off the street for a job?" He pursed his lips in contempt. "They are only to clean the domes and not touch the items. Seems when they were cleaning this one and started to put the dome back down over the item, a gem fell off." Martinez stood there nervously tapping his lips. "Anyway, I closed the exhibit this morning when I was notified of what transpired last night. Then I got authorization to seek outside help and called you." He cocked an eye at me. "Your listing said you were bonded, not merely bondable." There was a hesitation. "You are bonded, aren't you?"

"Yes, I'm bonded," I said while at first thinking to ignore the slam but then deciding to take the bait. I let my index finger play on the glass dome. "You never noticed it as a fake?" I asked.

"Excuse me?" He stood there staring at me with a frown of indignation. "Do you think all I have time to do is walk through the museum making sure that every piece is the

18

original? I think my last visit into this particular room was over four months ago and that was to validate a possession as being on display for insurance purposes. I may have glanced at these items but I didn't notice anything at the time."

He stood there watching me while I surveyed the scene.

"Det. Hargrove, I really need to re-open this section as quickly as possible. With all the discussion about 2012... well, this exhibit is very popular right now."

I stroked my chin in thought. "Being honest here, I didn't know it was a fake and truly doubt most visitors would realize it. A trained eye? Yes, possibly. I see no reason not to re-open. Set the alarms and let the visitors in."

"Thank you, Det. Hargrove, I think you might have the right idea there," Dr. Martinez said. He placed the item back on the pedestal, spending quite a bit of time adjusting the position. It was then that I perceived he was purposely hiding the missing jewel. He carefully put the dome back down. "There, ready to be armed again."

"So you think the cleaning crew did the switch?" I asked. "An inside job, so to speak?"

"Actually, no," Martinez said. "When we realized it was a fake we immediately reviewed the security tapes."

"Ah, yes, the security tapes?" I repeated.

"Even with alarms, we still have motion monitors and video tapes," he replied. "The minute you walked into this museum you've been under surveillance. They, the cleaning crew, used a hand signal to notify the security staff when they were ready to clean this area. The alarms were turned off across the board for the room. When each dome was replaced, after a ten second delay, it automatically re-armed that particular item."

"So how is it the crooks, a.k.a. your cleaning crew, made off with the real one?"

"We figure they swapped it when dusting and polishing

the domes of fingerprints."

"Fingerprints?" I interrupted. "Did you check for prints? On the dome?"

"Detective," Martinez said. "Our cleaning staff use custom designed soft cotton gloves to handle the domes so they don't leave fingerprints. As I was saying, security has to keep watch on all the displays while the cleaning crews are working. It was supposedly a failsafe system."

"It failed," I said stoically letting the irony of my voice linger. "So why call me? Why not the police? Why not call in your cleaning crew and arrest the culprit?"

"As I stated, we reviewed the tapes and found nothing."

"Could I see the tapes, Dr. Martinez?" I asked. "Perhaps I could see something which might have been missed. You keep saying 'he,' but could it have been a woman?"

"I can have a copy made for you, if you'd like, but let me assure you, there will be nothing of any use on it," he replied. "Our security personnel have–" He paused. "A woman?" He tugged at his lower lip, and then shook his head. "No, no. We're quite sure it was a man. After all, as I was saying, security personnel have gone over that tape with the proverbial microscope and found absolutely nothing of use. Just our cleaning crew and the gem falling to the ground."

"Well, if I saw the hand signal, I could probably pull it off," I said. "How often do you change the code?"

I watched Martinez. He shifted his weight back and forth on his feet, all the while frowning and looking into a dark corner of the room.

"I believe we change it approximately every six months, yes, twice a year. Now, tonight, when the cleaning crew comes in, they will be notified of the new code for this room."

"This room?" I asked. "You mean the same code is used for all the items?"

"Why of course," he replied with an indignant voice. "Do

you have any idea how complicated it would be for each item to have its own code?"

"Do you realize how easy it would be for a person to happen by and see the code being displayed?" I retorted.

"The cleaning crew only works after the museum has been closed. I might add, at least two hours after the museum has closed, so for a patron to chance by is practically impossible."

I looked around the room at the different items on display. Then I glanced up at the cameras overhead and watched them as they slowly moved back and forth in sync to keep the whole room completely in view at all times.

Cameras? My mind raced ahead; I had an idea.

"Dr. Martinez," I started. "Can you tell me how many cameras are lost in the museum each day?"

"Excuse me? Lost cameras? I'm afraid that is out of my jurisdiction," he said with disdain. "If it is something critical, I am sure I can get the young lady at the information booth to help you with that."

"What if the suspect had placed a camera in this room to watch the cleaning crew then picked up the camera the next day?"

Martinez scanned the room looking at the possibilities. "Why would anyone do that? A camera, you say?"

"If you wanted to learn how the cleaning crew or anyone, for that matter, was able to get into the domes to clean..." I glanced over at the scepter. "A camera would record everything. In fact, I'd place at least two, if not more, to get as many possible angles." I waved my hand, encompassing the room. "Yeah, if I wanted to learn any secrets in this room, a lot of cameras would be the answer."

Martinez frowned. "I don't remember seeing anything on the tapes that showed somebody leaving any cameras. It would have been pretty obvious."

I thought for a few seconds. "It wouldn't be on that tape.

Think. When was the last time the cleaning crew did this room? It would be on that tape. How often do they clean? Weekly?"

"They do this room twice a month, on the second and fourth Tuesdays," he replied.

"Fine," I said. "So let me speak to the information person and see if any camera was found in that time period." I hesitated. "Would it be possible to get a copy of the tapes of last month's cleaning of this room also?"

"I'll check," Martinez said. "You'll have to specify the dates and times of the tapes you'd like copied. Now, if you'd like to speak with the information person, follow me."

Martinez turned and motioned for us to leave the room. I headed out and he followed, closing the door behind him. There was a soft click as the latch fell into place.

"Excuse me," Martinez said softly. He placed the key in the slot and locked the door. "There," he said. "Secure."

I frowned, feeling my eyebrows knit together. "I thought you were going to leave the exhibit open to the public?"

Martinez stood there with the key before him and an awestruck look on his face.

"Why, yes, I do believe we had mentioned that." He tittered uncontrollably. "This whole thing is so nerve wracking; I totally forgot. Habit I guess."

He unlocked the door.

Chapter 4:
Security

Mayan Date: 8 Chuen 14 Mac ~ 12.19.19.17.11

*"Father Sun, I offer my blood and beseech
your help with the strangers."*

*Prayer of Chac Tun B'alam
Ruler of L'akam Ha*

Museum: 3:10p.m., Wednesday, December 12, 2012

Feeling like the new pet puppy, I found myself following Dr. Martinez, dogging him as we finally entered the grand foyer of the museum. Now I could see our destination on the far wall where the words 'Information / Tours' were proudly engraved in the marble over the small inset window. The window was closed but near it was a polished mahogany desk with a young lady sitting behind it.

Dr. Martinez approached. "This is Miss Jennifer Morrow," he said motioning to the young lady sitting at the desk.

She stood and extended her hand and I quickly did my

usual appraisal: early twenties with a very large rock on her third finger; engaged, not married.

"Detective Barry Hargrove," I said taking her offered hand.

"What can I do for you, Detective Hargrove?"

Her voice was soft, low, almost sultry but very clear and extremely soothing. It was obvious to me that she was hired to have a calming voice during chaotic moments with groups and possible irate patrons.

"This is going to seem like a strange request," I started and grabbed my handy notepad, flipping to the calendar. "Is it possible, sometime last month, around the fourteenth or twenty-eighth, I believe, that anyone happened to report a lost camera?" I hesitated. "Or maybe even a found camera?"

She gave a quick frown. "If you give me a minute, sir, I'll check." She sat down at her computer and I could hear the keys softly clicking as she typed.

"The fourteenth?" she asked. "Is that correct?"

"Or there about," I replied. "Give or take a couple of days."

"Oh, yes, I remember this," she said pointing at the monitor. "A very strange thing and oh, by the way, Detective Hargrove, you're correct, it was on the fourteenth. Two cameras were turned in that morning; one by a young school boy at nine twenty-two and the other by the day cleaning crew for the night crew; that was at eight fifteen."

"Ah-ha," Dr. Martinez said. "You seem to be on the proper track, detective."

I smiled. Finally, something was going my way.

"Can you tell me where the camera was found by the cleaning crew?" I asked.

It was obvious to me that the cleaning crew's camera was probably one hidden in the antiquities room. At least, that is what I hoped.

"Aren't you the lucky one," Jennifer said. "Both cameras were found in the antiquities room of the Mesoamerican Exhibit."

"Lucky? Both?" I asked. "That is more than coincidental."

Jennifer giggled. "It's more than that," she said. "Only one person picked up both cameras. He came in that very same day."

"Only one?" I asked. "Are you sure?"

She strummed her finger on the keyboard nervously. "Oh, I'm quite sure," she replied. "See? Right here I have the name of the person and the item lost. Adam Montoya claimed both cameras. I remember, he was quite relieved to find they had both been turned in since they were mini-camcorders." She lowered her voice. "Actually I quite surprised they were even turned in since they looked quite expensive."

"That's fine," I said absently. "Do you remember what he looked like? Any outstanding features?"

"I can do better than that," Dr. Martinez said. He pointed toward the camera over Jennifer's shoulder and then pointed back over my shoulder to second one. "We obviously have got him on film both coming and going. Let me take you to Security."

"Thank you, Miss Morrow," I said. "You have been very helpful. Oh, I almost forgot. Do you happen to know what time he claimed the cameras?" I hesitated. "Did you say they were camcorders?"

She looked at her monitor. "Nine forty-two and yes, they were mini-camcorders. By the way, I have an address for Dr. Montoya, if you'd like it."

Both Dr. Martinez and I cocked our heads.

"An address? Doctor?" I asked.

"Of course," she replied. She fumbled through a couple of files down in the drawer. She looked at Dr. Martinez. "I thought you would recognize his name, Dr. Martinez. He comes here quite often and is one of our more generous benefactors." She pushed and pulled papers within a hanging file jacket. "I would say he normally comes in at least twice a month but I don't believe I've seen him since he found his cameras. Ah, here it is." She pulled a sheet from the file folder and sat back up. "Yes, this is it. Adam Montoya. He lives at 392 Avenue A. Apartment 10B."

"This certainly makes it easier," I said while writing the information into my notepad. "Of course, putting a face to the name will help, too. So, if you don't mind, Dr. Martinez, I'd like to check out those security tapes you were talking about."

"Follow me," he said and headed toward the back of the museum.

"Tell me, doctor, what exactly is this time scepter all about?" I asked. "Why would anyone, including Montoya, want to steal that particular item? It seems he spared no expenses. Really. Think about it... two mini-camcorders? I wonder how many other cameras he had in the room."

Martinez continued to weave a path through the museum; his voice was quiet but firm.

"The Scepter of Time? Why would somebody steal it – jewels, turquoise, jade? Probably for money or just put it into a private collection. I really don't have any idea why Montoya would have stolen it. But if you want to know more about the Scepter of Time, it was discovered in southern Mexico, at Palenque, inside the tomb of Pacal, one of most powerful of Mayan priests and ruler in Mayan history. That particular relic was old when the Mayans, including Pacal, used it in the ceremonies. When Pacal died, it was entombed with him. Strange how certain relics are discovered. You've seen the crystal skull we have?"

He peered back at me and I nodded.

"It, too, is old and woven into the tales of the three items we have displayed together." He stopped and leaned against the wall next to the door marked *Security*. "Tell me, Detective Hargrove, exactly what do you know about the Mayan calendar? Are you aware of the prophecy?"

"You mean that doomsday thing everyone is yelling about? The end of the world?"

"Exactly," Martinez replied. "The end of the world. As you know, according to the Mayan calendar, time will end on December 21st of this year. The skull was discovered at the Palenque ruins shortly after Alberto Ruz Lhuillier excavated Pacal's tomb in 1952." Martinez fidgeted. "With less than glorious details, the skull finally came into our hands at this museum. We've had the skull for years. There were other items located with the skull but it wasn't until the recent translation of the satchel that we were able put it all together. It took many years to ascertain the true meaning but the words were there for anyone to read: *At the time of no time, it is a girl of innocence, for her eyes to time will come.*"

I frowned and stared at him silently for a few seconds. "So what does that mean?"

Dr. Martinez smiled. "That's the tricky part about predictions, they're ambiguous at best, until the exact moment or immediately after, the fact. Then, they are right on the money and it is all so very crystal clear to everyone."

I played my index finger over my small moustache nervously as I thought about the so-called prophecy. "I guess they like confusing a person," I finally said. "No time? Time will come?"

Martinez continued to lean against the door casually. "It took a lot to get the translation from the satchel, and I feel it is a solid one, although cryptic at best. Still, the three items go together; at least that has been my contention from the beginning. The skull was found in Pacal's funerary and beside it, in an urn was hidden the scepter with the satchel wrapped around it. Of course, the skull was immediately hailed as the great find and the urn lay stowed in a crate for the next forty-odd years. That was how I found it in a dusty storage room here at the museum. Whoever had packed the urn away was very methodical and precise since they placed a note with the urn stating it was found right next to the crystal skull. I decided to work on the urn since it had inscriptions on it. I found the translations to be incursive and illogical, they kept referring to a scepter within. The vase was sealed so I finally decided to have an x-ray performed. There was indeed something inside the urn. It was filled. I received the permission to open and if needed, to destroy the urn. I was able to break the seal and therefore easily open the urn. Gold, jade and turquoise beads, thousands of them, spilled from the vase and flowing out with all those beads came a beautiful jewel encrusted scepter."

"And the satchel was wrapped around the scepter, right?" I added.

"Correct," he said. "It took another two years before I realized the design on the satchel could be translated. The rest is history, as we say." He laughed. "Ready to go into Security?" He punched the keys on the pad and pulled the door open. "Shall we find out what Mr. Montoya looks like?"

I nodded my head and followed him into the room. A myriad of monitors flashed views of the museum, switching camera angles and displaying different actions happening inside and outside the building.

"Perry?" Dr. Martinez called. "Could you please bring up the video for last month, the fourteenth."

"Yes, sir," the man at the desk said. "Do you have any particular angle or time?"

Martinez smiled at the man. "Information Desk. Jennifer said it was around nine forty something."

Perry punched keys on the computer keyboard and pages of filenames dashed across the screen.

"How about we start at nine thirty that morning?" he asked

and flipped a switch.

Before anyone could reply, the large screen above his computer burst alive with a display of Jennifer from the back and a group of small children who were assaulting the desk.

"This was at nine thirty-one," Perry said and pointed at the flashing time marker in the corner.

The children were hustled away by the teacher and an assigned guide. Dr. Martinez nodded approvingly. Perry sped the video up and a man popped onto screen. Perry slowed the display, reversed it until the man had walked backwards out of the screen.

We watched in total fascination while Jennifer greeted the tall, distinguished gentleman. I was caught off guard when the man cocked an eye to the security camera and winked. I was sure I saw a small smile cross his lips.

That concerned me.

The man spoke and used his hands to describe what he was obviously talking about; the cameras. Jennifer nodded and retrieved the two items from a covered box very nearby her desk. The man was elated and we could tell he was thanking her profusely. She sat back down to her computer, typed and I noticed her glancing up at the clock. She was typing the information into the computer.

I had my man, or at least a lead that I didn't have earlier. Dr. Montoya put the cameras into his case and then he looked directly up at the camera, smiled and winked again. This time there was absolutely no doubt about it. It was a deliberate action. I watched him saunter out of the museum, his single gold canine tooth etched into my memory.

"Well," Dr. Martinez said. "He seems to be quite amiable enough." He looked at me. "Don't you agree?"

I stood there in the dimly lighted room hoping my jaw wasn't gaping open too far. "Dr. Martinez," I said. "He may be a pleasant man but you must remember, he is our main suspect;

actually, the only suspect. You do realize he is probably the one who stole your Scepter of Time. Now, do you still think he is a pleasant man?" I stood there watching Perry and Dr. Martinez.

"A thief. Oh, yes, he is most certainly our thief," Dr. Martinez replied. He was flustered, that was evident. "What I meant was he just didn't look like the type. Very distinguished and all that."

The screen continued to show people approaching the desk. I frowned and knew my eyebrows were nearly one furry caterpillar at the moment. I nervously tapped my index finger on the desk before me. Something was niggling at me.

"Perry," I started. "Could you rewind that again? I'd like to review Mr. Montoya's entrance."

Perry played with the buttons and the screen blurred as he moved the video back to our man's entrance. I watched again with a more discerning eye this time. He strolled onto the screen from the right.

"Hold it," I said. "Freeze that frame, please."

Perry pushed a button and Montoya was frozen in position.

"What is the problem, detective," Martinez asked. "What are you seeing?"

"Exactly where is the front door from Miss Morrow's position?" I asked pointing at the screen.

"Why it would be..." Martinez started to point.

"Right here," Perry said and thumped the screen above him. He pointed to the lower screen where a set of doors were partially open.

"And our boy Montoya is coming from the right," I said putting my index finger on him. "Why would that be?" I hesitated. "Unless he had already come into the museum, went to the room, found the cameras missing and was hoping Miss Morrow would have them or know of their whereabouts."

"What's this?" Perry said and pressed a button.

A box appeared on the screen and he moved it over Montoya, then he enlarged the box, pressed another button and the screen blurred and re-focused as it zoomed in on the designated boxed area. A small camera hung from a lanyard on his hip.

"Either he has a camera fetish or he had more than two cameras," I said. "I wonder how many he has in those pockets?" I pointed to the coat pocket and pants pocket on screen. "He certainly seems to have more cameras than the usual tourist."

Martinez stumbled backwards clutching his chest. I grabbed him.

"My God!" he exclaimed. "So blatant."

"A good thief usually is," I said. "Are you okay?"

"Just caught off guard," Martinez replied. "I'm quite fine now, thank you." He grabbed a chair and sat down.

"Now, Perry," I said. "Could you show me last night's... wait a minute." I jerked out my notepad and looked at the calendar again. "How about the night of November 27? Can I see the security tapes of the crew cleaning that night?"

Perry typed furiously and a new video popped up on the monitor. I watched four men enter the antiquities room and begin cleaning. I couldn't make out the face of the cleaner lifting the lid to the scepter but we could see him carefully polish the glass and remove any possible fingerprints.

"Can you go back to where they enter the room? Maybe we could see their faces." I was hoping my intuition was working on full charge.

Again the screen blurred and we saw two groups of cleaning staff move through the hallway. The first group passed the door to the antiquities room and the next four walked in.

"Would you like me to slow it up?" Perry asked. "I didn't really see their faces with those hooded suits on."

31

"Re-run it again," I said.

This time I scrutinized the first group. The four of them moved quickly yet I could see their faces. When the next group came into view, Perry slowed it down. Three of them were talking animatedly together; I could make out two of the three faces for details. The fourth member kept his head down. *"Fourth?"* I thought. My mind raced. Four in the first group, four in the second group. "I really don't think Montoya is our suspect any longer," I said. Martinez jerked his head to stare at me. "Take a close look at your cleaning crew for that night."

Martinez and Perry stared at the screen.

"So what do you want me to see?" Martinez asked. "It's the cleaning crew."

"Yes, two groups of four each," Perry added.

"They work in two groups of–" Martinez stopped and stared at the screen, slowing moving his hand to the screen as if touching each person validated them.

"You said you have seven on the cleaning crew, but that night you had eight."

"Oh, my god!" Perry yelled. "It was right there in front of us all the time. I should have caught that! Eight!"

"One too many," I said. "Look closely at the second group, the one who doesn't seem to fit. I don't need to see a gold tooth, I can tell by his stature, walk and height. That man is Montoya. Right now I'd call him our perp. No if, ands, or buts about it."

Perry still remained seated. In the low light I could see him nodding his head in agreement, all the while staring at the screen and the eight cleaning people revealed there. Martinez was again seated and breathing deeply.

"Gentlemen," I said. "Thank you for an interesting afternoon. I do believe I need to go visit Dr. Montoya and see what is transpiring." I nodded to Dr. Martinez.

Martinez slowly stood up, turned and followed me out of

the room. The door clicked shut behind us.

"Please be discreet," Dr. Martinez said while putting a hand on my shoulder like a confidant. "I'd like to keep this as hush-hush as possible. For the museum's sake, you understand. Also, as I stated in my office, your daily fee of five hundred dollars and extraneous expenses will be covered. I will have a check made out for the minimum five days and it should be ready tomorrow morning." He cautiously looked around. "It is imperative the museum recover the artifact." He hesitated. "At any expense."

I nodded my head in acknowledgment. "Don't worry. If there are any extenuating circumstances or extreme cash amounts, I will attempt to notify you first. I understand."

I turned and left. Jennifer smiled and nodded at me as I briskly passed through the entrance foyer. I had a mission.

Chapter 5:
Finding Mr. Montoya

Mayan Date: 8 Chuen 14 Mac ~ 12.19.19.17.11

*"K'inich Ahau, Ah Pukuh, K'ul'uklan, I call on you.
Give me, your faithful servant, a sign."*

> *Prayer of Chac Tun B'alam*
> *Ruler of L'akam Ha*

Metro City: 4:12p.m., Wednesday, December 12, 2012

My stomach had growled when I left the museum, so I had located the nearest food vendor. Now, about twenty minutes later, I found myself wishing I hadn't had the street vendor special, but one can't beat a $5 meal of dog, chips, and a drink. I'd held off on the kraut and onions this time. I slugged down the last of the soda and was about to toss the can into a bin when a street vagrant snatched it from my hand. I shrugged my shoulders; let him redeem it for the money.

I gazed up at the apartment building. Definitely a better neighborhood than I lived in but then again, he was a doctor; I was a working stiff. I tried the front door and as expected, locked. I buzzed for 10B, the one marked "A. Montoya" but there was no response. I wasn't about to be put off by that and decided there had to be a manager so I buzzed the one that was labeled "Res." to see what would happen.

"Who's there?" a gruff voice barked.

"I need to see Dr. Adam Montoya," I replied.

"Well, ring his number, I'm not him." A harsh click followed.

"I tried that. He doesn't answer," I said and realized I was talking to myself. I buzzed "Res" again.

"What?" the voice snarled.

"Dr. Montoya isn't answering the buzzer and he was expecting me at three thirty," I lied. "He could be injured."

The buzzer droned and I pushed the door open. A young lady strolled down the corridor twirling a clutch of keys on her index finger.

"His apartment is upstairs," she said. "Follow me."

"Who was I talking to? Your father?" I asked.

"No, that was me," she replied innocently. "I use a voice box to alter my own voice." She smiled. "It sounds much more impressive, don't you agree? Besides, it keeps the baddies at bay."

You had to hand it to the girl. She knew her stuff.

"So you have an appointment with Dr. Montoya?" She eyed me suspiciously.

"Uh, yes," I replied.

"Here we are," she said and rapped loudly on the door. "If he is asleep, this should wake him up, wouldn't you think?" She absently twirled the keys. "Two knocks and then I can enter the premises for security and safety reasons."

She rapped again on the door, this time even louder.

Standing there watching her, I could tell that she was mentally counting off some imaginary timer which she had established. I silently waited and watched.

"There," she said. "That should be plenty of time and he hasn't answered." She hesitated and gave a quick scrutinizing look. "You *do* have an appointment?"

I nodded. There was no doubt in my mind she was questioning my actions and I really was starting to feel a little guilty about them.

"Right," she said and shoved a key into the door. "Hopefully, if he is home, he hasn't put up the security chain. That could present some problems." She snickered.

The door opened. Beyond I could see the lavish setting Montoya lived in and I pressed by the young girl and walked into his world. Tropical plants were everywhere and the white gauze curtains wafted in a slight breeze coming through the small slit of an open window.

"Dr. Montoya!" she yelled and closed the door behind us. "It's Melanie. Are you here?"

I glanced about the area then walked into the dining room and finally into the kitchen. He wasn't there but the elegance was. The highly polished mahogany dining table, eight captain's chairs and a monolithic hutch gleamed under the immense crystal chandelier. I headed for the bedroom but Melanie was already standing at the doorway.

"I don't see him in here," she said. "Strange. I've never known of him to forget an appointment in the three years I've managed this building. Are you sure you had an appointment today?"

I peeked into the room noting the jaguar skin covering the bed. One closet door was ajar and I saw very little inside.

"Excuse me," I said and eased myself by her. I opened the closet door. It was basically empty. I opened the door to the bathroom. It was not only clean, but seemingly sterile. Nothing personal was in sight. It was like he lived here on a part time basis. I was confused.

"Hellooo?" a feeble voice called. "Who is in here?"

"It's just me," Melanie said leaving me alone in the bedroom; I followed her out. "Oh, Mrs. Tweiller. I'm sorry. Did we bother you?" She approached the old woman, gently grabbed an arm and assisted her to one of the many plush chairs.

"Oh my," Mrs. Tweiller said noticing me. "Is this the gentleman who will be sub-letting Dr. Montoya's apartment?"

"Sub-letting?" I said. "This is available for sub-let? I thought this was Dr. Montoya's residence."

Mrs. Tweiller placed her index finger to her chin. "Let me think," she said. "I get so confused these days. I may have forgotten." She frowned and shook her head as she fought her mental battle. "No, I'm sure. Dr. Montoya said he was leaving for a few months and I asked him if he was going to sub-let. He laughed that grand laugh of his and said I could pick the person as long as I kept his plants alive." She smiled at us, satisfied with her memory. "Yes, that's what he said. Now let me get a good look at you, young man." Her bony index finger waggled in the air motioning for me to come closer.

Melanie glared at me. "Is that why you're here?"

I vehemently shook my head. "No." I mumbled. I'm sure my wide-eyed expression of surprise confirmed my denial. I glanced about quickly. "I don't think my meager income could afford something this nice." I bent down and kneeled beside Mrs. Tweiller. "Did Dr. Montoya happen to say where he was going?"

She tapped her lower lip in thought. "Mexico," she said. "No wait. Was it New Mexico?" She sat there frowning. "I can't ever keep those two straight," she said with a nervous giggle. "Is it the old one or the new one? Do they have pyramids there?"

"Excuse me?" I asked. "Pyramids? In Mexico?"

Mrs. Tweiller broke into a loud laugh. "You should have

37

seen his Halloween costume."

"Costume?" I asked. She was keeping me confused with all the topic changes with each sentence of conversation.

"Oh, I'd come to water his plants and he was wearing it. He looked so frilly in all those feathers. And that headdress!" She blushed and lowered her head to hide her eyes. "Oh my, those tights! It was strange to see him in those skeleton tights." She covered her eyes with her hand. "It was so very revealing. But those feathers! Why I was reminded of my days back in vaudeville." Her eyes glazed and she sighed loudly. "Oh my, those were the days, indeed." She suddenly looked about. "I met Fanny Brice when I was seven years old. I have pictures, you know. I was such a high kicker." She wrung her hands and took a deep breath. "The theater; it was wonderful."

"Yes, Mrs. Tweiller," Melanie said. "So you think Dr. Montoya went to New Mexico?"

"Did you know that he said his costume was for December, not for Halloween. Now just how strange is that? Do people in New Mexico celebrate Halloween in December?"

The lunchtime newscast blasted into my memory.

"What color were the feathers? Where they dark?" I asked.

"Oh my." She sighed. "They were all different colors but mostly black. There were some blue and green and white and–"

"Thank you," I said cutting her off. "Perhaps I was wrong about the date of my appointment. If Dr. Montoya is in Mexico or New Mexico he certainly won't be here now. If you'll excuse me."

I stood up and headed for the door. My man was in Mexico, of that much, I was sure. Now I needed to notify Martinez of my travel plans to Mexico. *"I think an extra three thousand should cover my expenses down there,"* I thought.

Chapter 6:
Mexico

Mayan Date: 10 Ben 16 Mac ~ 12.19.19.17.13

"I have seen the bright bird in the sky.
The shadow people continue to wander our village.
K'inich Ahau, your travel of today is almost done.
Protect your people. Bolontiku, I implore you,
show me your night visions of guidance."

Prayer of Chac Tun B'alam
Ruler of L'akam Ha

Palenque City: 2:12p.m., Friday, December 14, 2012

The flight to Mexico City and the jump to Villahermosa was interesting but exhausting. I rented a car and drove to Palenque. The jungle was magnificent with its lush growth and humid heat. I had the windows up and the air conditioner turned on full blast, and yet I could hear the myriad of birds and the howler monkeys; they were everywhere. Barbara, whom I'd met on the flight to Mexico City, was a plethora of information since she'd been to Palenque a year earlier. She'd given me all the details and directions to a hotel on the outskirts of town. I slowed the car and found the turn she had described. The cobblestone street was perfect. She'd told me about and the "T" in the road and the next thing I knew, I was at the hotel and all the quaintness that came with it. After checking in I decided to walk back to a little cantina I'd seen.

I sat there in the dead heat, sweating, enjoying my orange juice-based drink. It was refreshing and since the alcohol content was zilch, I'd keep a level head in any future encounters. The large palm leaf fan circulated the air but it didn't really cool. I could see why siestas were so popular. I wanted to close my eyes and sleep.

"More?" the waiter asked and pointed to the drink.

"No," I replied, slightly startled. "Just enjoying the afternoon." I grimaced; it was obvious the man didn't understand me; we'd struggled just to get the drink ordered. In reality I was stalling, trying to figure out the best way to approach Montoya. Of course, first I had to locate him, but I was pretty sure he would be doing another sacrifice within the next few days. I'd have him then.

The waiter nonchalantly held out his hand to be paid; that I understood. I pulled out a dollar and the young man's eyes widened and he smiled. He nodded vigorously and took the bill.

Suddenly there was a loud commotion and a small body came running out of the building next door. The child looked about quickly and then dodged a path through the pottery and baskets toward me. He cowered near my table, hiding behind the tablecloth.

"Shhh," he whispered and placed his index finger to his pursed lips. "Señor, ¿por favor...?" Then he folded his hands as if in prayer to me. His eyes, big, wide and brown pleaded and I was ensnared.

I smiled, gave a small nod then lifted my glass and sipped my drink.

"Juanita?" a gruff voice yelled. A large, brutish man stormed out the door of the building. "¿Juanita, dónde estás?"

The little boy pulled deeper into the folds of the white tablecloth and hid. I glanced over at the man and he scowled at me, and then said something that seemed aimed at me.

I nodded politely and pointed at myself. "Americano," I said and took another sip. He moved on to continue his search.

I had my man to find; he had his. I felt my table's covering move and realized the boy was now hiding under the table.

"Please, señor," he whispered. "No tell him."

"Just keep silent," I hissed. "And he won't know."

The man rampaged around the front of the store pushing boxes and lifting up large baskets. He stood, breathing heavily and wiped the sweat from his brow. He scowled while he surveyed the area. I quietly sat there watching him as he seethed and fumed. Finally, he stormed down the empty cobblestone street toward the encroaching jungle.

"He's gone," I said. "It's safe to come out."

The boy stuck out his head and pulled off his straw hat. A short mop of unruly hair bounced on top of his head and flopped down over his ears. Big brown eyes stared up me.

"I am orphan, señor," the boy said. "My name Juan–" He hesitated. "Si, my name is Juan. That man says he is my uncle. His girlfriend runs that store," he pointed at the door where he had originally come, "and he make me work there. I never see him before and he no look like my father. I lived in orphanage, he come." A tear welled up. "I no want to be with him." He looked about. "I no want to go back to orphanage."

The tears flowed and I was afraid that I was being hustled, but I felt there might be some truth to the story.

"How much do you need?" I asked. I'd heard about the

Mexican urchin hustles; Barbara had been quite vivid in her descriptions.

"Señor, ¿por favor...?" he said. "I no want money."

"Well, Juan," I said. "Your uncle went that way so you're safe for now." I motioned to the waiter and headed out. I had to figure out where Montoya was hiding after the fiasco he pulled on the steps of the ruins.

"Señor?" Juan followed me. "You look like a good man. I stay with you? I cook."

I stopped in my tracks and stared down at the rugrat before me. He was a little dirty, the clothes a little scruffy but it was the eyes. The child had eyes that sucked one in so quickly.

"How old are you Juan?" I asked.

"Twelve, señor. I clean house, too."

"Twelve? You certainly don't look that old. How is it you speak English so well, Juan?" I continued my stroll back to my hotel and he toddled along beside me.

"I live in Juarez with my mama and poppa. There was accident, a shooting, and they were killed. I go to school in the U.S. of A. and learn to speak English very good."

I nodded my head while listening to his story. It seemed plausible. "Are you really twelve?"

He paused. "No, señor, I am ten; but almost eleven. My uncle came to orphanage, now here," Juan said. "Please, I show you the city. Si?"

"Juan, I think I'll let you keep me company since I don't speak Spanish all that well. You can be my translator and I will pay you one American dollar a day to help me. Does that sound like a good deal to you?"

"I speak English good," Juan said and beamed at me.

"Let's get out of here before your uncle or his girlfriend sees you. Do you have some other place to stay?"

"Señor, ¿por favor...?" Juan said. "I know a place. Follow me."

He grabbed my hand and pulled me down the street and away from all the bad memories. I knew I was walking on very thin ice believing this child, but I had a new friend – and possibly a resource.

"You have room, señor?" Juan asked me when we were visually clear of the cantina. "My friend, Lupe... her real name Guadalupe, anyway, her mama has a spare room and rents to strangers."

"Thanks," I replied. "I've got a room." I pointed at the hotel. "So where does Guadalupe live?"

"Very near here," Juan said. "I stay with her, her mama like a mama to me. Very nice."

"Tell you what, Juan," I said. "Tomorrow morning I plan to go to the Temple of Inscriptions. Do you want to go along?"

"Oh, yes, señor."

"Fine," I said. "Meet me in front of my hotel around eight a.m. I'll even buy you breakfast. How's that sound?"

"I like fajitas, señor. Breakfast fajitas with lots and lots of scrambled eggs."

"Please, Juan," I said. "Call me Barry."

"That is very good, señor Barry."

I laughed. This child was more than street savvy. He was a very mature ten-year-old. I decided to humor myself.

"Did you hear about what happened there the other day at the temple at the ruins?"

"You mean the killing of the goat? Yes, Lupe's mama told us of it."

"What did you think?"

"Lupe's mama said it is our heritage, señor Barry. It was necessary to help our god, K'inich Ahau."

I cocked an eye of wariness at the lad before me. I couldn't consider him a street urchin any longer. Juan was a font of knowledge.

"Do you know who the man was?"

43

Juan's face lit up. "I bet Lupe's mama would know him. She knows everyone." He grabbed my hand again and started to tug me. "Come! She tell you."

I was tempted to follow Juan to this wonderful woman who knew everything then realized I was talking to a ten-year-old boy. Yes, maybe Lupe's mother might have the information but I really doubted she would be the great and powerful Oz he thought her to be.

"Here," I said handing him a quarter. "I'll see you in the morning. Fajitas, right?"

"With scrambled eggs?" Juan's eyes reflected his excitement.

I roughed up his hair and winked at him. "Yes, I know, with lots of scrambled eggs. In the morning, buddy."

Chapter 7:
Lupe's Mama

Mayan Date: 11 Ix 17 Mac ~ 12.19.19.17.14

*"Oh Mighty K'inich Ahau, may my blood offering
guide you across the sky. Ah Pukuh, show
me the way of these shadows. Bolontiku,
give me the vision to see my future."*

*Prayer of Chac Tun B'alam
Ruler of L'akam Ha*

Palenque City: 7:50 a.m., Saturday, December 15, 2012

I sat on the bench just outside the main door of the hotel. I was in the shade yet it was already warm outside.

"Do you wish a taxi, señor?" the attendant asked.

"No, I'm waiting for a friend," I replied. This time it wasn't a lie. I noted his name: Diego; I liked it. A newspaper lay beside me so I picked it up and glanced at the images. It wasn't in English and therefore I stared blankly at the headline. In the lower corner was a picture of a mob at a pyramid. I didn't need a translation to realize what the article was about; obviously, the sacrifice performed a couple of days prior.

My mind wandered. Two days ago I trudged the slushy winter streets of the city and tried to ignore the icy blasts of frigid, arctic air. Today, I sat in the shade of a reasonable hotel with a very warm breeze. From the wintry north to equatorial heat in twenty four hours – amazing. Even though I was in a short sleeve shirt and slacks, I was already starting to sweat. At least I wasn't wearing a heavy coat, sweater and gloves. A satisfied smile curled my lips.

"Señor Barry?"

I looked up and there was Juan smiling at me. He had his hair combed, parted down the middle and was wearing a clean tee shirt and jeans. Today he didn't appear quite the urchin I remembered of yesterday, but there was something that niggled at the back of my mind. Something just wasn't quite right. I tousled his hair. It helped; he looked better.

"Ready for breakfast?" I asked.

He nodded agreement vigorously and I stood up. A young lady with a small girl stood about half a block away, watching us. I nodded to her. She turned and pulled the child with her as she walked away.

"Is that your friend and her mother," I asked.

Juan nodded and waved at the little girl who kept looking back as they walked away.

"Let's go get those fajitas and scrambled eggs," I said and headed into the hotel.

Juan followed but seemed cautious.

"Table for two," I said and the waitress lead us to a small table at the edge of the patio where amongst lush plants, a huge fountain cascaded water and koi streaked about in the clear basin waters. The swimming pool, not a lavish Olympic sized one, lay nestled among the deep tropical foliage. Two blue-and-yellow macaws bobbed up and down with each other. She placed a small menu in front of each of us.

Juan's eyes were like huge saucers. "This is magnifico," he whispered. "I have never seen anything this beautiful before. It is like heaven."

"Trust me, Juan," I said. "This is not heaven, not anywhere near it."

It was a nice view but I had seen better in Vegas, New York, Chicago, and a hundred other cities. Still, for thirty-five dollars a night, it was an impressive sight.

"Buenos dias," she said approaching the table. "May I take your orders?"

"My companion would like a breakfast fajita with lots of scrambled eggs," I said and scanned the menu. "I would like a cup of coffee, black, a bagel and..." I saw the breakfast fajita and read what it consisted of. "Actually, skip the bagel, make that two breakfast fajitas. Would you like some milk, Juan?"

He nodded his head. "Chocolate?"

"And two orange juices please?"

"That will be two orange juices, one black coffee, one chocolate milk, and two orders of breakfast fajitas." She glanced at Juan. "With scrambled eggs. Will that be all?" She stood there smiling, holding her order pad even though she had written nothing down.

"That should cover us for the moment," I said. "Gracias."

"I'll be back with the juice, coffee and milk," she said, turned, and left.

"She is very pretty, no?" Juan said.

"Now are you going to try and hustle me with pretty girls?"

I glanced about the open indoor patio area. The restaurant took up one side while the other three sides of the patio were open to the hotel and a few patrons milled about in the shadows of the overhanging veranda. Suddenly, I saw the young woman I had noticed outside earlier. She still had the little girl in tow. She was watching us.

The waitress returned with our drinks, placed them on the table, smiled, and left.

"Señor Barry? Would you consider her? You know, as a pre-dater?"

"Excuse me. What?" My attention had been elsewhere.

"As a pre-dater, would you consider her?"

"Consider who?" I asked totally confused by the question. "What is a pre-dater?"

"You know, señor Barry," Juan said. "If you are a pre-dater, would you consider her? She is not a child but would you?"

"Whatever are you talking about?" I asked. "What is a child pre-dater?" I stopped. Suddenly I realized what Juan was saying. I was appalled. "Where did you hear that? Child predator? Are you calling me a child predator?"

"Yes, that is the word," Juan said, smiling. "Predator. Are you a predator? Lupe's momma told me to be careful."

"Of course not," I said indignantly. "Whatever possessed you to think that..." I stopped and scanned the area for the woman and little girl. That had to be Guadalupe and her mother. Obviously the woman was only trying to protect Juan.

"Here's your food, gentlemen," our waitress said. "If you need anything, let me know."

"Eat, Juan," I said bluntly. "I need to take care of something and will be right back." I looked at the waitress and read her nametag. "Rosa? Would you watch my companion for a couple of minutes?" I looked about the area. "I need to go back to my room for an item."

"No problem," she said with a smile.

I dashed out of the restaurant and quickly made my way around the veranda to where I had last seen the woman and girl. She stood there hiding behind a tall stand of bamboo and large green fronds of some plant. I could see her holding on to her daughter. I took a chance.

"Hi Lupe," I said while kneeling down beside the little girl. "Would you like to have some fajitas, too?"

The woman turned and I saw the woman's grip tighten on the little girl's hand. She pulled the child closer to her. Then she started to push her way by me to escape.

"Please," I said. "My name is Barry Hargrove. Won't you join Juan and I for breakfast? Trust me, Guadalupe's mother, I am not a child predator. I am a detective hired by a large museum to locate a stolen item."

She struggled against me, pushing me away. "No speak English," she screamed.

I held a finger to my lips, grabbed her hand and gently pulled her with me as I stepped backward away from the bamboo and palms that hid her. Juan was on the other side and saw me, then her. He waved.

"Señor, ¿por favor…?" she said. "English, no good."

"It's fine," I said softly. "Juan can translate those words we don't know. That's why I hired him to help me."

She frowned. "Juan? You mean Jua…"

Lupe said something cutting off her mother. I really did wish I knew the language. A short battling conversation ensued between them with Lupe's mother finally smiling at me. "Si, Juan."

I led them back to the restaurant and we were graciously moved to a larger table for four. Rosa quickly took their orders, more breakfast fajitas with extra scrambled eggs. She returned almost instantaneously with the food.

"I am sorry," I said. "I didn't get your name and feel silly calling you Guadalupe's mother, or Lupe's mom." Juan quickly spoke and she looked at me. Again, a little conversation ensued between Juan and the mother. All the while he tore his fajita in half and held it in his hand. I felt silly holding a fork at ready over my fajita while they ate with their hands. Dropping the fork, I grabbed up my fajita in preparation of eating it.

"What did she say?" I asked Juan. "Who is Juanita?" I took a bite of fajita.

"That is her name for me, little Juan," he said, his cheeks getting red with embarrassment. "Her name is..."

"My name Benita Angelina Gonzales Hernandez," she said and extended her hand.

I dropped my fajita and wiped my hand. "Barry Hargrove," I said and shook her hand. "Now, about this child predator thing."

Juan started to translate.

Chapter 8:
The Palenque Ruins

Mayan Date: 11 Ix 17 Mac ~ 12.19.19.17.14

*"O Mighty K'inich Ahau, I offer up my blood.
Help me to understand. The shadow people move
about my father's village. Today I touched one."*

*Prayer of Pacal Tun
Son of Chac Tun B'alam*

Palenque Ruins Backroad: 9:42 a.m., Sat., Dec. 15, 2012

I tried to keep my stomach down as we rumbled over the back road to the pyramids. I had wanted to take the tour bus but Benita was quite adamant her uncle could drive us there. When I told her I had a rental I could use, she protested even more. So her uncle won. Pedro was a pleasant enough man but he replied to everything with a "Si, si, señor." which I was finding almost irritating. I quickly realized he had no idea of what I was saying and spoke even less English than Benita. Juan attempted to translate what I asked, but still, it was always the same rehearsed answer.

The barely-painted truck skidded to a stop and road dust floated around us. Thick jungle overgrowth was everywhere; birds flittered among the leaves. I watched a flurry of hummingbirds attacking a red hibiscus bush and a toucan clacked its bill in an argument with a small parrot over a clutch of berries.

"We are here, señor Barry," Juan said after Pedro had stopped talking.

"We're here?" I repeated and again scanned the area for anything that might resemble a ruin or excavation dig.

"Yes," Juan said. "Uncle Pedro says the park is over there." He pointed.

Why was I here? I had no idea but figured it would be the best place to start. I got out of the truck and Juan followed me. Pedro yelled something and Juan responded back to the old man.

"He will wait for us," Juan said with a beaming smile.

I reached into my pocket and pulled out two bills. "Here, Juan," I said. "Take this back to Benita's uncle. Give him one and you keep the other. I want you to go home to Benita and I will see you tomorrow."

Juan hung his head. "Did I do wrong, señor?" he asked.

I grabbed his chin and made him look at me. There was a tear and I gently wiped it away.

"No, you didn't do anything wrong," I said. "Let me just wander around and absorb the magnificence of this place. If it is half as fantastic as everyone has told me, I'm quite sure I will be back tomorrow. Is that okay?"

He shrugged his shoulders, turned and scuffed his way back to the truck.

"Hey!" I yelled. "See you for breakfast? Bring Benita and Lupe if you want."

He ignored me but I could see him give the money to

Benita's uncle. The old man put a hand on his shoulder but he pulled away and buried his face in his arm that he had on the open window's edge. I was pretty sure he was crying. I felt like a heel.

I wandered into the lush overgrowth following the small worn path through it. The howler monkeys cried in the distance. Suddenly a clearing on my left opened up and I saw a pyramid – a magnificent structure of stone. It rose into the sky and was breathtaking. I strolled onto the green lawn before it and watched others mill around, walking up and down the steps and coming in and out of the doorways. I held still. There was no gate, no guards, nothing. I was sure that there had to a proper entrance; visitors didn't just wander in from the jungle. Pedro must have come on a back entrance road used by the archeologists and workers.

Suddenly it hit me. I'd sent Pedro back home. I looked about for a bus; there had to be tour group here somewhere. There just had to be.

A large group ambled onto the opening and headed for the steps of the pyramid. I looked back at the pyramidal structure. There, in the bright sunlight, a man stood with outstretched arms, dressed as a skeleton in a feathered robe. The sun glistened on the golden headdress and the wind fluttered the long feathers attached to its top. I'd seen this scene before.

Montoya was here!

I headed toward the pyramid. I had to corner Montoya before he got away. The mob engulfed me and then I was behind them, following. What was going on?

A siren sounded startling me. Three scooters charged by in pursuit of the mob. Five officers raced onto the lawn from the right in an attempt to cut the mob off.

I slowed up. I didn't need to get involved with this melee. Suddenly a native in ceremonial garb raced toward the pyramid. I was in his way and he passed through me. Literally the man passed through me like a ghost. I froze in my tracks and felt the shiver slowly course up my spine leaving goose bumps in its wake.

"What is this, señor Barry?"

Startled, I jumped. "What are you doing here, Juan?" I asked stooping down to my little shadow. "I thought I told you to go home with Pedro." My heart still raced but I'd been distracted.

"I only wanted to help you, señor Barry." He held his head down knowing full well he had done wrong and disobeyed me. "Here," he said and held out the dollar bill I had given him.

"Did Pedro leave?" I asked.

"I do not know," Juan said. "I jumped out of the truck and left him. What are they doing?" He pointed at the mob.

I glanced up at the temple pyramid. I could see Montoya and several other natives at the top. It was very impressive, especially with the mob shouting from below. Montoya stood there with his hand in the air. I knew what was coming next. I turned Juan away from the scene. The mob and the officials were in conflict as Montoya continued his sacrifice.

"Did you get that?" I heard a woman ask. "Did you hear me? I asked did–"

"Get what?" I snapped then noticed that she was talking to the man with her.

She briskly walked by barely noticing us. "I just wish he had let us know a little earlier so we could have gotten all of it properly. Tell me, Emil, what did you get?"

"With all this running, very damned little," the man said huffing by with a camera on his shoulder.

I looked up at the pyramid again. Montoya had completed the ceremony and could no longer been seen, he had quietly disappeared into the mob. I didn't understand how somebody dressed as lavishly as he had could sneak away, but he'd done it.

Suddenly there was a man who popped out of the mob and was discreetly walking away from the group. He had a duffel bag. The woman and the cameraman changed direction from the pyramid to the escaping man.

I watched the man. It was Montoya. I grabbed Juan's hand and started toward the trio.

"Is that the man you are looking for, señor Barry?"

I tripped. I had totally forgotten, even though I had his hand in mine, that Juan was with me.

The woman who I had snapped at earlier hailed Montoya and he stopped to talk. I could tell he was nervous and kept a wary eye on the mob and police at the Temple of Inscriptions. Back on my feet, I hustled Juan forward. I had to meet this man.

"I'm sorry, Miss Camal," Montoya said. "It would seem that I need to be on my way." He watched me with concern as I approached.

"Dr. Montoya!" I yelled. "Wait."

He turned and dashed into the lush growth of the jungle a short distance away.

"Did you just call him doctor?" the woman asked in perfect English. "My name is Lucia Camal. I'm a newscaster with..."

"Yes, Miss Camal," I said watching the leaves of the one tree finally come to a halt. "I recognized you from an earlier newscast a few days ago."

"Are you really her?" Juan asked.

"What a special child," Lucia said and kneeled down to him. "Tell me, do you like Lucia Camal?"

"Oh, yes," Juan said. "Some day I grow up and be just like you."

I frowned down at Juan. What the hell was he saying?

Juan looked around frantically. "I mean, I want to be newsperson, too. To travel and see all kinds of things."

"Oh, how cute," Lucia said standing up and shoving the mike in my face. "Is he your son?"

"No," I replied. "He is my translator I hired."

"How interesting," Lucia said. "Child labor?"

I glared at her. She was not about to put me on the spot and make me her new pet project for the viewing audience.

"Actually, Miss Camal," I said. "He came to me, wanted me to protect him from a supposed uncle. Juan is an orphan and from what I could tell, was already in a slave situation. I have confirmed most of the story with a mutual adult friend of Juan's. I pay him to translate but mostly he is just a companion. He was suppose to be headed back to town with Pedro but as you can see, he didn't listen to me." I smiled innocently at her and waited.

"I see," she said.

I smiled. "But, really, are we here because of Juan? What do you know of Montoya?"

"It would appear you know more," Lucia said. "I only know him as Ah Pukuh and this is his second sacrifice."

"Let me check and see if Pedro is still here," I said. "If not, you give us a lift back to Palenque and we can share information. Is it a deal?"

"You have a deal," she said and stuck out a hand to shake. "Your name is?"

"Barry Hargrove," I replied.

"I will check, señor Barry," Juan yelled and was sprinting across the open area to where Pedro had dropped us.

He quickly disappeared into the overgrowth surrounding the open area. Lucia, her cameraman and I headed back to their transportation.

Juan came dashing back onto the lawn and quickly joined us. I grabbed and lifted him into the air with his own energies, swung him in a circle and then put him down.

"That was fun, señor Barry," Juan said. "My father did

that when I was younger." A tear welled in his eye.

"So was Pedro there?" I asked to change the topic.

"Oh, yes," Juan said. "He talk with a stranger. I told him we go with señorita Lucia."

"A stranger?" Lucia asked.

"Yes," Juan replied. "He very nice man. I think Pedro give him ride somewhere."

"Can you describe him?" Lucia asked.

"He has gold tooth." Juan pointed at his canine tooth. "He had funny thing on chin." Juan pointed at the area below his lower lip. "And two pretty scars. Like this." He made small zigzag movements with his first two fingers across his cheek.

"That was Ah Pukuh," she said.

"You mean, Dr. Montoya," I corrected. "The scars must be new, I think."

Chapter 9:
Cohorts Anonymous Split

Mayan Date: 11 Ix 17 Mac ~ 12.19.19.17.14

"Mighty K'inich Ahau, today I saw my father's priest become two. A shadow moved from Chimalpopoca during the sacrifice. Is this a good sign? Both Chimalpopoca and the shadow offered you a beating heart. I now offer you my blood."

Prayer of Pacal Tun
Son of Chac Tun B'alam

Palenque Ruins Road: 10:37 a.m., Saturday, Dec. 15, 2012

Lucia filled me in on what she had learned about Ah Pukuh and other tidbits her assistant was able to find. I informed her of what I knew about Dr. Montoya. What I didn't tell her was the theft of the Scepter of Time from the museum. I was pretty sure Miss Camal was holding a trump card also so I didn't feel guilty about it.

"So why are you trying to locate this Montoya person?"

Lucia asked.

She sat in the passenger seat and had her back turned partially away from Juan and I. Emil drove the van and we sat in the rear on equipment boxes that transferred each bump of the road in its entirety to my butt.

"I was hired to locate him," I said. "Seems he was doing some shady business at his apartment and the manager wants him back there."

"Uh-huh," she said. "Now, what is the real story? I didn't get where I am by buying into a crappy story like the one you just told me. The truth this time, Mr. Hargrove. I do believe you were hired..." She shook her head at me. "But not by some apartment manager."

I sat there with Juan watching me. I saw Palenque coming into view. I calculated just how long I could put her off.

"Where do I drop you off?" Emil asked.

I couldn't have asked for a better queue; Emil was my out. "I enjoy walking," I lied. "Find a corner and stop, we'll get out."

Lucia glared at me. "You can run," she said. "But you will still have to answer me at some point if you want me to help you with Montoya. Here is my card with my phone number. Call me when you want to talk."

"This will be good," I said and pointed at a corner we were quickly approaching.

Emil pulled over. Juan and I got out of the van. Lucia rolled down the window and leaned out.

"You do realize Ah Pukuh lets me know when he is going to perform his sacrifices," she said as the van started to pull away. "Call me."

So that was her ace, she knew the where and when he would be available in public. If I wanted to know, I either shadowed her or I shared knowledge.

"Señor Barry?" Juan called. "Why you no tell her the

truth?" He stood there with questioning brown eyes.

"Was it that obvious?" I asked. "Any idea of which way we go?"

Juan pointed to the left. "A long walk, señor Barry. Follow me." He headed off and since I really only had one choice, I followed. I didn't realize Palenque was such a large city as it suddenly appeared to me.

"So you knew I wasn't telling Miss Camal the whole truth?" I asked casually taking time to notice the neighborhood and hope I could make the full walk of unknown length.

"You carry a secret, yes?" Juan asked. "Why you want this man?"

I stared down at my little companion with a new admiration. For one so young he was very knowledgeable beyond his years.

He glanced up and an innocent smile beamed at me.

A phone rang. I stopped dead in my tracks.

"What is wrong, señor Barry?" he asked.

"A phone," I replied. "I need a public phone. Well, actually, a phone book." I glanced around me looking at the different shops in the area. "There," I said and pointed at what appeared to be a pharmacy or store of some sort. "I bet there is a public phone in there."

I grabbed Juan's hand and practically pulled him across the street to the store. I looked at the outside of the building and didn't see anything remotely appearing as a phone booth so I grabbed the door and shoved Juan in first. There was a coolness inside but I was very sure it wasn't air conditioning. Even with minimal cooling it hit me big time and my sweat chilled me. The temperature change left me reeling.

"Do you see a phone?" I asked Juan.

"¿Tiene un teléfono publico?" Juan yelled.

A man standing on a ladder put down the can he was dusting and pointed to the back of the store.

"Muchas gracias," I said and hustled to the back. "I hope there is a telephone book."

"¿Tiene un directorio?" Juan asked aloud.

"Sí, sí, por teléfono," the man replied and waved his free hand absently at us.

I grabbed the book and flipped through the pages finally locating 'Montoya' and it was like a listing of 'Smith' back home. So I scrutinized for Adam. There wasn't a listing for him. I grimaced.

"You look for who?" Juan asked.

I looked down at my small companion and patted him on the head. I couldn't help but smile.

"I am looking for the phone listing of the man I need to find, Adam Montoya," I said. "Miss Camal would love to know his full name, of that, I am very sure."

Juan grabbed the phone and punched numbers on it.

"What are you doing?" I asked, quite surprised by his sudden action.

He held up a finger for me to wait.

"Cuál es el número de teléfono de Adam Montoya," he said into the receiver. "Por favor."

He grabbed a pen from my pocket and wrote the number down on the back of my hand.

"Si, si," he said. "Muchas gracias." He hung up the phone. "There, señor Barry." He held up my hand for me to see. "This telephone number Adam Montoya."

I was flabbergasted. This little boy in mere moments had gotten me a contact number for the man I was down here searching after.

"Okay," I said. "Here's the plan. First, let's get out of here. Get a cab. Get you home. Get me back to the hotel. And, finally, I call Montoya."

Juan looked at the floor and scuffed his foot. It was quite obvious my plan didn't sit well with him. I re-evaluated.

"How about you come back to the hotel with me?" I asked.

He looked up at me with a sparkle I hadn't seen of late. "Oh, si, señor Barry," he exclaimed and ran down the aisle of the store to the door.

The man on the ladder was about to yell something at Juan but realized the door had already slammed shut and Juan wouldn't have heard it anyway. I strolled down the aisles and noticed a small packet of milk candy. I truly enjoy milk candy so I grabbed a bag and headed to the counter.

"Oh, señor, un minuto," the man on the ladder said.

He put the can back on the shelf along with the feather duster then hustled down the steps and hurried across the store to the counter. I handed him an American dollar. The gentleman looked at it then reached into a drawer below the counter and handed me some change, which I stuck in my pocket. The front door opened.

"Señor Barry," Juan yelled at me. "Hurry."

I sauntered to the door, enjoying the last remnants of coolness before I hit the street again. The door opened and I saw the cab sitting at the curb just beyond Juan. This kid was good.

Chapter 10:
Calling Mr. Montoya

Mayan Date: 11 Ix 17 Mac ~ 12.19.19.17.14

"Mighty K'inich Ahau, your journey of the sky nears end yet you have not shown me the path to knowledge of these shadow people. I seek your guidance. The Bolontiku have hidden their visions. Blood fell from the sky at K'inich Janahb' Pacal's long sleep house. Do you wish a sacrifice?"

Prayer of Chac Tun B'alam
Ruler of L'akam Ha

Palenque City: 5:20p.m., Saturday, December 15, 2012

I sat there on the bed next to the small nightstand, staring at the number scribbled on the back of my hand. The numbers glared back at me. The evening meal had been filling and Juan had enjoyed eating at the restaurant again. Of course, I did have some difficulty in getting him to eat something other than fajitas, breakfast fajitas.

"What you do with number?" Juan asked between chews

on the milk candy I'd bought.

I sighed deeply then glanced over at him.

"I'm about to call this number," I said. "I think Montoya will be quite surprised to hear from me."

Grabbing the phone, I scanned the dialing instructions and punched in the numbers that Juan had written. There was some static, a buzz, a few clicks, a snap then I heard the familiar ringing sound as it connected with my party.

"Bueno, residencia del Sr. Montoya," a woman said.

"Hola," I replied. "Is Mr. Montoya in?" I asked.

"Si, un momento," she replied.

There was a soft click. Now I started to wonder if I had done the right thing; the man had music on his phone system. Soft music played and I realized my foot was tapping in tempo to it. A D.J. cut in and startled me. I listened to him hype on about a product when I heard another distinct click.

"This is Mr. Montoya." His voice was deep, resonant and powerful sounding.

"Good evening," I replied. "My name is Barry Hargrove." I hesitated, watching Juan crumble up the empty candy package.

"Yes, Mr. Hargrove?"

"I'm sorry," I said. "I would very much like to talk with you. I believe you have an item of mine." I decided not to play games, and instead just put my cards on the table.

"So you're the gentleman I saw at the ruins today. I was informed about you. What is it you think I have of yours?"

I smiled. So Camal had taken the initiative with the information I'd given her. She must have called him immediately after dumping us out of the van. I'd have to remember she was more aggressive than I originally thought.

"Rather than discuss this over the phone I think we need to meet," I said.

"You realize, Mr. Hargrove, that I can't be opening my

doors to every person who wants to talk to me. A person of my position in the community, I prefer to remain a private entity."

"That may very well be," I retorted, "but you seem to have a flair for bringing attention to yourself. Old lady Twitter or whatever her name was truly enjoyed your December non-Halloween costume." I pulled my notebook from my pants pocket and flipped pages. "Yes, a Mrs. Tweiller. She wanted to know if I was looking to sublet your apartment."

"Oh, I see," Montoya replied. There was a pause that dragged on. "Dear, dear Mrs. Tweiller. So you believe me to have in my possession, a particular item of yours? I will be taking a wild guess here; are you a museum official?"

"No. I'm–" I hesitated, wondering how to approach the topic. I'd already thrown my cards on the table so I decided to cast caution to the wind. "I'm a detective hired by them."

"Ah, Detective Hargrove, I am honored. Unfortunately I am quite busy with some errands I must attend to this evening. If you'd like to meet me at the ruins tomorrow morning, say around seven thirty, I am sure we can work something out."

I frowned. What was he up to?

"Do you remember the road Pedro used today?" he asked.

"Not really, but I am sure I can find it." I made a mental note to ask Benita about the road and how to get there.

"Good," Montoya said. "I will meet you where he parked his truck. Will you be bringing your little friend along?"

"*Little friend?*" I thought and sat on the edge of the bed completely stunned. How did he know about Juan? Then I realized he had mentioned Pedro. Perhaps it wasn't Camal who had tipped him off but instead, was Pedro. I was very sure they had spoken on the return trip, especially with the two of them speaking the same language. With no language barrier, I was positive Montoya probably now knew more about me than I about him.

"Uh, at the present time, most likely, yes."

"You decide, Detective Hargrove," he said. "Now, if you will excuse me, I must be about my meetings."

He hung up and I sat there holding the phone to my ear, listening to the silence of a dial tone.

"Señor Barry? Is everything okay?" Juan asked.

"Fine," I said absently as my mind raced to figure out the situation now before me.

"Tell me, Juan, do you know the road Pedro took us on today?"

I watched him from across the room; again, there was something, that something which niggled at me, something that wasn't right. His hair was parted down the center, the bangs were different, yet there was an air about him that had changed.

He smiled at me and nodded his head. "Oh, yes, señor Barry, we all know the back road. The highway is for the tourists and the buses."

I nodded my head absently. "Good," I said. "Can you be here tomorrow morning very early? Seven?"

Juan nodded his head vigorously. I considered having him stay the night but with the predator issue still fresh in my mind I decided it was not the best avenue right now.

"Tell you what," I said. "How about we get you home and I talk with Benita about tomorrow morning? In fact," I grabbed his hand. "We'll take my car and you will show me the way to Lupe's house so I can talk with her mother. Okay?"

Juan frowned momentarily then smiled that innocent smile of his. His dark eyes sparkled.

It only took a couple of minutes and I had the car and was on the back streets of Palenque. Juan pointed and I turned as he directed. I just had to remember how to get back and I was starting to think it might be more difficult than I hoped.

"There," he yelled. "Lupe's."

I squinted in the still bright light of the evening. A small, plain building stood amongst the other non-descriptive structures. I could see Lupe playing with a couple of other kids and she looked up as we approached. Juan waved frantically at her and she smiled and waved back. She spoke to her friends and they waved and giggled at our arrival, surrounding the car.

Benita came to the door and then rushed out, admonishing the girls and pointing back to their toys. The three girls hung their heads and slowly sulked back to where they had been playing.

"Good evening, Señor Hargrove," Benita said with difficulty.

"Miss Hernandez," I replied and nodded my head.

"I teach her English," Juan said proudly. "She learn good, yes?"

I tussled his hair. "Yes," I said.

Benita pointed to the house and offered me to come with her. She led the way and Juan followed along, waving to Lupe and her friends.

"Would you like to play with them?" I asked although I knew no respectable young boy was going to play with three other girls.

"It would be..." he hesitated. "You need me. Lupe mama no speak English." He waved a final time to Lupe and stepped through the entrance behind me.

Benita offered me a seat and I sat down. She poured me a glass of water and gave it to me then she stood against the wall with her arms folded in front of her, watching me.

I explained to Juan what I wanted him to convey to her about me picking him up at seven the next morning. He spoke with her and their was a flurry of talk between them when finally he turned to me.

"I go if you take her and Lupe. She remembers the road."

I frowned, slightly perplexed. "I thought you said you knew the road?" I asked.

Juan smiled sheepishly. "Most, yes," he replied.

"Fine," I replied and sipped some water. "But no breakfast. You eat before I pick you up."

Juan spoke again with Benita. I couldn't tell if she was agreeing or not, but finally, he stopped fighting with her.

"She say she bring lunch for us." Juan shrugged his shoulders while giving me a sheepish grin.

"Why lunch?" I asked. "I'm going to meet Montoya in the morning. He speaks English and I am only taking you because he asked about you and you know the road."

"She say we..." He wrinkled his nose and frowned. "How you say? Enjoy the ruins." He hesitated. "All day." Again, he hesitated. "If you agree."

I thought about the situation. It appeared that if I didn't take the group for a picnic then Juan wasn't allowed to go with me. If Juan didn't go, I didn't have directions although I was sure they could provide such at the front desk. I mean, if a small boy knew the way, I am sure the manager, desk clerk, even Diego would know the route. I glanced at Benita. She remained stoic, standing defiantly with her arms crossed, watching me, calculating. Maybe she still considered me a predator and this was another test. I could feel my lips tightening under the pressure. There were few options, I nodded and Juan grinned. A day wandering around the ruins could be fun.

"Sure," I said. "A picnic sounds fine. We all go."

Chapter 11:
Sunrise

Mayan Date: 12 Men 18 Mac ~ 12.19.19.17.15

*"O Mighty Sun God, K'inich Ahau, today I offer
you much blood for your journey across the sky.
May our enemies blood please you and guide me to
know the path of action with these shadow people."*

*Prayer of Chac Tun B'alam
Ruler of L'akam Ha*

Palenque Ruins: 7:20 a.m., Sunday, December 16, 2012

I grabbed the bag with our lunch from the trunk and handed it to Lupe. Another bag carried our drinks, and Juan reached in and got it. He hefted the bag with a grunt, so I reached over to assist.

"No, no, señor Barry," he said. "I do it."

I let go and suddenly Benita was there to take the bag out of the trunk. She smiled and said something. Juan let go. She also had the bag that Lupe had grabbed. Benita spoke in a soft voice to Juan.

"She say we go to the ruins of the palace and be in the courtyard until you come."

Benita, Lupe and Juan scurried up the path and were quickly hidden from sight. Suddenly I was alone with only the howler monkeys to keep me company. The sun had been up and it was already starting to warm the day. Still, in the shade of the jungle I found it to be cool and refreshing. I watched the light play through the foliage, sparkling here and there, highlighting for a mere instant a section of tree or overgrowth only to be dashed into shadows just as quickly as the sun continued its upward climb.

I heard a cry, looked up and there in a ray of sunshine, a bird spread its wings in a stretched arc above its head. He had his red crest completely fanned out and it radiated in the sunlight. The tips of the feathers, both in the wings and the fanned tail were aglow, the colors iridescent in the morning light. My heart lifted at the sight. It appeared the bird was about to ignite and burst into flame like the legendary phoenix being reborn.

"Magnificent, isn't it?" Montoya whispered behind me.

"Stunning," I replied softly not wanting to break the magic.

"It is a moment like that when an Mayan priest realizes the fullness of communing with the creatures of the forest. You and I are of the modern world, the one filled with hustle and bustle, steel and concrete; but if you allow yourself to drift back a thousand years and know nothing but nature, what would you think?" Montoya asked.

It was an instantaneous thought. "The bird is an omen," I whispered, knowing full well it was the answer he was searching for.

"It is still an omen today," he said. "That is the Northern Royal Flycatcher and it is sacred. Now, look beyond to the next tree. Do you see it? The red-breasted bird in iridescent blue-greens and those two long tail feathers? It's called a Quetzal. One of the rarest birds in the jungle and most sacred to the Mayans." Montoya waved his hand in an arc at the trees. "Now it is up to me, a priest of the Mayans, to decipher what this very fortuitous omen is. Come, let us talk."

He motioned me toward the ruins. We crossed the small growth of jungle that hid the road from the ruins. Suddenly the path turned and again, like before, the ruins spread before me with all their splendor gleaming in the early morning light. I could see Benita and the kids moving toward the palace. A few other tourists wandered the grounds. A cool, early morning breeze tickled my neck, and then was quickly replaced by the heat of the rising sun.

"Appears to be another hot day," I said hoping to break the silence.

"So you think I have the Scepter of Time; is that correct?" he asked casually then cocked an eye in my direction.

"Oh, please," I replied. "I know you have it."

I wasn't about to start playing games. Obviously, he wanted to. I glanced at my companion when I noticed something moving in his hand, twirling like a baton.

"Is that—"

"Yes, Detective Hargrove," he replied proudly. "This is the scepter."

He held it out for me to view. Now that I could see the real one in the sunlight, it was quite obvious the one at the museum was so very fake. The inlaid gems glittered in the natural light, and the jade and turquoise were exquisite. I reached out for it. Montoya snatched it back from my reach.

"I'm afraid I can't let you have it," he said. "At least, not yet."

"Señor Barry!" Juan called and waved from the stairs of the palace.

I felt a shift, a change. The ruins were gone; not the

structures, but the deterioration. In their place stood beautiful buildings. The compound was crowded, but not with tourists. Instead, natives pressed forward and I was carried in a wave of excitement by the group headed to the pyramid. There, atop the stairs, stood one person in full ceremonial regalia with a bound warrior before him. I realized it was Montoya standing there; his eyes were wide and his face was frozen in blissful commitment. He held the obsidian knife above him, and then it slammed down into the victim. There was blood everywhere as he pulled the heart out and showed it to the crowd. I felt drops splatter me. A priest rushed up the stairs to receive the heart and raced back down to place it on the altar in a bowl to burned as an offering.

Then it was gone. I staggered and caught my balance with an outcropping of stone.

"Are you okay?" Montoya asked grabbing my arm.

"Did you see that?" I asked.

I looked wildly about the surrounding area. The ruins were back; Juan, Lupe and Benita were at the palace and my little buddy stood there waving at me.

"The time shift?" Montoya asked. "Of course. Each time I have offered up a sacrifice I have felt this change." He looked about. "Still, it has never been as strong as this. I felt a power move me today." He rubbed his hands absently as if they were covered in something.

I looked at him; his eyes were afire with excitement. He held the scepter close to him, hugging it to his chest.

"You do realize I need to return the scepter," I said, and once again reached out to take the item from his grip. "Dr. Martinez was quite adamant. It is mandatory I return the scepter within the next few days."

He turned away, protecting his prize from my prying hands.

"I'll make you a deal," Montoya said. "Allow me to keep

possession of the scepter and I will return it to you at the end of the week."

I stopped in my tracks and stared at the man. He was attempting to cut a bargain. He certainly wasn't Wimpy from an old Popeye cartoon, and this wasn't a hamburger being haggled over until a future payday. The facts were facts; Montoya had stolen an artifact, a very valuable item, and it needed to be returned to the museum. That was my job.

"Today is Sunday," Montoya said holding the scepter out for me to view. "As I see it, by next Sunday you would have this back in the museum."

"Actually," I said once again grabbing for the scepter, "if I take it now I could have it back in the museum no later than Tuesday." I smiled at him while my finger closed around empty air as Montoya pulled it away. "I need that artifact!" I demanded.

"And you will get it when I am finished," Montoya retorted.

"Why do you need it?" I asked. "You owe me that much."

More people wandered onto the open area; a busload of tourists no doubt. Montoya appeared nervous, turned and headed toward the pyramid.

"Come with me," Montoya said. "I'll show you what you need to know. It's up here in the Temple of Inscriptions. I discovered it last year."

"You discovered? Are you an archeologist, too?"

"My doctorate is in archeology, detective," he sneered. "If you'd investigated, as a good detective would normally do, you'd had known that."

I wasn't about to rise to the bait. "Actually, I wasn't sure if your studies had been in thievery or in janitorial duties," I replied. "You looked rather professional in the tapes. I guess I never really gave it a thought beyond that. I'm just chasing an artifact which happens to have a thief attached to it."

"I see," Montoya said.

We approached the temple and began the climb up the stairs. I looked up to see the Northern Royal Flycatcher and Quetzal fly to the roof of the temple. Tourists behind us 'oohed' and 'awed' and cameras clicked, but to me, it was obvious. An omen.

Chapter 12:
Temple of Inscriptions

Mayan Date: 12 Men 18 Mac ~ 12.19.19.17.15

*Chac Tun B'alam stands atop the temple watching
two ghostly figures move up the stairs toward him.
He slowly pulls the knife down the inside of his
thigh, blood traces around the blade and down his leg.
"Mighty K'inich Ahau, I offer you my blood.
I see shadow people approach.
They come; I feel akin to one while
the other appears as K'ul'ulkan."*

*Prayer of Chac Tun B'alam
Ruler of L'akam Ha*

Palenque Ruins: 7:50 a.m., Sunday, December 16, 2012

"This way," Montoya said and slipped around the corner of the temple.

From a distance the Temple of Inscription steps were easily seen as steep but now that I was up close, they were very steep. I was winded from the trek up the stone stairs. The worst thing was that I felt like a sheep being led off to slaughter as I blindly followed everyone. Perhaps I should be asking questions, or at least analyzing the situation a little closer. Instead I was just going along with the actions of others. Juan had his agenda, Benita had hers, Lucia knew what she wanted and even Montoya had his plans. I was here because of Montoya but yet it was under Lupe's mother's rules. Me? I was just following; I was the sacrificial lamb.

"Here," Montoya said. "How familiar are you with the Mayan language?"

I cocked an eye at him and was more than sure my sarcastic look told him all.

"As I expected," he mumbled. "My apologies. I do tend to forget Mayan is not a common language like French or English. Anyway, if you look at this inscription you'll notice these two characters represent K'inich Janahb' Pacal; not necessarily an exact name for him, but a synonym, a nickname, if you will."

He looked at me and I nodded my head to acknowledge what he was saying. "Go on," I finally said, trying to look interested.

"It states he demanded the crystal skull, the scepter and its satchel be buried with him. We are very fortunate to have located his tomb when we did."

"So, do you think that it was luck, or destiny?" I asked. "You seem to think that the scepter is necessary..." I hesitated.

"Yes," Montoya said. "The Scepter of Time is a mandatory item as time comes to an end, so to speak. That is why I took it from the museum. I needed it here for the ceremony."

"Ceremony?" I repeated.

"The inscriptions here are explanations of what will happen," Montoya said bluntly. "I know others have attempted to transcribe what is carved here but they are not on the proper page of knowledge to correctly interpret what is written. They think it must tell of K'inich Janahb' Pacal's achievements." He looked directly at me. "They are wrong!"

"Excuse me, but exactly why are they wrong and you right? Wasn't this all translated by a group? Therefore, I find it a tad bit difficult to believe that only you have correct translation." I folded my arms in front of me and waited. I knew he had to be seething.

"I thought if I brought you into my confidence you'd realize what I was doing." He stood there glaring at me. He leaned against the wall, his hand rested on one of the inscriptions; a finger tapped gently against the stone.

"Is that how you see it? I'd be swayed to your way? Agree to the theft?" I asked.

"It could be worse, you know." He smiled and cocked an eyebrow in my direction.

"Tell you what, Montoya. Just give me the damn scepter and let me go back home. How's that sound? Workable?"

"Look at this," he said. "See how this curls here?" He pointed to the inscription at eye level. This is where I interpret it to say: *calls on the crystal skull*. They have interpreted this to be: *found the crystal skull*. Here." He pointed at another image further down. "This says: *moves through time* where they think it to be: *goes to time*."

"Okay," I said. "You say this and they say that. Why should I believe you, or even care about what you're saying?"

He placed an arm over my shoulder like a confidant. Montoya slowly turned me to face the jungle.

"Look out there." Montoya swung his arm in an arc to encompass the vastness before us. "See the deep greens? The monkeys? The birds? The jaguar? The Mayans lived with nature; they thought differently than today's man. That collaboration of scientists translated with the mindset of today's modern man, not like a person – a Mayan – who lived with the earth. The way a tree grew was important to them. If a bird chirped differently it meant something to them; it was an omen. The world around them was their life; all of it had meaning. Today we have forced the world to conform to us." He smiled at me. "At least we are naive enough to think we have controlled how the world is."

I stared out at the overgrowth, the wealth of jungle that encroached on the temples and buildings which was being excavated. Suddenly what Montoya was saying made sense; I wanted to believe this man.

"Okay, so what exactly is your translation?" I asked.

He smiled at me. "Come by my house tonight, about eight, and we can go over a full translation of what is here at the Temple of Inscriptions. Will that work for you?"

I nodded absently.

"Señor Barry?" Juan called. "Would you like some water?" He stood beside me with a bottle offered up.

I took the chilled water. "Thank you."

The jungle disappeared, receded into the distance. Now natives milled about the compound, some carrying wood, others with urns. I stood at the edge of the Temple of Inscriptions. I could hear chanting to my left and I turned. There a Mayan priest stood with his arms outstretched, calling to the mass of natives at the base of the steps. The priest turned to me and raised both hands with palms lifted upwards. "K'ul'ulkan," the priest shouted. I felt the wind flutter the feathers on my headdress and a small hand tighten on mine. Looking down I saw the robe of feathers I wore. A jewel-encrusted gold harness of leather and fabric hung from my waist. A hand clenched mine; a small child, the face smeared in blue and white staring back at me with wide eyes. A necklace of turquoise and jade beads was draped around the child's neck and glistened on the white fabric of the tunic. In the distance, standing on a terrace of the palace, a woman and small girl were watching. I waved and called out to them.

"Señor Barry?"

I staggered backwards as the jungle zoomed in to once again consume the pyramids and temples. Much of the city was gone and the multitude of natives had disappeared. I blinked my eyes to re-focus on the views about me.

"What happened to you?" Montoya asked. "What did you say? What was the language?"

"Excuse me?"

"The language! What language did you just speak?"

"I didn't say anything." I frowned at him.

"But you did, señor Barry," Juan said. "You waved and said some funny words." He massaged his hand.

"Why are you doing that?" I asked and pointed at his hand.

"You squeezed it," Juan said and continued to massage it. "It hurt."

I kneeled down. "I'm sorry," I whispered, taking his small hands into mine. "Did I really say something?" I gently rubbed his hands.

He nodded his head. "Si, señor Barry. It hurt when you held my hand, and the words made no sense."

I searched his eyes; there was fear. "What else?" I asked softly. "Did you see something – something that didn't make sense?"

He slowly nodded his head. "I saw strangers and was afraid. Then you changed and squeezed my hand." Juan slowly massaged his hand. "It hurts." A tear formed in the corner of his eye then traced a path down his cheek. "I want to go home, señor Barry."

I hugged and held him close. In the distance I saw Benita and Lupe.

"How about we go get something to eat?" I asked. "Would that make you feel better?"

Juan smiled and nodded.

"I will see you later tonight," I said to Montoya.

He nodded agreement and we quickly joined Lupe and her mother. I spent an enjoyable afternoon with them learning about the ruins of Palenque. Still, all day long I felt a pull at me and constantly glanced at the Temple of Inscriptions hoping for an answer.

Chapter 13:
An Evening with Montoya

Mayan Date: 12 Men 18 Mac ~ 12.19.19.17.15

*Chac Tun B'alam paced the courtyard watching
K'inich Ahau set in the distant horizon. He looked over
at the temple and watched the shadow people mill up and
down the steps. He was still confused by the one that
appeared as the tales described of K'ul'ulkan. He knew
that as time ended, all would come together. He awaited
the great moment; K'inich Ahau would reign.*

*"Please come to meal," his wife pleaded. "I have
prepared maize, tasty turkey and xocolatl to drink.
The shadows will await your return."*

"A vision tonight, Bolontiku. I beg you."

*Prayer of Chac Tun B'alam
Ruler of L'akam Ha*

Palenque City: 8:20p.m., Sunday, December 16, 2012

I sat in the room trying not to gawk, but it was impressive. Some of the items I was very sure were contraband, or at least damned excellent copies. My mind wandered back to the early morning meeting and fought a small battle. *"He said he was an archeologist,"* I thought. *"No, he said his doctorate was in archeology."* I let my fingers glide over the small four-inch square glyph. It felt real to me yet I was reminded of a coaster that one would use for drinks. I picked it up.

"Please, Detective Hargrove, do be careful with that," Montoya said striding into the room.

"Not a coaster, eh?" I replied while carefully placing it back down on the table.

He snickered and sat down behind the desk, kicking up his feet.

"Have a seat, detective," he said.

"So, doctor," I started. The chair I plopped into was very plush and I sunk deep into its recesses. "Exactly what were you hinting at this morning?"

I was uncomfortable; the chair was too plush. Looking around I noticed another chair that didn't appear quite as soft. It had a padded seat and was more reminiscent of a dining room captain's chair. I eased out of the plush chair and moved over to it.

"Ah," Montoya said, watching me. "You are a man with similar likes to mine. I find that chair quite detestable." He pointed at the one I'd abandoned. "But my designer insists it is perfect for the room. I demanded on a match to my desk chair." He dropped his feet and swiveled in his chair. "Of course, mine spins and yours doesn't."

I smiled, not sure why we discussing furniture. In fact, his demeanor reminded me more of a little boy and his toys. He leaned back and slid his slippered feet back onto the desk.

"Detective..." he hesitated. "First, would you mind if I called you by your first name, which is Barry, right? I find titles and all that flim-flam just too formal, and it tends to put up boundaries we really don't need."

I eyed him suspiciously. Did I really want to be friends with this person? Going on first names might bring us together on a common level but I might lose some professionalism if I wasn't careful. I frowned.

"Oh, please," Montoya said. "You can call me Adam and it will make the conversation so much easier. Trust me."

"Fine, Adam," I replied. "Now back to the issue at hand. You promised to explain to me why you needed the scepter. At the present time, I really feel my obligation is to retrieve the item and return home and give it back to the museum. So..." I spread my hands in his direction. "What are your thoughts?"

He opened a desk drawer and pulled out the Scepter of Time and laid it on his chest. I could feel my jaw drop open.

"You don't keep it locked up?"

Montoya gave me an innocent glance. "Why should I? Who knows it is here?" He shrugged his shoulders and smiled. "Well, of course, both you and I know I have it. I really don't even think that even my retainers at the house here know I am in possession of it. Of course, there are those people back at the museum..." He gazed at the ceiling. "No – they're not here. So why would I lock it up?"

"But one of your servants could take it," I said.

"Please, Barry. Servant indicates a slave connotation and I really don't consider any of my staff that. If you noticed, I called them retainers. I have a housekeeper, a groundskeeper and a mechanic handyman. If they were going to steal, I am sure they would have done it long ago. After all, the housekeeper alone has been with my family almost forty-five years. She was born to my father's housekeeper."

"I didn't mean to implicate your staff, Adam. But, what if

83

somebody attempted a break-in?" I glanced about the room and waved my hand to take it all in. "I realize there is much here of value; but still, open a drawer and voila! A jewel encrusted staff."

Montoya sat there with hand covering his mouth; he was obviously considering my words. He finally nodded in agreement. "A valid point," he said. "I will have it placed in the safe when we are done." He glanced at the door. "Come in, Ix'iloom."

The woman who had answered the door and led me to this room now stood in the doorway with a tray of food and drinks. The scent of the steaming items didn't strike a familiar cord but they did smell delicious. She placed the tray on a small table beside Montoya's desk.

"Please," he said waving his hand at the food. "You'll find these to be melt-in-your-mouth delectable." He grabbed a handful and popped one into his mouth. "Mmm. My gods, Ix, you still have the talent for making these."

The old lady smiled warmly and spoke softly; I could barely hear her.

"Your daughter made these? Fantastic," Montoya said. "It is good the old ways are not lost. Please, Barry, do try one."

He again motioned for me to try something from the tray. I leaned in and picked up a dark, oblong item. There was a warmth to it, but the item wasn't hot when I picked it up. I wasn't sure exactly what it was but decided this woman had no reason to kill me; I stuck it in my mouth.

It melted, flavors bursting on my tongue. I knew my eyes widened in surprise. There was mint, lemon and a mixture of fruit before I felt the lump. A nut? It mashed as my tongue pushed it up into the roof of my mouth. A chocolate wave smothered my tongue. Eating this delicacy was more than an epicurean experience; it was a sensual assault of gastronomical proportions. Then I heard it.

"Mmm..."

It was me! I could have sworn it was more of a moan than a statement. Montoya sat there smiling at me.

"As you can tell, Barry," he said. "The Mayans definitely know how to cook."

Suddenly I was alert. Mayans? I leaned back against the chair and watched my host closely. The last of the fruity nut mixture slid down my throat. Again the word he had used surfaced: Mayans.

"Why did you say that?" I asked. "You called her a Mayan."

"She is," he replied and popped another nugget into his mouth and closed his eyes. He swallowed. "Ix'iloom is a direct descendant of the Mayan race. In fact, all my retainers are of the Mayan race; just like your little friend is a Mayan. Although for the life of me I don't understand why you insist on using the name Juan."

I frowned. Just that quickly, he was once again the condescending doctor of earlier today. I was sure our moment of buddy-buddy was over.

"Now, I promised you a lesson in translations," Montoya blurted. He grabbed another handful of morsels and lifted the goblet of liquid. "Do make sure you taste the drink." He stood up.

I tossed him a questioning look.

"Please," he said. "It is non-alcoholic–" he hesitated. "And non-poisonous," he added with an impish grin. "Actually you'll find it to be quite refreshing."

I selected two more of the oblong treats and three of the round ones that Montoya had been eating. I lifted my goblet and could smell a faint hint of chocolate. The vessel was a little warm, not hot, but carried a hint of heat. I tasted it. It was mildly warm but the liquid burst on my taste buds like a crashing surf. It was sweet, it was chocolate, it had a hint of

85

vanilla. And was there a spice? It was a flavor I wasn't familiar with. It was delicious.

Montoya watched me. "Another Mayan treat," he said. "It's called tascalate. They had the ability to combine flavors and textures in their foods. As you can see, the Mayans weren't the savage beasts the Europeans thought them to be."

"I never thought that," I replied then cringed, knowing full well I considered most of these people just Mexicans.

"Well, enough of the culinary education," Montoya said. "You wanted to know how I knew the others had mis-translated the glyph. Come with me."

He headed toward what appeared to be a small section of library shelving. He pushed it to the side; it rolled very easily. Just as quickly, a key appeared in his hand and he opened the door that had lay hidden behind moveable shelf. It was the entrance to another room.

"Welcome to my laboratory, Barry," Montoya said. "Come in and let me show you my life's endeavor."

He eased back and held the door open for me. Beyond I could see books: open books, stacked books, shelved books and what appeared to be thousands of pictures strewn about a huge room. I strolled in and was awestruck by the myriad of glyphs in the room.

The door closed behind my host and I heard a distinct click. Montoya strode by and into the room, spinning with outstretched arms. "This is my life," he whispered. "This is my future." He stopped and stared at me for a moment then motioned for me to come to him. "Look at this one," he said. "See? Here's what I was speaking about this morning. The curl?" He pointed at the glyph.

I walked over and examined what he was talking about. He grabbed a book and started to flip pages. He stabbed his index finger at a page.

"This is the translation that 'they' came up with – blah,

blah, blah, a stick in time, blah, blah. What were they thinking? Stick? This glyph is about the scepter. It's not *stick in time* but *Scepter of Time*, and that is because of the curl."

I nodded my head like I totally understood, but then decided it would behoove me to be honest. "I have no idea what you are talking about. I don't understand glyphs."

"Fine," Montoya said and guided me to a table with a couple of chairs. "Let me give you a crash course. Did you have plans for the night? If so, I would suggest you cancel them; this is going to take some time."

I sat down and he slid a book in front of me. He opened the cover, and then flipped a switch on a small black box.

"Ix'iloom, please bring refreshments into my lab," he said. "I hope you don't mind, it will be a long night."

"I think I'm up to it," I said.

"I wasn't talking to you," he said. "I was apologizing to Ix'iloom since she will be bringing us the nourishment to make it through the night. Those treats we had earlier are freshly made, not something you pick up at the local supermarket and zap in a microwave."

Chapter 14:
Facing Reality

Mayan Date: 13 Cib 19 Mac ~ 12.19.19.17.16

Chac Tun B'alam strides to the base of the temple. He watches the shadow people warily. Chimalpopoca approaches, leading the prisoner and guard; a full sacrifice to K'inich Ahau. Chac Tun B'alam narrows his eyes and watches the three trudge up the steps.

"O Mighty K'inich Ahau, accept this full blood sacrifice to help you on your path. Help me to see the meaning of the shadow people."

Chimalpopoca plunges the knife into the victim, then the head is severed, displayed and finally tossed to the cheering crowd below.

Offertory of Chac Tun B'alam
Ruler of L'akam Ha

Palenque Ruins: 7:20 a.m., Monday, December 17, 2012

"Quiet," Montoya whispered. "Do you hear it?"

I listened to what I could hear. Howler monkeys, macaws, birds, insects. The sounds blended, blurred and then the jungle was gone. Once again the magnificence of Palenque spread before me. No, this was not Palenque, this was L'akam Ha, the city of K'inich Janahb' Pacal. The courtyard glistened in the early morning sun. The Temple of Inscriptions was before me. I watched three people slowly ascend the steps, two in regal headdress, one painted in the sacrificial blue. Mesmerized as I watched, I couldn't believe the young man to be sacrificed followed with a dignity. Even from this distance I could tell he wasn't a native of L'akam Ha, but instead a prisoner. He never struggled. There was a group of natives anxiously moving about at the base of the temple. As I stood there watching, a breeze moved the feathers of my headdress and I was reminded of where I was. Beside me, in similar regalia, Montoya stood regally watching the ceremony. The group arrived at the top and the priest turned to face out at the crowd. An altar suddenly appeared at the top of the temple. The guard eased the prisoner onto this altar. The priest moved behind the altar and rested a reassuring hand on the prisoner's head. An obsidian knife lifted above the priest's head, the ornately carved jaguar head of jade shining in the sunlight. The black, chipped blade glinted and a flash of reflected sunlight blinded me momentarily. The knife came down and pierced the abdomen of the prisoner. I jerked my head to clear my sight. Everything vanished.

"You saw it!" Montoya yelled as he stared at me. "You were there, too!"

I nodded my head. There was no way I could deny the emotions I was feeling. There was a loathing of the sacrifice yet a rush to have participated in assisting K'inich Ahau to complete his travel of the sky.

"You saw it yesterday, too," Montoya demanded. "You heard them call you K'ul'ulkan. You spoke the native language."

I shook my head. I didn't want to get wrapped up in Montoya's delusions.

"What did you say? What were you saying when you spoke? You spoke the Mayan native tongue; something not heard in almost two thousand years. My god, man! Do you have any idea of the significance?" He wrung his hands. "If only I could have been a part of yesterday's vision."

I glared at Montoya. He stood there raving at me, yet I had just witnessed a brutal killing. He wanted me to remember what I had said and I just wanted to forget everything I had seen.

"Okay you two," the woman's voice said. "You want to sneak around and leave me in the dark, that I can understand. If you two want to collaborate, again, I understand. But trust me, boys, that doesn't mean I'm not coming after you."

I turned to see Lucia Camal approaching us.

"Montoya... or should I call you Ah Pukuh?" She shrugged. "Whatever. So why haven't you called to let me know when the next sacrifice was going to be? And you, Detective Hargrove, why haven't you been a little more forthcoming with details?" She looked around. "What gives? What are you two up to?"

"Señor Barry," Juan shouted and came dashing up past the cameraman. He embraced me. "I thought you had forgotten me, señor Barry."

"How'd you get here?" I asked unwrapping his arms from me.

"I found the little urchin at your hotel," Lucia said. She stared at me for a few seconds. "Don't forget, I'm a newsperson, Detective Hargrove. I get my information.

Anyway, Juan" – she slurred his name – "was sitting on the bench in front of your hotel waiting for you to come home. With just a little bribing I found out the two of you had a meeting. So we checked your home, Dr. Montoya, and since the two of you left there early this morning, with some simple deductions, here we are."

"Wait a minute," I said. I was totally confused. "Juan was at my hotel this morning?" I gazed down at him. "What time did you get there?"

"Eight, like always," he replied. "Lupe and her mama waited a little while then they left."

"Then you went to Montoya's place then here?" I glanced at my watch. 9:12 a.m. "Holy shit! Adam, do you see the time?"

Montoya stood there shaking his head. "Seems we lost about two hours with our little visit."

"You're okay with that?" I asked. "Two hours while we watch a dream?"

"What the hell are you two talking about?" Lucia snapped and gave me a calculating look. "You starting to smoke some of the local stuff here?"

"Don't worry about it," I said and waved my hand to dismiss the conversation. "We came out here to ascertain certain aspects of Dr. Montoya's translations."

"That's a snazzy looking toy you have there, Dr. Montoya," Lucia said in her business voice. "Exactly where does the Scepter of Time come into play here?"

I stared at her, all the while knowing full well my jaw had dropped in surprise.

A slight smile and glint in her eye, she watched us. "Like I said, boys. I am a reporter and I have many resources available to me. Is that the one stolen from the museum? It looks real."

She reached for the baton but Montoya pulled it back from her grasp. He held it close to his chest and watched her, his eyes flaring. He suddenly seemed possessed with a demon.

Again, there was a shift and the jungle disappeared. A small hand grabbled and held on tightly.

I could feel the weight of the headdress and when I looked down, I once again had on the native trappings and sandals. To my immediate right was Juan but his hair was much longer and pulled back. He wore a full cotton tunic. Beyond him was Lucia, she stood there with a haughty appearance, her long dark, hair tumbling down to cover her naked breasts. I could see the traditional markings and tattoos on her face. To my left was Montoya and he had on the dark feathered robe and large headdress I had seen him wearing when he appeared on the television news. I was slightly disturbed by the skintight skeleton body suit he wore and remembered Mrs. Tweiller's comment. My mind raced to think back how long ago that had been when he was making his first sacrifice.

"K'ul'ulkan!"

The voice jolted me and I looked at the man who had shouted. He strode swiftly across the open area toward me. Scurrying before him were two wiry men who couldn't be bodyguards but were more likely servants. They wore only a minimum of a loincloth.

"Chac Tun B'alam has called you to attend," the man said. "Do you not listen?"

I heard Lucia say something and then Juan's hand dropped from mine as she pulled him away and they stood to one side.

"K'ul'ulkan is a god, Chac Tun B'alam," Montoya said and pointed at me. "Do you demand of a god? Let not his anger rest upon your head. The feathered serpent never sleeps."

Chac Tun B'alam lowered his head in a nod of obeisance. "Ah Pukuh is right. K'ul'ulkan is called for an offering to K'inich Ahau." Chac Tun B'alam cocked his head so he could look at Montoya then to me. "Bless us with your presence, mighty K'ul'ulkan..." He glanced at Montoya. "And you, mighty Ah Pukuh, as time..."

Chac Tun B'alam jerked back to stare at Montoya. His eyes were locked on the Scepter of Time that Montoya held to his chest.

"You have brought us K'inich Janahb' Pacal's Eyes." He reached out to the baton. "The Eyes of Pacal. Where is the Conscience of Pacal?"

"The eyes of..." I said before the vertigo hit me.

The jungle quickly encroached and once again the ruins of Palenque stood before us. Gone was the clarity of the city of L'akam Ha. Gone was Chac Tun B'alam.

I glanced over to Montoya; he still clutched the scepter. Juan pulled at my hand to get my attention.

"Señor Barry," Juan said. "Again you scare me with this magic world you take me to."

"Magic, shit," Lucia spat. "What kind of hocus pocus you pulling here? I don't do drugs and that was one hell of a trip."

"Better yet," Emil started. "How about you all explain the language the four of you were muttering to one another. I couldn't figure out anything you said..." He patted his camera. "But I got it all on tape. At least I didn't lose my focus."

Lucia twirled and faced Emil. "Let me see what you got. Maybe it will be useful." She moved closer to peer into the small viewer.

Montoya and I quickly joined her and four adults stared at the screen, watching as we spoke our parts in the performance a few minutes earlier.

Emil stood there playing with his camera, adjusting buttons. We watched a static-laden screen filled with snowy images and a squealing sound track. I had managed to make out Lucia, and then Montoya popped on the screen. I knew this because I'd participated; to others it would be no more than shadowy non-descriptive figures bouncing in and out of focus.

"What the f..." Emil yelped. "I swear you guys were

93

talking some sort of gibberish. I didn't understand a single word."

"Well this won't be of any use," Lucia said. She looked about the group. "We did see the same thing, right? Chac Tun B'alam?"

I looked at my watch. My stomach growled; I was hungry. Ten after twelve. Almost another two hours had been lost.

"So what are you two going to do next?" Lucia asked.

"I want to verify my findings at the Temple of Inscriptions," Montoya said while looking at me in a sheepish way.

I nodded my head in agreement. "Me, too."

"I will stay with señor Barry," Juan said and stood close to me.

Something again niggled at my memory. I could see Juan in the dream and wondered about the tunic he wore. It was him, yet he appeared slightly different. I frowned.

"Well I'm going back to the station," Lucia said. "Got a little research of my own to do." She glanced over at me. "K'ul'ulkan, eh? This story gets better every minute, just too damned bad I can't get a frigging handle on it." She glared directly at Montoya. "But I will and you know I will."

"That, Miss Camal, I am quite sure," Montoya said. "Be very careful with the knowledge you discover."

"C'mon, Lucia," Emil whispered. "Let these two whack jobs go play their games." He tugged at her arm, pulling her back with him in his retreat.

Lucia jerked her arm out of his grasp and stormed back to us, standing firmly in front of Montoya. "You said you were a doctor and I respected your professionalism," she hissed. "You have your doctorate in archeology, Mayan archeology." Lucia planted her hands on her hips. "How many items have you stolen from these digs? What secrets have you gleaned you won't share with your colleagues? Very few in your particular field are as rich as you apparently are."

Montoya cast a side-glance at her. "I come from a wealthy family, Miss Camal. Seems you haven't done all your research, yet." He stepped around her. "Now, if you will excuse me, it seems I have more treasures to steal, as you are so quick to accuse."

I stood there totally perplexed. I had seen Montoya's residence. He did, in fact, appear to be quite well to do. Also, many artifacts appeared, on the surface, to be authentic and priceless. Now I questioned if they were replicas or real.

Montoya stopped and turned to face me.

"Barry, if you feel I have misled you, please feel free to join Miss Camal on the return trip to Palenque."

A small hand grabbed mine. "I believe him, señor Barry. I think he is honest man."

"What makes you think that, Juan?" I asked.

"A sign. You see Quetzal bird there?" He pointed at the bright bird with the twin long tail feathers that sat in the tree above us. "It is the bird of great leaders. See the blue green feathers? They are for royal family only. We put our faith in leaders. Señor Montoya is leader, yes?"

The Quetzal, at that particular moment, spread its wings and lifted from the branch and flew up to hide in the lush growth above. I stared down at the small lad. For one so young, he continued to amaze me with his great insight into the human psyche. If a small child could see this much, how could I not agree? I slightly clenched my hand around his and followed Montoya.

"So, Barry, do you think Miss Camal will be doing her research? I am willing to bet she is already searching for our names – especially K'inich Janahb' Pacal."

I grunted my agreement and followed him to the Temple of Inscriptions. The palace already had become busy with tourists milling about the different levels in the high mid-day sun. I shook my head, the morning had started out simple enough then without warning, time passed in the blink of an eye. I let my mind wander about the character of Chac Tun B'alam and realized how suddenly overdressed I felt in my short sleeved shirt and khaki pants. I felt this overwhelming desire to be dressed in the harness and feathers of K'ul'ulkan. A shiver coursed through me.

"Is there a problem?" Juan asked looking up at me with those dark brown, innocent eyes.

I smiled down at him. "No problems," I said.

The world shifted.

Chapter 15:
Chac Tun B'alam

Mayan Date: 13 Cib 19 Mac ~ 12.19.19.17.16

*Chac Tun B'alam watched the shadow people who,
only mere moments earlier, had been Ah Pukuh and
K'ul'ulkan. He knew he could touch them but now,
once more, they were of the shadows. If he,
Chac Tun B'alam but had the Eyes of Pacal
and the Conscience of Pacal.
They were shadows no more! They were back.*

*Thoughts of Chac Tun B'alam
Ruler of L'akam Ha*

Palenque Ruins: 12:25p.m., Monday, December 17, 2012

Again, like earlier in the morning when I first arrived I could hear the howler monkeys, a myriad of birds and insects. The sounds once more assailed me then the jungle was gone. I stood in the main plaza by the palace. I was again in L'akam Ha. It was a Shangri-La except I wasn't the haphazard tourist who accidentally fell from the sky. I was an American private detective who was hallucinating in the jungle heat. *"Perhaps I have malaria,"* I thought.

"That man is coming again," Juan whispered.

I looked up and saw Chac Tun B'alam coming toward us. I was a few steps behind and to Montoya's right. He motioned me to join him, but then said, "Wait."

Chac Tun B'alam walked majestically toward us, his gait strong. There was no doubt he was a leader. The air about him radiated his rightful arrogance.

"Lord Ah Pukuh and Lord K'ul'ulkan," Chac Tun B'alam said. He bent to one knee and bowed his head to us. "Forgive my outbursts. It has been many k'atun since last you walked with us. I am honored for you to walk with me at this time of ending." He stood.

"Is it not written we shall join you at the final Bak'tun?" Montoya asked.

I shot a questioning look to Montoya. Exactly where was he going with this?

"It is written, Lord Ah Pukuh," Chac Tun B'alam replied.

"Show me your words," Montoya said and spread his arm slowly out to indicate the chief should lead the way.

I held tightly to Juan's hand; I could feel his nervousness. I smiled down at him.

"Is this the child sacrifice you desire, Lord K'ul'ulkan?"

I had been gawking elsewhere and hadn't noticed Chac Tun B'alam approach me. He now snatched Juan's hand from mine. He had already motioned for one of his henchmen to approach. Juan struggled and fought to get loose. Chac Tun B'alam was raising his hand to strike at Juan.

"An honor is bestowed upon you, child. Do not disgrace yourself," the chief said to a screaming Juan. His hand came down. "You are in the presence of Lord K'ul'ulkan."

"No!" I yelled.

My hand grabbed Chac Tun B'alam's wrist in mid-air and

held it from striking Juan's face. I could tell my eyes held anger and my voice carried a conviction I was sure the chief had never heard spoken to him before. He was the ultimate decision-maker; obviously no one had stopped him from performing an action before. There was a hesitation, a quick questioning glance, then he dropped to one knee. I let go of his wrist.

"I beg forgiveness, Lord K'ul'ulkan. I only wish to serve and please you."

I didn't know exactly what to do but figured a bit of amnesty might help. Stretching out my arm, I rested my hand on his shoulder and firmly gripped the man before me.

"Your eagerness to serve is noted," I said and smiled at him then quickly took Juan's hand back in mind. "This child is not for sacrifice."

"As you wish, Lord K'ul'ulkan." He looked at Juan and his eyes widened. "I did not know," he whispered. "Now I understand."

Chac Tun B'alam again bowed his head before standing up. He stared at Juan and quickly motioned to dismiss the henchman. He slowly glanced about the plaza to see who had seen me reprimand him.

"There is no need for a sacrifice," Montoya said. "We are here to help you. Have you not been requesting K'inich Ahau's aid?"

Chac Tun B'alam eye's flashed wide and a smile slowly curled the sides of his lips. "You were sent by Lord K'inich Ahau? My prayers have been answered."

"Again, show me the words," Montoya said and motioned for him to lead us.

Perhaps Montoya was enjoying this display of godhood but I was starting to get nervous. A glimpse, a short moment of possible lunacy was fine but we were now living the parts. I looked at my watch then realized such an item wouldn't exist in this world. Chac Tun B'alam led us to the Temple of Inscriptions and began the trudge up the steps leading to the top. My stomach growled and the chief turned at the sound.

"Again I fail you," he said. "The gods visit me and I lack the courtesy of a meal." He clapped his hands and sent one of his men racing down the steps toward the palace. "They will return with a meal and tonight–" He guardedly watched us. "If you remain, I will have a large feast prepared in your honor."

"Time moves mysteriously," Montoya said. "We may or may not stay. We may or may not return."

"As it is," Chac Tun B'alam replied calmly. "Come."

He led us into the temple, grabbed a burning torch and headed down the steps to where K'inich Janahb' Pacal lay. He pointed into the tomb at a nearby shelf.

"There is where the Eyes of Pacal and the Conscience of Pacal resided as commanded by the words of K'inich Janahb' Pacal. Now they are gone yet you, Lord Ah Pukuh, I see have the Eyes of Pacal."

"At the proper time, Chief Chac Tun B'alam, I will return the Eyes of Pacal to you."

The chief nodded and then turned to the wall opposite the tomb and placed the torch in a holder. He then put his hands on a matching set of glyphs on the wall near the torch holder. He pushed, straining his muscles. I watched his arms tighten and the arms bulge in the strength he used to move the block back.

Suddenly there was a click, a faint but still deliberate sound. The wall opposite K'inich Janahb' Pacal's tomb moved, sliding slowly to the right. A small opening, an entrance, to a hidden room opened.

"Come," the chief said and stepped into the dark opening. I saw the torch lift and suddenly another torch was aflame. I stepped into the room and pulled Juan behind me. Chac Tun B'alam walked across the flickering darkness and put the torch in a holder there.

Montoya was following me; I could hear his breathing. "My god," he whispered. "The lost treasures of Pacal. I thought them only to be legend."

I could see items in the glowing light. Polished jade and turquoise reflected and glittered in the flickering flames. Headdresses of gold and iridescent feathers lined the shelves. I watched Montoya walk over and reverently touch a breastplate of jade beads; obviously the old chief hadn't worn it for war. It was then I noticed Chac Tun B'alam. I could see the clouds of doubt and question in his eyes.

"You wanted to see the words?" he asked when he noted I was looking at him. "Behold!"

He held a smaller unlit torch. He lifted it to the flames of the large torch and it burst into fire. Chac Tun B'alam moved it to the wall. "It is written," he said and his hand moved across the glyphs.

At the time of no time
In the alignment of the stars
A girl of innocence
Will bring a new beginning

"I have heard words very similar," I said before realizing who all was listening.

"What does that mean?" Chac Tun B'alam asked. "These are the words of Lord K'inich Ahau, spoken to K'inich Janahb' Pacal. Were you not there, Lord K'ul'ulkan?"

"Let K'inich Ahau smile on us," Montoya said and headed for the exit.

It was a subtle hint but one that Chac Tun B'alam understood. He doused the small torch then reached for the larger one. I followed Montoya out of the room and could hear the chief dousing the second torch. Then there was a faint clicking sound. Chac Tun B'alam stepped out of the room and the stone wall moved back into place.

"Señor Barry," Juan whispered. "I think Lupe's mama will be worried."

Suddenly we were standing in the dark shadows at the bottom of stairwell. Gone was the weight of the headdress and the flutter of feathers. We were still in the Temple of Inscriptions, just outside the tomb of Pacal. Juan ran up the stairs and slipped under the cord that barred tourists from attempting to go down the perilous steps to K'inich Janahb' Pacal's tomb. Montoya and I tread carefully up the steps, attempting to keep as quiet as possible so as not to be noticed by the authorities. I breathed deeply the fresh air when I reached the top and noted the lowness of the sun. My stomach growled loudly. I looked at my watch. Five forty-seven. Over five hours had passed while we were with Chac Tun B'alam.

"I very hungry, too, señor Barry," Juan said. He stood there rubbing circles over his stomach. "Can we get fajitas?"

"Fajitas, eh? Take care of your young cohort then join me at my home later tonight," Montoya said. "I'll drop you off at the hotel. I need to research this Conscience and Eyes of Pacal our young chief has mentioned."

Chapter 16:
Meeting With Lucia

Mayan Date: 13 Cib 19 Mac ~ 12.19.19.17.16

*Chac Tun B'alam watched the gods disappear to once
more walk with the shadow people. His eyes narrowed.
Why would Ah Pukuh and K'ul'ulkan wish to see
the words? Why did Ah Pukuh touch
K'inich Janahb' Pacal's items.
Were they truly gods?*

*Thoughts of Chac Tun B'alam
Ruler of L'akam Ha*

Palenque: 7:32p.m., Monday, December 17, 2012

Montoya dropped me off in front of the hotel. Juan had
pointed at a corner that he said was close to Benita's house. I
was a bit reluctant, but let him go. Now, I was watching for
him as we approached the hotel to see if Juan was anywhere to
be seen. He had said he wanted fajitas but suddenly decided he
wanted to go home. I didn't see him lurking about, so I figured
he had to be with Lupe and her mom. Montoya was all a-

103

twitter about what Chac Tun B'alam had shown us. He hoped to go back tomorrow and see if he could find the correct glyphs and open the secret room. I wasn't as excited by that since we seem to have a good working relationship with Chac Tun B'alam and I didn't see any reason to jeopardize it. I was still haunted by Chac Tun B'alam's questioning look while we were in the secret chamber.

"See you later," I said and stepped out of the car.

"About nine," Montoya said. "I think I have an idea of what the Conscience of Pacal is but I'm not positive." He leaned over and stared up at me. "This is all very exciting. Do you have any idea what we have done for archeology today?"

"Do you realize I should be arresting you and dragging your ass back to the museum?"

"Ah, Barry, you devil you." He smiled. "You do believe me."

I shut the door and tapped the top of the car. "See you later."

Montoya sped off and I slowly stretched my arms and realized just how tired I was. Meandering over to the doorman, I asked in the best Spanish and sign language I could muster.

"Moi." I pointed to myself and then placed my hand out at about Juan's height. "Amigo? Juan?" I pointed down at the ground. "Here?"

"Si, señor."

I shook my head wishing I knew more Spanish than I did. Juan was a lot more helpful to me; I had to admit that.

"His friend and her momma stood over there for a long time until the newspeople came and Miss Camal talked with him."

I stared blankly at the man before me.

"Si, señor, I speak English pretty good. Your Spanish is very bad. Moi? I believe it to be French."

"So, Lucia Camal did pick him up here this morning?"

He shook his head. "She asked me if I knew where you were. I did not. Then Juan told her that you had an appointment with Dr. Montoya last night."

"You seem to know quite a bit of what happened this morning." I looked at his badge. "Diego."

"Gracias, señor. Very few call me by my name. Miss Camal went in and spoke with Charita then asked Juan if he wanted to go with them to find you. They left together."

I stroked my chin thoughtfully. Lucia definitely was doing the footwork on this story and keeping tabs on every possible angle. She didn't strike me as the type who would settle for 'this is what I have, go with it.' She'd dig. Now I wondered exactly what she'd learned about our ghostly chief and the names he'd called us. I thanked Diego and headed for the restaurant; suddenly I was starving and a slight scent of something absolutely delicious wafted through the small shutter doors as a couple left for an evening stroll.

A quick glance at the menu and I ordered. The dining room was even more magical in the evening with small lights flickering in amongst the lush growth of the enclosed patio. Candles were being lighted on shelves and adding even more ambiance. My waitress brought a plate with heavenly aromas preceding it and my mouth began watering. She put the dish down and I stared at the two glazed pork chops before me. A pineapple and mango chutney cascaded between the chops and even the small pile of salad greens with tossed fruits looked inviting. She placed the tall fluted glass with white wine to the side. I breathed in deeply the scents, picked up the knife and fork, then felt the knife slide through the meat effortlessly. It was melt-in-your-mouth tender and blended with the juices of the chutney to slide down my throat. I was in heaven.

From my vantage point I could see a television; I couldn't hear it but I saw flashes of images and Mayan ruins. I didn't recognize any of them and then finally saw the words on the screen: Chitzen Itza. They kept showing the crowds and I got the impression as time was quickly approaching, mobs were starting to form at the great pyramids there. My mind wandered and suddenly I realized that each day there appeared to be more and more people at the ruins of Palenque. I smiled. If the public knew what I had learned the last few days, they wouldn't be gathering in Chitzen Itza but here instead. Still more images on the television flashed up showing a tent city at the ruins fo Chitzen Itza.

Finally, with my appetite sated and my stomach full, I pushed away from the table and enjoyed watching the faintest of sunlight dwindle away to leave only the twinkling miniature lights and candles to shed a soothing glow on the surrounding area.

"Fancy my finding the great god, K'ul'ulkan eating," Lucia said. She strutted up to my table, pulled back the opposite chair and sat down.

Her dark blue blouse and skirt blended into the shadows, her tanned skin and black hair glistened in the glow of the surrounding light; but it was her eyes that truly caught my attention. They were shimmering pools of amber, golden flicks dancing in the wavering candlelight. I was lost in the moment. I knew I had to be tired and exhausted but now that she was here. Suddenly, I was revived.

"What do you mean great god?"

"You, Detective Hargrove, are being considered by Chac Tun B'alam to be the reincarnation of K'ul'ulkan. The great feathered serpent god. I did my research like I promised I would. The strangest part of the K'ul'ulkan mythology is he was Caucasian."

"You mean white?" I asked.

"Other than being a tad short of K'ul'ulkan's mythic six foot stature and long flowing hair, Detective Hargrove, you meet the basic requirements in Chac Tun B'alam's eyes."

"I hardly doubt that, Miss Camal," I chastised. "To make things easier, how about you call me Barry and I'll call you Lucia?"

She knitted her brows together in a small frown. The flickering amber dwindled away.

"Is there a problem? I just thought it would be easier for us to talk."

I watched as Lucia nervously rubbed her index finger back and forth on the tablecloth. It was obvious she was thinking and considering. I realized she deliberated all decisions; some fast, some slower. This was a slow choice. I waited.

"Fine, Barry," she finally said. "Remember, I want to keep this professional at all times. Just because we are on first name terms doesn't mean we're buddy-buddy." I watched the flickering amber return to her eyes.

I reared back and frowned at her. *"Professional?"* I thought. "Have I in some way indicated to you anything less than professional?" Then I remembered my first encounter with Montoya and how I was hesitant to call him Adam.

The waitress hustled to the table, noted my finished plate and politely slid it off the table. "Would you like coffee? For two?"

"Two, I said. Black for me." I turned to Lucia. "How do you like your coffee, Lucia?"

She stiffened at my familiarity then relaxed. "Black will be fine," she said, hesitated, then added more instructions, but this time in Spanish.

"Si, si, señorita Camal," the waitress said and quickly stepped away.

I cocked my head and gave Lucia a questioning look. "And?"

"I asked for a little chocolate and other things to be slivered into the coffee." She looked at me. "It is a modern Mayan treat. I was bold and changed your order."

"Dr. Montoya introduced me to some Mayan delicacies last night," I said. I stifled a yawn. "Forgive my rudeness, Lucia. It was a long night with him and I've had very little sleep." I stared blankly at the empty table before me. "By the way, have you had an evening meal? I wasn't thinking. Would you like to order something?" I raised my hand to call the waitress back.

She smiled at me. "No, please..." there was a hesitation. "Barry." Lucia dropped her eyes. "I caught a quick bite on the way over here. I was sort of in a hurry."

The waitress returned with the coffee and again my olfactory senses were assaulted with scents arising from the cup. I leaned over and inhaled deeply.

"Coffee with chocolate, chilies and vanilla," Lucia whispered. "Taste it."

I remembered the experience from the night before at Montoya's home and picked up the cup to eagerly pull it to my lips in anticipation of the taste sensations. I sipped. The flavors exploded in my mouth and down my throat with the heat of the chilies playing with my neck muscles; I felt them constricting. The chocolate soothed, the vanilla softened and I breathed.

Placing both elbows on the table, I held my cup close to my mouth and inhaled the scents.

"Last night Montoya's staff made taz... tasca..." I shook my head trying to remember.

"Tascalate?" Lucia asked.

I nodded.

"Very tasty, indeed," she said then sipped from her cup. "I hope you like this."

I closed my eyes and slowly nodded my head. How could I not like it? A beautiful woman, a tasty drink, evening shadows, twinkling lights and ambient candle lighting. What more could any man ask for?

Lucia frowned, then smiled, leaned her head to one side

and gazed at me; her long, dark hair cascaded over her shoulder and her brown eyes once more caught the highlights of the burning candles. Music played softly in the background. I gazed at Lucia.

What more could any man want echoed again in my head.

Chapter 17:
Morning Surprises

Mayan Date: 1 Caban 0 Kankin ~ 12.19.19.17.17

Chac Tun B'alam watched the night sky and
Saw the stars shifting in their paths. He could
see the alignment coming; it was near.
Chac Tun B'alam knew the Eyes of Pacal and
the Conscience of Pacal would guide him to the
final Batun. The stars continued on their way.

Thoughts of Chac Tun B'alam
Ruler of L'akam Ha

Palenque: 6:11 a.m., Tuesday, December 18, 2012

The sound of running water from the bathroom awoke me. I turned on the bed to look; the door was closed but a woman's voice softly sang on the other side. My head hurt but I didn't feel like I had a hangover.

The door opened and Lucia walked out.

"Oh! You're up," she said. Her cheeks flushed. "I hope I didn't wake you. I was trying to be quiet."

I rubbed my forehead and pulled the blanket over my waist. The sheet had covered me but it was apparent Lucia was embarrassed by my situation. My mind raced to remember the night. We'd sat and talked at the table then moved to the enclosed patio. She'd ordered some sort of concoction that tasted very fruity but I knew it had to carry one hell of a wallop. Then we'd switched to wine and from that point, my mind went blank. I remembered a kiss but couldn't remember if it was in my wishful dreams or reality. I looked up. Lucia was in my room.

"Last night must have been good," I said in a monotone voice. I wanted to be as noncommittal as possible, since I couldn't remember anything of the night before.

"You passed out, Barry," Lucia said. "I had one of the waiters assist me getting you to your room. It was late. You were out cold and I had him put you in bed. I removed your shoes... and your shirt. The rest, for modesty purposes, I had performed by the waiter."

"But you're here," I said.

"You slept there," she said and pointed at the bed I was in. "I slept on the couch." She pointed to the lounge area side of the room.

I glanced out to where she pointed and could see the pillow and blankets there. I glanced about my bed – one pillow. I'd definitely slept alone.

"Now I need to get to work. Well, actually, back to my apartment, and then to work." She stepped back, analyzing me. "Did you actually mean what you said last night?"

My mind raced to find something, anything that could possibly be recalled about a conversation.

"You said you wanted me to come with you to Montoya's place today?" Lisa sat down on the edge of the bed.

"I said that?" I asked. "Don't see why you can't go. You going to bring your news staff with you?"

"If you want Emil and Maribel along, I can get them onboard without a hitch. Cameras, too."

"Pick me up at ten?" I took a deep breath. "Actually, pick *us* up at ten. I'm sure Juan will be with me." I smiled.

"See you at ten, Barry," Lucia said and mussed my hair. "Did you know that Juan likes breakfast fajitas?"

I laughed. "Very much. So, I'm guessing I was a perfect gentleman last night?"

Lucia stood by the door. "Yes." She opened it. "Now, get out of bed and clean up."

"Join me tonight for supper?" I asked.

"Would seven be agreeable?"

I nodded my head and watched Lucia disappear behind the closing door. The door clicked and I tossed the blanket and sheet back to get out of bed. I still had my slacks on. My guess was the waiter had his limits, too. I dropped the last of my clothing and headed for the shower.

Palenque: 7:41 a.m., Tuesday, December 18, 2012

Diego was standing duty when I strolled outside to wait for Juan. It was past seven thirty and in less than five minutes I saw Juan strolling toward us. Benita and Lupe were with him. He saw me and immediately starting waving frantically, then dashed toward me.

I nodded a greeting to Benita and Lupe.

"Would you like to join us for breakfast?" I looked at Benita. "I enjoy adult company."

Juan translated what I said and I saw Benita's cheeks flush in embarrassment.

"What did you tell her?" I asked and ruffled Juan's hair.

Diego came to my rescue and spoke in a flurry of words. Benita smiled and thanked him. She turned to me.

"Si, señor Barry. I like fajitas."

We headed to the restaurant and the waitress quickly seated us. Between bites of fabulous breakfast fajitas with extra scrambled eggs, I tried to explain what had occurred the day before. Benita had thought perhaps Juan was not telling her the truth and was creating a fanciful tale to keep him and me out of trouble.

"You? K'ul'ulkan? Si, si." Benita frowned. "Excuse? Usted es un hombre blanco y también lo es K'ul'ulkan. Eso también lo piensa el jefe Maya."

"What did she just say?" I glanced to Juan then stuffed another piece of fajita into my mouth.

"She said you are a white man and so is K'ul'ulkan; the Mayan chief thinks so, too."

Diego strolled into the restaurant and nodded at me before coming to the table.

"Señor, ¿por favor?, I know you here to study the Mayan. I am a follower, as is..." he nodded at Benita. "We are followers of the new priest, Ah Pukuh. I listen. Last night you spoke with Miss Camal about K'ul'ulkan, Ah Pukuh and the Eyes of Pacal. Do you truly have the Eyes of Pacal?"

"Tell you what, Diego," I started. Suddenly people were coming out of the woodwork to help me, if that was truly what it was. "Ah Pukuh has the Eyes; I knew the item as the Baton of Time. He stole it from a museum and I am a private detective assigned to locate and bring the item back. That was back..." I stopped to think; it seemed so long ago yet was only a couple of days. "...last week. I've learned about things which I knew nothing about and now have become involved with trying to save humanity according what your Ah Pukuh has taught me."

"The time is coming, señor Hargrove. It is necessary for the Eyes to be made available to our chief. Do you know where Ah Pukuh lives?" Diego asked.

I absently nodded my head. Diego and Benita conversed

quickly in hushed tones. Benita seemed somewhat defeated yet Diego was energetic in his speech. He turned his attention back to me.

"You must take Benita with you and retrieve the Eyes of Pacal. Our shaman talks with Chac Tun B'alam. Give the Eyes to him and he will make sure Chac Tun B'alam receives the Eyes of Pacal. This must be performed before December 21st or our chief will not be able to properly lead us to the new time." Diego stepped back from the table. "I have been too forward and beg your pardon." He bowed and quietly slipped away.

"¿Por favor?" Benita said. She stretched across the table and placed her hands over mine. "Es necesario que hagas esto, mi amigo."

I looked to Juan who had lost interest in the conversation and whispered with Lupe.

"Hey, Juan, what did Lupe's mother say?"

He spoke to Benita and I figured it was to ask what she had said; she spoke and Juan interpreted. "She said they need your help."

I grabbed Juan to make sure I had his full attention. "Okay, buddy, this is very important and I don't want you to screw up the translation. Comprende?"

Juan's eyes were wide. I'd never really used a stern voice with him before.

"Tell her to take Lupe and wait at her home." Juan started translating. "At ten this morning, Miss Camal will pick up you and me. We will go to the house of Ah Pukuh and I will attempt to get the Eyes of Pacal."

Juan finished then looked to me to see if I had more to say. When I said nothing, he spoke. "I told Lupe's momma exactly what you said."

Benita said something. Juan nodded his head.

"She says she will go home and wait. She thanks you for helping the Mayan people to find their heritage and their future." He waited, watching me.

"Gracias," I said. "More coffee?"

Benita declined, thanked me profusely for breakfast, then grabbed Lupe's hand and left the restaurant and hotel. Juan and I saw them to the front door and stood with Diego while we watched them walk down the street.

"You will not help?" Diego asked.

"I am going to help but not sure exactly how I am going to do it," I said. "But I do know I have to do it in my own manner. Comprende?"

"Si," Diego said. "I was not right to ask your aid. You are a guest and I am employee here."

"Diego," I said. "I am helping you. Tonight I wish to talk with you in my room. Is that possible? Around eight?"

He nodded his head excitedly. "Oh, si, señor Hargrove. Eight is fine." He hesitated, suddenly acting more like an awkward schoolchild. "May I bring Benita?"

Surprised, I absently nodded my head in agreement. Finally I found my tongue. "I think it would be good. Your English is..." I let the sentence go unfinished as I felt Juan's fingers tighten in my hand. "If I am not here at eight, just wait. Please?"

I turned to Juan. "Do you want to wait here? I need to get some things from my room and make a very important phone call."

Juan glanced at Diego. "I will go with you, señor Barry."

Palenque: 9:06 a.m., Tuesday, December 18, 2012

The hotel operator was efficient and quickly connected me with the international operator. It didn't take long for the operators to connect me.

"This is Dr. Martinez," he said. The familiar soft voice made me smile.

"This is Detective Hargrove," I replied. "Considering the..."

"Where the hell have you been?" he yelled. "I've been attempting to contact you since Saturday. Is this how you deal with all your clients?"

"I take it you didn't get my message I was in Mexico?"

"Mr. Hargrove," Martinez said. "I have more..."

The pronunciation and drama he used in speaking assured me it was more that just a snide commentary. I wasn't happy.

"That is *Detective* Hargrove, Dr. Martinez." I cut him off and raised my voice. "You sent me in search of some silly relic. I know where it is and hope to have it in my grasp by no later than this Friday."

My pacing the room didn't help to calm me. Juan sat quietly in the chair; he wasn't going to chance my anger.

"Well, Detective, since Miss Camal's last broadcast, we really have no use for your services any longer. She announced to the world that your buddy, Montoya, has the real Baton of Time and the two of you are validating its purpose. We've already started proceedings against your friend, Dr. Montoya." He hesitated. "Yes, I've contacted the police about this."

My legs weakened and my butt dropped onto the bed; I sat there totally stunned. One, Lucia had never mentioned any of her broadcasts or that I was in them. Two, had I moved to the other side? Was I really a *buddy* of Dr. Montoya?

"Dr. Martinez," I started. "I believe I owe you an apology and..."

"Consider yourself terminated, Mr. Hargrove," Martinez yelled.

For a flighty, nervous Nellie type of person, he had suddenly found gumption and less tact than I remembered. There was no doubt about that when he called me 'Mister' instead of 'Detective.'

"I was going to ask if you knew what..."

"Good day, Mr. Hargrove. The museum will cover your expenses through today but from midnight tonight, any debts incurred will be of your own restitution. Enjoy Mexico."

The phone clicked loudly when he slammed it down.

Fired. I'd never been fired before. My mind was numb.

"Is everything not good, señor Barry?"

I looked over at Juan huddled in the chair by the window. Knees pulled up, arms locked around them and his chin resting atop; he was scared.

"I'm fine, Juan. Just fine." I knew I had to get things done, especially since Martinez was such a snit and hadn't allowed me to ask my question. Something told me in the long run I was going to come out of this with a better understanding than even Martinez could ever have anticipated. I grabbed my laptop and waited for the connection to the internet. "Let me see what we can find online, eh Juan?"

Juan slid off the chair and stood beside me at the table. "What do you look for?"

"I'm going to do a quick search for K'ul'ulkan, Ah Pukuh and Conscience of Pacal, little guy. Everyone around me seems to know more about this than I do, even your ghostly Mayan chief, Chac Tun B'alam. I bet his name translates into something like Me Big Chief."

"Chac Tun B'alam," Juan repeated the name. "It means Red Stone Jaguar. Jaguar very strong." He growled and pretended to scratch with claws in the space between us. "Red is strong. Stone is strong. Jaguar is strong. This chief very strong and wise."

"Yeah, right," I said. My voice was distant as I scrolled the results of the search. "Will you look at this? There is a crap load of stuff about 2012 out here."

I punched keys, I read, I learned. Glancing at my watch I noticed it was almost time for Lucia Camal to show up. I was ready. This time I hoped to have the upper hand.

"Ready to go, Juan?"

"Lupe's momma say I tell you all truth." Once more Juan was sitting in the chair by the window, hands folded neatly on his lap and a very concerned look on his face.

"Can you tell me the truth later? We really need to get a move on." I held the door open for us to leave and motioned for him to get a hustle on.

"She say I tell you soon or she tell you and I no help you." Juan remained in the chair, head down.

Well," I said and closed the door. I walked quickly across the room and kneeled before him. "What is so important you must reveal it to me before we leave?" I placed my fingers below his chin and lifted his face so I could see his eyes. It was then I noticed the tear trickling down his cheek. "Hey, what's the problem, little buddy? Did your uncle find you?"

"He no uncle," Juan said, his voice cracked. "I no tell you the truth."

My stomach dropped. Something told me I was going to be in more trouble than I could imagine. My mind raced to guess how many laws I might have broken.

"Lupe's momma is my real aunt," Juan said softly. "Lupe is my cousin."

I sighed relief. My room phone rang startling me. I grabbed the handset.

"Hello?"

"I thought you'd be waiting outside when we got here," Lucia said. "Get your butt down here. Now!" She hung up.

"Let's go," I said to Juan and grabbed his hand and pulled him from the chair.

"There is more," he said.

"Later, Juan," I said. "Miss Camal is waiting for us. There is much to do today. Okay? We can talk later."

Juan quietly nodded in agreement.

Chapter 18:
More Surprises

Mayan Date: 1 Caban 0 Kankin ~ 12.19.19.17.17

*"O Mighty K'inich Ahau, I call upon you for guidance.
I offer you my blood. You have sent me Ah Pukuh and
K'ul'ulkan. Are they truly the gods I have been taught?
The days are less; help me."*

*Prayer of Chac Tun B'alam
Ruler of L'akam Ha*

Palenque: 10:37 a.m., Tuesday, December 18, 2012

Emil pulled into the cobblestone plaza of Montoya's home. In the daylight I could see it was more of an estate than a small house. I'd come at night, and even though there had been plenty of decorative lighting, I was intrigued by the spaciousness of the hacienda called home by Dr. Montoya. Blooming hibiscus in shades of coral stood before a backdrop of an unknown vine with white flower clusters. In front, studded every six feet was a beautifully attended white rose bush. In the dark, I'd only noticed shrubs and lights.

A bird's beautiful warbling caught my attention and I turned to see it in the fountain. I watched it flit and hop about the three-tiered splashing fount of water in the center of the court. More roses, this time in shades of deep red, circled the fountain. The small amount of grass was well trimmed.

Lucia wasted no time hustling me to the front door.

"Let's get on with this," she said and rang the doorbell.

I glanced at her and hoped my frown indicated my concern. "What is your problem today?"

"Nothing," she said and looked down at the walkway. "I just have a lot on my mind right now."

"So do I and don't need this attitude. Is it about last night?"

"Oh?" Emil asked.

Juan and Maribel watched us. The door opened.

"Buenos dias." Ix'iloom said. "Ah, Señor Hargrove. Por favor! Come in. Come in." She waved us in with her illusive smile that made Mona Lisa appear like a grinning idiot.

"Is Dr. Montoya in his office?" I asked.

Suddenly a little hand gripped mine and held tight. I smiled reassuringly down at Juan.

"No. Un minuto." Ix'iloom held up her index finger. "Un minuto." She hustled over to a small table and retrieved an envelope lying there. She held it out for me. "Para usted."

"She says it is for you, Señor Barry," Juan whispered.

I took the envelope and noted it was not sealed. I slipped the flap out and retrieved the folded note from inside. I read the scribbled note from Montoya.

"Es del Dr. Montoya," Ix'iloom said. She held her hands together in front of her white apron, very prim and proper.

"She says it's from Montoya," Lucia said then turned her attention to Ix'iloom. "¿A dónde está el Dr. Montoya?"

"No sé, Señorita Camal."

I looked down at Juan.

"Miss Camal asked where Dr. Montoya was and the other lady said he is gone."

"You can question her all you want, Lucia," I said. "I don't think she is going to give you any more information. If she does know where Dr. Montoya has went, she won't betray him and I'm more inclined to believe she doesn't know." I held the note in the air, waving it gently. "He has gone in search of the Conscience of Pacal."

Ix'iloom, ever stoic, fought a curling of the left side of her lips. She may have even been part of his research to understand what the item truly was.

"So, folks, let's go home," I said and motioned them back out the door. "Dr. Montoya will not arrive back until late tomorrow." I hesitated a moment. "If he can do it that fast."

Lucia stopped at the entrance, turned and faced me. "How do you know that? And what you do you mean by that crack?"

"Because he says so in his note. Here, read it."

She snatched it out of my hand and read the quickly written, barely legible words.

Gone to get 2nd part of Pacal.
Back tomorrow night, cops willing.

"What the hell does 'cops willing' mean, Barry?" she asked.

I opened the door and ushered them through the opening, the cool air of the hacienda rushing out into the warming day. "Simple," I said. "He has gone to retrieve what he feels to be the other half which Chac Tun B'alam mentioned yesterday."

"And the cops willing?" Emil repeated. "You haven't explained that."

I deadpanned a glare at Emil. "If he don't get caught," I said. "What did you think it meant?" I massaged my forehead. "Take me back to my hotel. I need to get things packed and

121

find a new place to stay." I glanced at Lucia. "Since you were so eager to broadcast the event, my client has terminated my services. So, for all practical purposes, I no longer have a job or income." I smiled at Lucia hoping to not scare her away since I still thought there might be a chance between us. "I'm a simple man with simple needs."

"You can't blame me for this," Lucia said. "I'm a reporter and the news is the news."

"Fine," I said. "Just get me back to my hotel. I'll figure it out." Maybe I was wrong about the connection between us. It wouldn't be the first time I'd misread the opposite sex.

We piled back into the station's van and Emil drove us back to my hotel; an uneventful and very quiet trip. It was nearing noon when he pulled up to the hotel.

"Welcome back, Señor Hargrove," Diego said opening the doors of the van. He pulled down the brim of Juan's ball cap and nodded politely to Lucia and her staff. "If you will, the front desk needs to speak with you."

I knew very well what the problem was. There was no doubt in my mind the museum had notified the hotel of my termination. With Juan in tow, I ambled over to the desk.

"Ah, Mister Hargrove," the young lady said. "We have been notified by Mr. Alvarez Martinez that they will no longer be paying for your accommodations."

"Are they paying through today?" I asked.

"Mr. Martinez was quite adamant your expenses would only be paid through midnight tonight; so yes, they have covered your stay for tonight." She smiled politely at me. "Will you be checking out tomorrow morning?"

My mind raced ahead calculating the expenses. This place wasn't all that expensive and my bank account still had a substantial balance. It wasn't as bad as I originally thought.

"Perhaps I should enjoy a nice evening meal and charge it to my room," I said.

She grinned. "As you wish, Mr. Hargrove."

"I think I will continue to stay here at least another night. Is there a problem with me doing day-to-day extensions?"

"No problem at all, sir. Just keep us informed of your wishes. Do you have a credit card I may use?"

I reached into my hip pocket and got my wallet out. She took the card I offered and made some notations on the computer. "Have a nice day, Mr. Hargrove." She handed me back my card.

I turned and saw Lucia, Emil and Maribel standing with Diego. The van was gone. I motioned for them to come in and join me.

"Just a few details I had to clear up," I said. "Shall we get something to eat? I'm famished." I hesitated a second. "Of course, it will be Dutch. Do you understand what that means?"

Lucia laughed. "Of course we do. It means you're cheap and we have to pay our own way. How about I treat on the station's account?"

Juan pulled on my hand. "Señor Barry? Do I get a dollar today? Will it be enough?"

I winked at him standing there holding his cap then reached into my pocket and handed him a dollar. "You're covered by Miss Camal. Okay? So save your money." I ruffled his hair, which always managed to fall back into place.

Chapter 19:
More Than Research

Mayan Date: 1 Caban 0 Kankin ~ 12.19.19.17.17

"Mighty K'inich Ahau, you are at the height of your travel.
The shadow people still haunt me but Ah Pukuh has not
appeared to make his sacrifice. K'ul'ulkan does not come.
Where are the Eyes and Conscience of Pacal?
Have I failed the gods?"

Prayer of Chac Tun B'alam
Ruler of L'akam Ha

Palenque: 1:37p.m., Tuesday, December 18, 2012

"Everything we've discussed is conjecture," I said. "Until I can confirm what you're telling me, I really don't want to jump to any conclusions."

"Fine!" Lucia said jumping up from the table. "You have a laptop up in your room. We'll go up there and get this all straightened out." Her arm was extended and the index finger pointed to the exit. She took a deep breath. "Emil. Maribel. You two go back to the station and whip up some gibberish for me since the Montoya story isn't going to fly today."

"Hey, Emil," I added. "Could you drop Juan off at his place?" I pulled another dollar out of my wallet and handed to Juan. "You go with them and be back here tomorrow morning for breakfast, okay?"

"But I want to help you, señor Barry."

"Nothing happening today, little guy." I kneeled down to be level with him. "Today I'm just going to enjoy the luxury of doing nothing. Lucia and I are going to do a little research then I'm going just do nothing."

Juan's eyes filled with tears but I was able to brush them away; his pout was another thing. I could tell he was upset but I really wasn't going to need his help. He got up from the table and hugged me.

"Tell your aunt I said hello and if they want to come for breakfast, that will fine." I headed him for the exit. "And no tricks, you hear me?"

Lucia nodded at Emil; he took his queue to depart with Maribel. He reached out to take Juan's hand but Juan pulled away.

"I will walk, it is not far," Juan said and glared at Emil. "I don't need a ride."

"Fine with me," Emil replied. "I'll just tag alongside just to make sure you're safe. I'll even have Maribel drive the van next to us so if you decide to ride, we can just hop in. How's that sound?" Emil glanced back at us as they left the restaurant and winked.

Palenque: 1:55p.m., Tuesday, December 18, 2012

Lucia's nails softly clicked on the laptop keyboard as she searched the internet for any documentation to confirm our suspicions. Perhaps her furious typing was to reinforce her statements made earlier in the day when she spoke of K'inich

125

Janahb' Pacal, the legends and such.

"So why not just type 'pacal' into the engine and see what comes?" I asked.

"I tried that yesterday, idiot," she snapped. The scorn was more than evident. "There were almost a quarter million hits. I'd still be searching for Pacal's world ending prophesy when it happened and still be needing another two or three weeks beyond that to finish."

"So what are you using to search?" I asked.

"I've entered 'Ah Pukuh,' 'K'ul'ulkan,' and 'Mayan calendar myths' with 'Pacal' to see what I will get."

"Well, I checked on K'ul'ulkan this morning," I said. A few stray hairs on Lucia's cheek caught my attention and I gently pushed them back behind her ear with my index finger.

She grabbed my finger, wringing it. "What the hell do you think you're doing?"

I winced in pain and pulled back. "Just some stray hairs," I whispered trying to keep my voice from revealing the real discomfort.

"Fine. Just because I stayed here last night does not mean I'm interested." She let go.

I pointed at the screen. "There. That one. It states Pacal's legacy with references to the Mayan calendar."

Lucia continued to click on the keyboard and leaned in.

Suddenly I was assailed with orchids and vanilla. The scent was heady and I inhaled deeply while realizing the room spun.

"K'ul'ulkan! K'ul'ulkan!"

I opened my eyes and was no longer in the room. A small opening in the trees above me let in the bright sun. Lucia leaned over me shading my eyes yet I could still see the lush growth of the jungle. The sun now framed her braided hair and head in a soft glow. I could tell my eyes were tired and my eyelids wanted to close.

"Now is not the time," she whispered. "Chac Tun B'alam will be coming. You are a god. Do not reveal your mortality to him." She grabbed my hand and held it to her breast. "I am your chosen. Listen to me. I, Sak Ek' Janahb, beseech you."

"My White Star Flower," I said and softly stroked the side of Lucia's face. "I will never leave you." My eyes closed again.

I felt her necklace and then soft, braided hair when she laid her head to my chest to listen for my heartbeat.

"K'ul'ulkan, stand up! It is time. I can hear Chac Tun B'alam coming. Stand up!"

As I raised myself to my feet, the chief strode into the small clearing that we had taken refuge in. He cast a questioning look at me, frowned, and then motioned his attending guards to surround us.

"Where is the one called Yax Ek' K'ahk'? She will soon be needed. The time of no time is coming. The prophesy of K'inich Janahb' Pacal demands her presence as well as the Eyes and Conscience of Pacal."

Lucia moved in front of me, placing herself between Chac Tun B'alam and myself. "When Ah Pukuh returns, so will Yax Ek' K'ahk'."

I pushed Lucia to the side. "I can speak for myself, Sak Ek' Janahb. Who is this Star Fire of Blue-Green you seek? Who is Yax Ek' K'ahk'?"

Chac Tun B'alam stood there, silent. His eyes once more glanced about the open area, checking his guards and the undergrowth. He cast an eye to the sky to watch the sun then raised his hands.

"K'inich Ahau! I beseech you. Before your travel ends, give K'ul'ulkan back his memories." He glared at me. "You are the god, K'ul'ulkan?" He touched my skin. "You appear as K'ul'ulkan. You must be him."

He dropped his arms to his sides like a beaten man and

hung his head. It was his sigh that made me look at him and wonder.

"K'ul'ulkan," he said and placed a firm hand on my shoulders. "You must find your memories in two nights. On 4 Ahau 3 Kankin you must assist Yax Ek' K'ahk' with time or Ah Pukuh will devour all and release the Bolontiku. The buried words have spoken. You must remember."

Chac Tun B'alam turned and walked away. His guards quickly gathered and followed him into the jungle as the howler monkeys growled their concerns in the treetops.

Sak Ek' Janahb stood once more before me and I gazed into her eyes. She reached her arms around my neck, our lips meeting in a fervent kiss. She broke and stepped back. "You must remember, K'ul'ulkan," she said.

Again she embraced me. I held her tight and close. This time our kiss did not stop. I felt her long, soft hair in my hands. My mind reeled as we stepped apart.

The room steadied and Lucia stared at the walls, as did I. We were no longer in the jungle but back in my room. She no longer was scantily clad and I no longer wore the trappings of a god.

"This can't be," Lucia whispered. Her eyes searched mine. "What is happening?"

I stepped closer and embraced her. She hesitated then wrapped her arms around me. We kissed, this time with a passion of a love, not of the moment, but of one suppressed over centuries. I had never felt this way about a woman before. My breathing deepened and hands slowly massaged her bare shoulders and moved to caress her breasts.

Chapter 20:
In Search of
Chac Tun B'alam

Mayan Date: 1 Caban 0 Kankin ~ 12.19.19.17.17

"Mighty K'inich Ahau, your journey is over. The shadow people leave yet K'ul'ulkan has not returned. The prophesy will come. As will the Bolontiku."

> Lament of Chac Tun B'alam
> Ruler of L'akam Ha

Palenque: 4:09p.m., Tuesday, December 18, 2012

The drawn curtains filtered the light into the room and the paddle fan above the bed cooled the room. The feather moved in the slight breeze and I leaned over and pulled it from the dried arrangement on the nightstand. Its blue-green colors glistened in the movement as I lay there twirling the small feather between my thumb and index, a smile curling my lips. I rose up and traced the feather down Lucia's cheek, across her jaw and down the length of her beautiful neck. I slowly played a twirling pattern between the mounds of her breast, tickling her.

Lucia placed her arm around my neck and pulled me to her. I bent in and we kissed in the embrace.

"So, this is how it is to be with a god, oh mighty K'ul'ulkan."

"And you are Sak Ek' Janahb, my white star flower," I said. "Promised to me by Chac Tun B'alam."

Lucia turned on the pillow to stare at me, her dark eyes searching mine. "You say the name and it sounds so beautiful to my ears. Am I really your white star flower?"

"You're everything to me," I whispered. "Shall I order room service?"

"Barry," Lucia said. "I think it time to realize you have obligations. You have Diego coming tonight." She pulled the sheet about her and stood up. "I think you two can talk much better if I am not around."

"I have a question," I said. "If you are Sak Ek' Janahb, do you have any idea who Yax Ek' K'ahk' would be?"

Lucia sat down on the bed while adjusting the sheet around her like a sarong.

"I have a better question," Lucia said and smiled. Her eyes twinkled in anticipation. "What did he mean by the buried words have spoken?"

I glanced at my watch. "Get dressed," I demanded. "Hurry. We can still make it to the ruins before it gets dark. I have a hunch and I hope ol' Chac Tun B'alam shows up!"

Lucia stood with the sheet wrapped around her watching me slip back into my clothes.

"Hey, get a move on if you want to go," I said. "I think I have the answer." I buttoned my shirt and started to tuck the tails of it into my pants.

Lucia slid into her blouse and skirt and quickly fluffed her hair with her hands. She slipped into her flats and stood there looking at me. "Ready?"

I hung up the phone and twirled the keys on my finger. "Got the car coming. Time to head out." I bounced quickly over to the door and held it open for her.

"You going to share your secret?" she asked walking out of the room into the hallway.

"Think about the last time at the ruins," I started. "Remember I told you we were down below in the Temple of Inscriptions? He opened the secret chamber. What stands out in your mind?"

We hurried down the hallway and I could see Diego driving the car under the portico. Lucia was frowning in thought as Diego held the car door open for her.

"I promise to be back in time for our meeting," I said to Diego as I got in the car. "If I am running late, just wait for me, okay?"

Diego nodded his head in agreement and I could see him waving at us in the rear view mirror while I drove away.

"Okay, Lucia. Try this. We go down the steps to K'inich Janahb' Pacal's tomb. At the bottom of the steps we turn and there is the entrance to K'inich Janahb' Pacal's room. What do you do? Think of each thing you'd do going into the room."

"Okay, I turn and down some steps to the floor which is stone and... there are steps," she said. "Is that what you mean?"

"Exactly. How many steps are there in the secret chamber?"

Lucia frowned momentarily then her eyes got wide in the realization of the fact. "You never mentioned steps. You said you stepped over the threshold and were in."

"Now you're thinking. Montoya wanted to see the words. Chac Tun B'alam read what he could show us but I think there is more. Remember, he even stated the buried words have spoken."

131

I raced down the rough road to the ruins under the canopy of jungle trees, vines and assorted flowers. The howler monkeys were quiet yet an occasional one could be heard. My mind wandered and I considered the beauty of the moment, the simplicity, the oneness with nature. I was a city dweller; an inhabitant of the steel and cement world where pigeons were the wild creatures. Why was I drawn to this rawness of nature?

"Barry? When we see L'akam Ha in its Mayan splendor, things are as if they were new and maintained. If what you are assuming is true, why would this secret chamber be filled with dirt. It sounds more like an pre-excavation dig?"

I almost stopped the vehicle. Lucia had broken my momentary reverie. She had a point. Why would the chamber have a dirt floor, all the rest had stone? I'd described the room to her and even while I spoke, it never dawned on me.

"We will know shortly," I said and sped the rental car bouncing down the road.

"There!" Lucia shouted. "That was the turnoff."

I slammed on the brakes and revved the wheels in reverse then slowly pulled into the side road and all its ruts. It was slow progress but finally I saw an old pickup and knew we were very close to the workers' entrance. Lucia and I jumped out of the car.

"I hope this works." I glanced about. "Shit! I forgot a shovel, spade, anything I could use to dig with."

Lucia stepped on the rusted running board of the nearby pickup and leaned into the cargo area. "Here," she said. "This should work." She handed me a small spade.

I grabbed the instrument and wondered how she knew it was there.

"Think about it," she said. "Obviously the workers' truck, so I figured it should have at least something useful back there."

I laughed at my stupidity and headed for the temple. The

sun was rushing toward the horizon to finish the day and light would be with us for a short length of time only. Time was running out.

"Oh my god!" Lucia exclaimed. "Up there!" She pointed at the top of the Temple of Inscriptions, where we were headed. "Isn't that him?" She glanced down at herself and then me.

"I see him, too," I said. "But we're not in native garb; we're still in regular clothes."

We rushed up the stairs where Chac Tun B'alam stood waiting for us. He spoke but I didn't understand a word. I looked questioningly at Lucia. She shrugged. Again the chief spoke something in Mayan and pulled a wicked appearing knife from its sheath.

"Lucia, let's go below," I said and turned away from the Mayan chief.

Once more Chac Tun B'alam spoke but this time I understood two of the spoken words: K'inich Ahau and K'ul'ulkan. I turned in time to see him lunge at me. The knife was targeted for my chest but I raised my arm to deflect it. The knife sliced through my arm and into my chest. I could feel the weight of it yet there was no pain. I gazed at my wounds; there were none. No blood, no damage.

Chac Tun B'alam cast the knife aside and fell to his knees. He kneeled there beating his chest and wailing words into the air. The only ones I recognized were again K'inich Ahau and K'ul'ulkan.

I was unsure of what to do and began to place my hand on his forehead. At the last moment I decided instead to place my hand on his heart. My hand felt the sensation of his chest but it continued into the flesh and I could feel the beating of his heart. The sensation was mind-boggling; I could feel the blood of the chief coursing through my palm as I held his heart. The look on Chac Tun B'alam's face told me he could feel my hand, too. There was absolute fear in his eyes. I smiled then removed my hand from inside his body. There was no blood. I touched my forehead, then my chest over my heart and then spread my hand, palm upwards toward him. He slumped back on his legs and stared at the setting sun behind me. His face was ashen.

"K'ul'ulkan," he whispered.

I turned to Lucia. "Let's go," I said. "Not sure what I've done but I'm pretty sure I've established my godhood to him."

I slipped under the ribbon at the top of the stairs and started down toward the tomb of K'inich Janahb' Pacal and the hidden room. Lucia followed. I still carried the shovel and was continually checking to make sure that I wasn't wearing feathers. My shoes scuffled down the steps, with small pebbles chasing their way before me.

The glyphs appeared totally useless to me. I stared at them trying to ascertain which ones Chac Tun B'alam had pressed the day before. I remembered they were mirror images of each other; they had a loopy thing with dots all around it.

"Muyal," Chac Tun B'alam said and pressed the two stones. He had quietly followed us.

As he said the word my mind filled with a blue sky and a single white cloud.

"Cloud?" Lucia whispered beside me. "I saw a blue sky with a cloud."

"Muyal," the chief repeated. "Muyal."

The stone slide back out of the way and the secret chamber was once again revealed. Chac Tun B'alam stepped in and proceeded to light the torches. I stepped in feeling the grit of the room slide between my foot and sandal. I was wearing my trappings as K'ul'ulkan. The chief no longer appeared quite so transparent and I could place my hand upon his shoulder and feel his flesh without passing through.

"Read me the words," I ordered.

Chac Tun B'alam stood full stature and slowly recited:

At the time of no time
In the alignment of the stars
A girl of innocence
Will bring a new beginning

"Now read me the buried words," I said.

The chief kneeled before the glyphs and reverently brushed the sand and dirt away from them. I stepped in closer with the shovel and quickly scraped a large shovel full away. Chac Tun B'alam grabbed the shovel from me and eagerly moved the dirt and debris away from the hidden glyphs. His hands brushed the collected dust from the glyph before he eased back to let me see what was revealed. He solemnly pointed at the images and spoke.

Blue green a star's fire
To raise Pacal's conscience
And see through his eyes
A day of harmony

"Whoa! Hang on a minute," I said. "Did you just say Yax Ek K'ahk'?"

"No," Chac Tun B'alam replied. "She who is not with you is Yax Ek K'ahk, she is Blue Green Star Fire. I read to you K'inich Ahau's words: Blue green a star's fire."

I tried not to frown but could see the doubt once more in Chac Tun B'alam's eyes. He had read me the words and I didn't understand them. I could hear the gears of his mind slowly grinding to a halt with the thought once more that I wasn't K'ul'ulkan. If I was a god, I should have known the prophecy and be acting appropriately. Montoya's interest in K'inich Janahb' Pacal's vestments hadn't helped.

Lucia had remained silent and very inconspicuous but now she fidgeted.

"K'ul'ulkan," she said and bowed her head reverently. "K'inich Ahau nears his journey's end. We must leave soon."

I looked into her eyes, which revealed more than the words she spoke. A slight nod of her head and cautious glance at Chac Tun B'alam reinforced my thoughts. Then she motioned ever so slightly toward the exit and I realized what she meant: it was getting dark.

"Join me, mighty K'ul'ulkan," Chac Tun B'alam said. The words had been sneered. He bowed quickly. "I shall have a meal prepared in your honor. Follow."

The torches had been extinguished. He quickly stepped around me and out the exit into the fading sunlight. I stood there in the dark with Lucia.

"Looks like we're eating here," Lucia whispered and headed out the exit.

"We shall join you," I said loudly and headed for the door.

Chac Tun B'alam grabbed Lucia's arm. "You are not K'ul'ulkan. You are an imposter." He slammed his fists on a glyph.

The stone door slid shut. I stood alone, in the darkness, inside the chamber.

Chapter 21:
Chac Tun B'alam's Trap

Mayan Date: 1 Caban 0 Kankin ~ 12.19.19.17.17

"Mighty K'inich Ahau, your journey is ended.
K'ul'ulkan is a false god. I have sealed the imposter.
I prepare an offering for you. Tomorrow your
journey will be with a blood sacrifice
at your first rays."

Lament of Chac Tun B'alam
Ruler of L'akam Ha

Palenque Ruins: 7:32p.m., Tuesday, December 18, 2012

I stood there in shock. I'd been trapped in a web of my own doing by pretending to be somebody I wasn't. What possessed Montoya to think I could pull off being K'ul'ulkan? My mind flashed over the pages I'd searched on the internet. I was suppose to be a god, to know what mortals thought and, at all times, be ready and at least one step ahead of the natives.

K'ul'ulkan, the serpent god, the earth shaker, the white warrior, the harbinger... of war. I was a war god! I walked with

K'inich Ahau in all his flaming glory of sunlight.

I turned, leaned against a rough glyph and slid down to sit on the dirt floor of the room. There was no light, no sun. I was trapped; I wasn't a god and things weren't looking too good for Lucia. There was no doubt in my mind what Chac Tun B'alam would do at sunrise. A beautiful young maiden, Sak Ek' Janahb would be offered up to K'inich Ahau. Lucia would be gone.

"*What was that?*" My mind's inquisitiveness noticed a glow, small and almost insignificant, but still, a glow. I got up and walked across the room in the almost pure darkness; the glow guided me. Cautiously I reached up and realized it was the torch. Heat still emanated from the smallest ember; surely K'inich Ahau was smiling on me. I softly blew on the ember and it brightened with the added air. I blew again. The ember became larger. I blew once more and a small flash of flame burst forth and I was bathed in the yellow glow of a torch's fire.

My mind raced to follow a thought sequence. I was in a small room with no idea of exactly how airtight it was. I watched the flames. They danced and I saw no indication they were burning the last of the oxygen from the room – although there was that possibility.

I threw caution to the proverbial wind since there wasn't any wind in the room and took the torch to light the one by the exit. The more light I felt I had, the better to possibly see an escape route from the sudden tomb I now found myself in.

A glyph stared at me.

Muyal.

Cloud. I heard the word in my head. Lucia had spoken it. Chac Tun B'alam had spoken it. It was the key to open stone door. There had been two. I started to check each glyph, to see if I saw a pattern. My hands played over each stone, not so much to clean the dust, but to see if it was loose or could move.

Each glyph was tightly arranged in the wall.

My mind sparked and I leapt over to the torch. Carefully I pulled on the handle, pressing it downward, hoping it would give and the door would slide open. I was wrong. Shrugging my shoulders, I couldn't help but think it always worked in those adventure movies. The room was not going to beat me. I stepped back to examine the wall. It was then I heard the words.

Oh-chee-bee. My mind flooded with an image of an open road just beyond door. *Oh-chee-bee.*

"*It couldn't be that easy,*" I thought. Softly, almost reverently, I whispered the words.

"Och-bi," I murmured into the flickering light of the room.

There was no way I knew what the Mayan words meant but I said them nonetheless. When Chac Tun B'alam had pushed the stones outside and said the word 'muyal' I had seen a fluffy white cloud in a blue sky.

"Och-bi," I repeated louder with a stronger affirmation in my voice.

Still nothing happened. I shook my head.

"You dumb-ass idiot," I yelled. "He said the word to let you know which stones to push. This isn't *Aladdin* and an 'Open Sesame' isn't going to open the door, you stupid shit. Find the glyph!"

I scrutinized the carved stones before me. The one directly down and to the right of the torch had what appeared to be a car wheel with a hubcap. I knew they didn't have cars back then but the image of an open road came to my mind when I saw it. It was a long shot but I had to try; I pressed the stone. It wiggled but it didn't really move. I placed my left hand on it, moved right to stretch my left arm and then stretched my right hand out. Easing away from the wall I checked the glyph to see what they were. I laughed. My search had started at the very top yet the torch was barely shoulder high. Again I had been deluded by the floor. I estimated I was almost three feet higher than the original floor. Therefore, naturally, the trigger stones would have been lower.

A quick drop to my knees brought me into an almost perfect alignment with the two trip stones. I pressed. Nothing happened. I pressed again, this time with more force. Nothing happened. In exasperation I bent forward and rested my head on the glyph in front of me.

Bee-ock! Captive!

I looked at the glyph I'd rested on. It was like looking out a doorway and seeing freedom with the sun and moon.

The stone door slowly moved, opening a small distance.

I jumped up and grabbed the opening stone with my hands and pulled. It moved a little more, and I could smell the fresh air. The door still wasn't open wide enough for me escape, but I now had an incentive. I could tell that the sun was close to setting, if it hadn't already set, by the darkness at the bottom of the stairwell. The sweet air allowed me to think that my chances of saving Lucia were now a reality. My first instinct was to press the glyph, and as I fell into the position necessary I realized it might close on a second push. I got up and wedged myself the best I could and pushed against the stone in an attempt to shove it back into the wall. It moved. I pushed with renewed energy. It moved again. Closing my eyes to the pain of rough stone scraping on my flesh, I finally was able to wiggle my leg and part of my shoulder into the opening. I pushed with all my might. The stone gave and moved about another foot. I slipped out and leaned against the opposite wall to gather my wits and strength. I was free.

Still huffing and puffing I glanced up at the glyph for cloud, stood up and stumbled over to them. Leaning against the wall, I pressed my hands on the stones and listened to the door slide shut.

Now that I was free I still had to find Lucia. As I slowly

trudged up the stairs from K'inich Janahb' Pacal's tomb I could hear my shoes grate on the stones; suddenly the sound was softer. I didn't need a mirror to know I'd changed. I was now in the garb of K'ul'ulkan. It was then the plan came to me and I turned to hastily walk back down the steps.

My fists slammed the cloud glyph and the stone door opened. The torches still burned and I put out the one on the distant wall then I grabbed the ornate jade battle dress of K'inich Janahb' Pacal. Montoya had been impressed with it; perhaps wearing it would work to my advantage against Chac Tun B'alam. I shook my head. I wished I were dressed in my regular clothes. Gone was the Mayan apparel. I was pleased with the instant change and grabbed in my pocket. My fingers wrapped around the one item I felt might help me pull off a renewal of my godhood. It was old and belonged to my father. He was gone but I kept it in perfect working order and now carried it for good luck.

Suddenly fascinated by the quick change, I thought about the Mayan trappings and saw my slacks disappear. I could control my apparel. K'inich Janahb' Pacal's vest was heavier than I originally thought but decided to wear it nonetheless. Completely garbed as K'ul'ulkan and in the warrior's vestments, I considered my regular clothes and they appeared as the Mayan trappings disappeared. I was almost ready; there was only the torch to deal with. It broke and crumbled into small pieces and I smiled; grabbed the burning torch, put it out, closed the secret chamber doors then gathered my supplies together. The chief was in for a little surprise of my own.

I slowly trudged up the stairs again, this time to the top. I strolled across the open area to the grand stairs and stood there. It wasn't quite full darkness but the stars were out and the plaza below was ablaze with torches. I carefully placed the torch on the first step down from where I stood. Across the way, at the Palace, I could see Chac Tun B'alam eating with

141

his family in the courtyard. Just behind him, tied and totally pissed, stood Lucia.

"Chac Tun B'alam!" I yelled. "I, K'ul'ulkan, demand you attend me."

"You are no god," the chief screamed. He raised a fist in my direction. "Go away!"

I held my father's lighter in my hand. I'd already slipped the wet cotton wad out and felt the liquid on my hand. I held my hand out to my side.

"Behold! I call on K'inich Ahau," I said and snapped my thumb on the lighter's wheel. The spark ignited the cotton and my hand was a flaming mass. My timing and aim had to be perfect. I tossed the cotton at the torch below me. It caught and I had a flood light of fire flickering below me. The fuel on my hand burned out and the flames flickered into oblivion. Still, I had stood not only in front of Chac Tun B'alam's view, but also many of the natives of L'akam Ha. They had seen my hand wide open, only to burst into flame at the request of K'inich Ahau. Flames were always impressive.

I could see the natives watching me from the open area between the palace and the Temple of Inscriptions. I was now highlighted by the flames of the torch at my feet. They all had watched me bring fire to my hand and transfer it to a stone step. I had brought fire from stone.

"You are a shadow people," Chac Tun B'alam yelled. "You are not K'ul'ulkan." He moved slowly toward me, carefully walking the steps of the Palace to the open space between the structures.

"I am K'ul'ulkan," I said. "I am the Feathered Serpent God." I thought of my Mayan apparel and could feel the change of trappings and the weight of K'inich Janahb' Pacal's armor. "Do I need to shake the land for you to believe? I am the War God. Do you not see my warrior's armor? Did you not try to cut me? Did I not hold your heart in my hand?" I paused.

"I am K'ul'ulkan!"

There was no doubt in my mind I now had total control. If not Chac Tun B'alam, the rest of the natives would accept me and offer their chief to me as a sacrifice.

Suddenly I felt a vibration but I couldn't believe it to be an earthquake.

The natives fell to the ground and groveled, praying to the mighty K'ul'ulkan.

"Bring Sak Ek' Janahb to me," I demanded.

Chac Tun B'alam hastened back up the steps to the Palace. His servants had already started to move her toward the wall and cut her restraints.

"She is free," the chief yelled. "I await your instructions, mighty K'ul'ulkan."

I carefully stepped down on the torch to put it out. The flames licked around the edges of my sandals but the fire extinguished. I gently slid the dead torch to the side, out of immediate eyesight, and then continued down the steps. Lucia was already running across the open space.

"Listen," I whispered when Lucia was near. "When I say 'think car' I want you to give it all you can. I am hoping we will disappear from their view."

Again I felt the earth move but this time much stronger than before. It was then I realized that the Temple of Inscriptions and many of the other structures were built to withstand these vibrations.

"I leave you now but will return tomorrow," I said loudly. "Now," I whispered to Lucia.

Both of us thought about the car and we were in the darkened shadows of the Palenque ruins. Lucia and I were back in our regular clothes. I felt a little dismayed at the loss of the people and torches but at the same time was quite relieved my stunt had provided the necessary actions. Chac Tun B'alam was not visible.

Chapter 22:
Meeting With Diego

Mayan Date: 1 Caban 0 Kankin ~ 12.19.19.17.17

"Mighty K'ul'ulkan! I offer you my blood."

Prayer of Chac Tun B'alam
Ruler of L'akam Ha

Palenque: 9:06p.m., Tuesday, December 18, 2012

I pulled into the hotel and jumped out. Lucia joined me and we quickly walked inside. Diego was sitting on a bench appearing very nervous.

"Oh, señor Hargrove," Diego said. "You said wait. I start to worry when you no return."

"Have you had anything to eat?" I asked, quickly trying to decide the next avenue of my plan.

"No, señor."

"Well, neither have I, but thanks for asking." Lucia added.

"We'll get room service," I said and headed for the hallway leading to my room. "We've got a lot to discuss."

"Wait," Diego said and dashed toward the front desk.

A few minutes later he strolled back to us with a very big shit-eating grin.

"I order and it come soon," he said while motioning us toward the room. "No charge you, Señor Hargrove." He shook his head no.

Lucia's cell phone rang as we entered my room. She moved to the chair and I could tell she was talking with Emil. I offered Diego the other chair and I sat on the couch where Lucia had slept earlier.

"No housekeeping today?" Diego asked looking at the bed beyond me.

"They did," I said sheepishly. "I took a nap earlier."

Diego glanced at Lucia then back to me with a smile. "Si, I understand."

I leaned back on the couch. "Earlier today you made a comment about an old Mayan priest in your village?"

"Chimalpopoca?"

Shrugging my shoulders, I made a face. "I guess that's his name; you never really said. But you did mention he can talk with Chac Tun B'alam."

Diego nodded. "I follow the old ways. Our shaman, Chimalpopoca speaks with gods and Chac Tun B'alam, chief of all L'akam Ha Mayans."

"You don't call it Palenque?" I asked.

Lucia snapped the phone shut. "What doesn't get called Palenque?"

"So nice of you to join us," I said. "Diego just referred to the ruins as L'akam Ha, the old name for Palenque. He also has a priest in his village who speaks with Chac Tun B'alam."

Lucia cocked an eyebrow toward Diego. "Maybe we should be talking to the priest about the items of K'inich Janahb' Pacal."

What she said made sense.

145

"I take you to Chimalpopoca. You go?" Diego smiled proudly.

There was a knock on the door. "Room service."

Diego jumped from the chair and was at the door in two leaps. He opened it and allowed the young boy with a tray full of covered dishes in. The lad placed the tray on the table and Diego waved him away. There was a small discussion between them then the boy left.

"I beg pardon if you no like," Diego said while removing the covers from the dishes. "I get us what the staff eat free. It is very tasty."

I glanced about the different plates not really recognizing anything as a dish, but I did recognize most of the basic items.

"Tortillas, beans, cheeses, cilantro, chilies, and shredded pork," Diego said pointing at different bowls and plates. "Also fish, rice, corn, salsa, different sliced fruits and a few other things. Enjoy."

Diego grabbed a plate and dabbled a little from each offering onto his plate and then grabbed two tortillas.

I watched as he used the tortillas to swab some of an item from his plate and then bit the loaded tortilla end. He was eating with a zest I found very catching and soon joined him with a plate of my own assorted items. I looked at Lucia and she wasn't hesitating to join the food stampede.

"So you follow the new religion of Ah Pukuh?" I asked between bites. I found eating with your fingers to be very catching; I wasn't too sure I wanted return to the big city and all its niceties. I glanced at Lucia; there were other reasons for not leaving Palenque that I found pleasing, too.

Diego scrunched up his face in disgust. "He attempts our religion. He no understand true method of sacrifice. Chac Tun B'alam sees this and questions his actions."

I jumped up from the couch while almost spilling my plate. "You know Chac Tun B'alam?"

146

Diego hung his head. "No, señor. I know of him. Chimalpopoca tells the people what he sees at the temple when Chac Tun B'alam performs the rituals."

"So, this shaman of yours sees the chief?"

Diego nodded his head while pushing a food-laden tortilla into his mouth.

"This could be a good angle for the news," Lucia said. She gave me a look and rolled her eyes denoting some form of exasperation. "Seems the station is a tad upset about my actions today so I told Emil what happened. He wished he could have gotten it on tape." She shrugged her shoulders. "But I don't know why since we all know how that went last time; no recording possible."

"So what does the station want?" I asked.

"They'd like an exclusive," Lucia whispered. "We'd have to set it up with the archeologists and somehow finagle an explanation–" She nervously held two fingers before her pursed lips knowing full well how the request was going to be received. "An explanation of how we learned of the secret room..."

"What?" I yelled, again almost spilling my meal as I jumped up from the couch once more.

"Calm down, Barry," Lucia said. "Sit down and eat. Chill. I can hold them off for a couple of days." She glared at me. "At least until you're gone; how's that?"

"When I'm gone? Guess I didn't realize I was leaving." I sat back down on the bed and tossed the near empty plate to my side.

Suddenly I felt strange. Just mere hours earlier Lucia and I had made love here, in this room, and now she seemed she was tossing me away like a discarded toy. I thought there had been some chemistry. A discarded toy? Was that what I'd been? Had I been taken on a ride, no pun intended, to give her a new story? I looked over at her and analyzed my situation, trying to read anything I could from her large, brown eyes.

She noticed me and frowned then wrinkled her nose at me. I continued to watch her. The room was silent and Lucia glanced over at Diego who sat in his chair staring at his plate. She looked back to me then quietly mouthed the word: *what*?

"This Chimmy shaman of yours..." I started.

"Chimalpopoca," Diego reminded me.

"Right, Chimalpopoca," I repeated. "What does he know about K'ul'ulkan?"

"Señor Hargrove, I bring him here or I take you to him?"

I hesitated for many reasons. If I went with Diego to see Chimalpopoca, I was pretty sure Lucia would tag along. If I stayed put and had him bring the shaman to me, I was almost positive Lucia and I would do one of two things. Either we would fight about the situation of her wanting a story or we'd land up in bed in a love-wrestling match. I wanted the latter but was pretty sure that wasn't going to happen.

"I need to get back to the office for a little bit," Lucia awkwardly announced.

I cocked a questioning glance at her. "Oh? I thought you'd want to go along with us to see Chimalpopoca."

"I'd love to, Barry, but I really need to get a little work done and Emil was adamant I pick up some video he has and look at it." She smiled at me. "You might find it interesting, too." She stood there like a little schoolgirl with a big secret just bursting to spill the beans.

Diego was quick to answer.

"We go, see video, and we go to Chimalpopoca. Yes?"

Again, I was being manipulated and told what to do. It was like Montoya all over again. I wondered just where he was and what he was up to? It was then I realized I could go to his house and take the stupid baton and go back to the museum, get my money and make Dr. Martinez eat a lot of crow and be done with this whole idiotic mess I'd gotten tangled in.

"Wait. Before we do anything," I said. "Exactly what does this shaman of yours have to say about K'ul'ulkan?" I was curious. Diego kept insisting this guy could talk with Chac Tun B'alam; I had to know how and what they talked about."

"Chimalpopoca knows you dress like K'ul'ulkan. Chac Tun B'alam not sure." Diego hung his head and I could see his eyes were closed. "Chimalpopoca not sure if you are a god. He meet you, touch you, then he know."

So I was being manipulated. It was Diego's job to get me to the shaman so he could validate my godhood for Chac Tun B'alam.

"Chimalpopoca also want see Sak Ek' Janahb," Diego added softly then looked up at me then to Lucia. He changed – there was a sense of dedication. No longer was there an awkward Mayan parking attendant before me. "I do what I am told," he said firmly. "No harm will come to you."

"Only Sak Ek' Janahb?" I asked while evaluating Diego's new demeanor. "Is that all Chimalpopoca asks? Who is telling you what to do?"

"Chimalpopoca. He seeks to reveal the truths. He needs to find who is Yax Ek' K'ahk'. I am friends with your guide, the one you call 'Juan' and Aunt Benita. I am only one of the many eyes and voices of Chimalpopoca. He knows Ah Pukuh is Dr. Montoya and does not truly believe he is a god. Chac Tun B'alam will never accept him as Ah Pukuh, death's god. But you – you have confused the great Mayan chief."

"I've confused him?" I was completely astonished. "How? Why me?"

"Did he not cut you? Did not the knife go through your body with no wound?"

I laughed. "Yes, that it did, indeed. I think it startled Chac Tun B'alam just a little."

"It is for Chimalpopoca to reveal the truths," Diego said. Again his demeanor changed, he was once again the backward parking attendant. "No laugh at our religion, señor Hargrove. It is very old, before your Christ."

"I'll get my car," I heard myself saying. I stood and put my dinner plate on the service tray. "We'll go to your office, Lucia, then on to the village to see the shaman. Is everyone agreeable with that?"

What was I doing? Suddenly I felt like an organizing Dorothy off to see the mighty wizard in Oz. Now the real question – who was Oz?

Chapter 23:
Chimalpopoca

Mayan Date: 1 Caban 0 Kankin ~ 12.19.19.17.17

"O Mighty Bolontiku! I offer you my blood.
Allow me to pass the levels of death
on the Tree of Life, the strong Celiba tree
as the stars allow."

Prayer of Chac Tun B'alam
Ruler of L'akam Ha

Palenque: 9:52p.m., Tuesday, December 18, 2012

The streets were basically empty and Lucia gave quick directions so I didn't have to swerve or slam on the brakes too often. The station was in a smallish building with nothing to make it stand out. I remembered the radio and television stations back in the big cities where I grew up; one could see the huge call letters and their station numbers flashing or gleaming in lights from quite a distance. I pulled up front and turned off the car's lights and motor.

"I'll be right back," Lucia whispered and jumped out of

the car. She took about two strides then turned back. "Do you two want to come in?"

I was out of the car; she didn't need to ask me twice. Diego was right behind me.

"Fine, boys. Just follow me." Lucia took lead and we followed like two little puppy dogs.

A couple of hallways, a twist and a turn and I watched Lucia open the door to an office and flick on a light that buzzed into existence overhead.

"This is it." She held out her arms and spun on one heel. "Welcome to Lucia's Lair. This is where I put together all the juicy crap you see me spouting on the screen."

I stared at the grey metallic partition walls with matching four drawer cabinets. A simple steel desk, mildly cluttered with papers and videos, was in the center of the room. A few awards hung on the walls; otherwise, the room was cold and sterile appearing.

She strutted over to the desk and started sorting through things. "Damn!"

I jerked around to look at her. "What's up?"

"Emil said he would leave the tape on my desk. I don't see it and that can only mean..."

"The boss has it," Emil said from the doorway. He had a silly grin. "I thought I heard somebody come in." He walked into the office. "Hey, look Lucia, I'm really sorry but the when the boss yanks it out of your hands, well, you know how he is."

"That's okay," Lucia said. "What was on it?"

Emil shook his head and raced over, grabbing her shoulders and lightly shaking her. "You won't believe it. I worked with the tape, you know, the one where you four were dressed rather scantily and talking gibberish? Well, I finally got the images to show. I had to slow down the video to see it then I had to separate out the audio. I had to speed up the audio to hear what was being said. Then I put the two separated segments together to create a new video. It was the one I put on your desk."

"Whatever possessed you to think of doing that?" I asked. "It doesn't even make sense!"

"But it does," Emil said excitedly. "It is the lightning and thunder syndrome. You see lightning then, depending on distance, you hear the thunder it caused. Light travels faster than sound so by slowing down the video and speeding up the audio I was able to bring them together in a new conjunction."

"A new conjunction?" I repeated. "What the hell does that mean?"

"Consider it syncing," Emil said. "We're in sync right now but when you guys went to the costume party, you were out of sync with the here and now. I re-synced and got the images and vocals."

"And the boss has them," Lucia said. "What's his plan?"

Emil gave her a skeptical look. "Are you sure you want to know?"

"Spill it." Lucia nonchalantly and shifted papers on her desk.

"He made Angela a newscaster." Emil nodded out the door. "They're filming the segment right now. He made Maribel her camera person."

"So what happens to us?" Lucia asked.

"We're going to make a comeback, Lucia," Emil said. "You said something about a secret room? That should put you back in the driver's seat and Angela back in her secretarial chair."

"Grab your cameras and come with us," Lucia said and shoved a few papers into a file folder. "Momma ain't about to let the triple-B get the best of me; at least, not yet!"

"Triple-B?" I asked.

"Bleach blonde bitch," Emil whispered and winked at me with a grin. "So where are we off to at this time of night? Do I need to get a van to get us there?"

"I'm guessing my car," I said.

"Chimalpopoca's," Lucia yelled back as she led us out of the small maze we'd come through.

The night air was cool and refreshing. Diego gave directions now and I didn't drive quite as fast as I had when Lucia was telling me where to go. Finally we were in the suburbs, the lights were less and the sky was clear above us. The Milky Way was stunning and I couldn't remember ever seeing it look the way it did tonight.

"We are close," Diego whispered looking up at the sky.

I slowed the car but couldn't see anything that appeared like a village.

"No," Diego said. "The village is still a little ways ahead. Go." He waved me forward then pointed at the stars. "We are close. In two nights it will happen."

"What will happen?" Emil asked.

"Time will pass to a new time," Diego said softly and reverently. "She will lead us to a new time and we will pass through the heart of the galaxy."

I slowed the car and gazed up at the sky. The Milky Way shimmered above me. It wasn't just a band of lights and clusters of stars but the whole sky was alive. It wasn't that the Milky Way was above me but more like it was engulfing me. I felt a part of the heavens; a oneness with the eternal cosmic universe.

"It is late," Diego said. "We have to get to the village."

My reverie lost, reluctantly I pressed on the gas pedal and we continued on the small road which led us to the village where Chimalpopoca lived.

"There!" Diego pointed to the side of the road.

I saw six, maybe seven small structures. That was the village? My mind raced to comprehend how so few buildings could be construed as a village. My grandfather's farm had more buildings.

In the dwindling light of a fire I could see a small figure shuffling toward us. There was a staff, which he appeared to use for support. He walked slowly and deliberately; like a man of many years who knew the realities of life.

"Chimalpopoca comes," Diego said. "We must get out of the car."

Diego kept his head bowed and I thought it best if I did so, too. I noticed Emil and Lucia also showed respect.

"So, this is K'ul'ulkan. Bah! Gods do not drive cars." He rapped me with the staff then turned to hobble away. "Follow."

I know my jaw hit the ground even though I never heard nor felt it do so. The shaman spoke English. Perfect English. And his voice didn't croak with age.

Diego pushed me forward and I was the first to follow Chimalpopoca. In the shadows I could see him better since he walked in front of me and the fire outlined him better. He was about five and a half feet tall, no real slouch although he did use a staff for walking purposes, it seemed. It took me a few minutes to realize Chimalpopoca wore a small cape of feathers. From the flickering fire I had trouble ascertaining a defined line on the shaman's shoulders and that was due to fluttering feathers.

"Stay," he demanded then continued to the other side of the fire.

I could see him clearly now in the firelight. I was surprised. The man appeared to be in his late thirties, perhaps early forties and quite strong. The finely chiseled facial features of a Mayan were obvious in him. He lifted an arm into the air and the feathered cape cascaded over his shoulder. His necklaces of beads and coin-like trinkets glistened in the firelight. I didn't understand the words but had heard the similar sounds before when Chac Tun B'alam spoke; Chimalpopoca was speaking ancient Mayan.

155

"He calls on Bolontiku," Diego whispered. "They are the nine gods of night and underworld."

"I thought Ah Pukuh was the god of the underworld," I said.

"You must understand our religion to comprehend our belief. We have many gods but we are not like the Greeks and Romans."

Chimalpopoca tossed something into the fire; flashes and embers flitted toward the sky in a heated race to escape. I looked upward to see the embers and saw the mighty branches of the tree above us. The small fire had barely illuminated the high branches over us.

"K'ul'ulkan! Come to me." Chimalpopoca ordered.

I slowly walked around the fire pit to the shaman. He stood there and stared into my eyes and each time I attempted to look away, he raised his hand to stop me. Finally he placed the tip of his index finger in the center of my forehead then slowly pulled it down over the ridge between my eyes, into the slight indent and over the boney section of the nose.

"Interesting," he whispered. "You deceived the chief. He told me you called fire from K'inich Ahau and held the sun in your hand."

I stepped back from the man, wary and unsure. Lucia made a small gasping sound of surprise. He knew about the earlier incident yet the only ones who could have possibly known were Chac Tun B'alam, Lucia and I. Even Diego didn't know about what had happened at the ruins.

"How do you know this?" I asked.

"I listen to the jungle. I am a shaman," he said.

He raised his hand and started to make an arc in the air before me. I grabbed his fingers and held them in my tight fist. I cocked an eye at him and stared him down.

"You may be a shaman, some sort of mystic for the Mayans," I said, holding his hand as still as I could while he fought for release. "I am not your backward peasant. Now you tell me how you know of this."

Suddenly Diego's hands were on mine. I'd never seen him move in. He unclenched my hand from Chimalpopoca's fingers.

"Never touch a Mayan priest," Diego said sternly. "Never."

Chimalpopoca slowly massaged his fingers and glared at me. "You have committed a sacrilege and must be held accountable."

"You forget I am K'ul'ulkan. I am a god." I stared back at him; he cringed.

A slow, twisted smile curled the ends of his lips and his eyes narrowed as he watched me. "So, you are K'ul'ulkan. You ask me how I know what you have done. You? A god?" He spat on the ground. "Chac Tun B'alam is right. You are a false god." He turned and started to walk toward one of the small buildings.

"Chimalpopoca!" I called. "Your English is exceptional for a village person. You speak better than Diego who works in the big city. Here, in the jungle with your eagle eye—" I snidely emphasized the word 'eagle' when I said it. "You claim rule as the shaman. Should I ask you who your alma mater is?" I waited mere seconds. "Or shall I, K'ul'ulkan, a god, tell you?"

The shaman turned and stomped back to the fire. He raised both hands, pushing the feather cape back over his shoulders, once again revealing the necklace of beads and coins. It was the one coin I'd noted earlier, silver with an emblem on one side – which I thought to be a glyph – while on the opposite side was in red and blue. It had caught my attention.

He grabbed some wood and tossed it on the fire. Embers danced and glinted in the heated air as they lifted to the darkness of the tree. The flames jumped into the night sky, lighting the area by reflecting back from the overhead tree.

"I am Chimalpopoca," he shouted. "I am the shaman of the Mayans, high priest to Chac Tun B'alam, last chief of the Maya during this b'ak'tun.

"I am Barry Hargrove," I shouted back and thumped him on his chest, pinning between his chest and my index finger the coin I'd noticed earlier. I leaned in closer. "The coin beneath my finger has a white A on a split background of blue and red. Do we talk or do I pronounce my findings louder?"

His eyes flared at me but I could feel him deflating in assignation to my demands.

Even the jungle was quiet.

Chapter 24:
The Alma Mater

Mayan Date: 1 Caban 0 Kankin ~ 12.19.19.17.17

"K'ul'ulkan again moves the earth.
Rest, my brother. Rest."

Prayer of Chac Tun B'alam
Ruler of L'akam Ha

Palenque: 10:23p.m., Tuesday, December 18, 2012

Chimalpopoca held his ground. Again, Diego grabbed my hands and pulled me away.

"You must not touch the shaman," he said and pushed me away from the man.

Suddenly the earth moved and I almost lost my balance, but felt comfortable with the action. Lucia dropped to the ground while Diego wobbled then found his footing; he helped Lucia to her feet. Chimalpopoca maintained his balance and stared at me for a few moments, studying my actions and definitely thinking over the situation.

"K'ul'ulkan shakes his tail and moves the ground. I find

this aspect interesting." The shaman gently pushed Diego back. "Allow K'ul'ulkan his freedom. He is a god and may touch a lowly priest."

Diego nodded his head and stepped into the shadows and obscurity. Chimalpopoca reached up and clutched the necklace and the coin I'd brought to his attention.

"My education was a wish of my mother," he started in a low voice. "She wanted me to be more than just another native in the jungle. I followed her wishes and went to American University in Washington, D. C. My course of study was Mayan heritage. With what I absorbed as a child growing up and what I learned at the university, trust me, Detective Hargrove, I have a very solid understanding of the Maya life, both current and past."

"And you knew of the secret chamber I was locked in," I added and smiled.

Chimalpopoca shrugged. "Perhaps."

Lucia moved up by me. "What's happening?"

"K'ul'ulkan and I have come to an agreement," Chimalpopoca said. "We will now move forward to address the issues of the next few days. Dr. Montoya has disappeared."

"He is in search of a specific item," I said.

"The Conscience of Pacal," Lucia added.

I frowned at her sudden and unusual eagerness in hopes she would see my displeasure. As usual, she ignored me.

"Yes," Chimalpopoca said. "I was aware of what he was doing. Ah Pukuh moves as he pleases in our world and we allow it. If I am not wrong, Dr. Montoya has gone back to his other home."

"You seem to know everything," I said. "Tell me this, what is the Conscience of Pacal? How does it work, especially in conjunction with the Eyes of Pacal?"

"Come with me." He headed back toward the small shanty, and then stopped. "Alone." He looked directly at Lucia.

"Diego? Show Miss Camal my office."

I frowned, curious as to what he meant.

Chimalpopoca leaned toward me. "Don't fret, it is my room where I perform my shamanistic magic for the locals," he whispered.

"Why are you doing this?" I asked while following him to the building.

He opened the door; the room was well illuminated. He obviously noticed my hesitation and finally motioned for me to enter. I'd been locked in a room before so I figured if I got trapped again, I thought I could get out of this one without too much difficulty. He motioned me to a small, well-worn couch.

"Have a seat. For convenience, call me Paul and I shall call you Barry. Is that acceptable?"

I shrugged my shoulders. "Sure, why not? After all, your house, your rules."

The first things I noticed in the room as I slowly took inventory were the books. A full wall, totally shelved from floor to ceiling. The rest of the room included a few pictures, some old furniture and a small altar in the one corner. Above the altar I saw his university degree and smiled.

He removed the feathered cape. "You are the first person ever to notice my alma mater coin." He fingered the coin on the necklace and held it out to admire. "Either nobody has the nerve to call my bluff or else they have no idea what it represents. My question to you is – how did you recognize it?"

"To tell you the truth, Paul, it was ten, maybe closer to twelve years ago, I dated a young lady from American University. She was a real sports nut and I attended enough games to recognize the emblem and logo from almost any distance."

He handed me a cup and poured from an old miner's coffee pot.

"Tascalate?" I asked watching the dark liquid pour into the

cup.

"Ah, you've had it? This isn't really tascalate but my own concoction, a variation. I hope you like it."

He poured himself a cup and put the pot back on the stove then sat in a wooden rocker opposite me.

"I have seen you and Dr. Montoya at the ruins. The fact you can appear in the garb of K'ul'ulkan intrigues me. Perhaps you truly are the incarnation of our Mayan god. From tonight's earlier show you have proven your godhood to Chac Tun B'alam. He has wavered about you since the first day you appeared. I'm not sure how you pulled off the knife stabbing."

I held up my hand. "Hold it. You're treating my actions like it is some sort of magic act. I have no idea how this is all happening. It seems I pass through planes of time and during that period I am not of either world."

"You have hit upon the proper idea. Time is coming together. The sun breathes just as K'inich Ahau breathes, although the sun's breath duration is 25,000 years. It inhales and 12,500 years later it exhales; another 12,500 years further on, it inhales again. Mayans have a very concise concept of time, which is tied to not only the astrological aspect, but also the astronomical. In a couple of days it will be December 21st in the year of 2012. The Mayan calendar ends with another Jupiter and Saturn conjunction." He smiled at me. "The sun will finish its exhalation. At that time there will be an alignment of our planetary system while at the same time, our galaxy will be at the exact centerline of the Milky Way. Such an auspicious moment, would you not agree?"

I stared at him; he sipped from his cup. I wasn't about to get sucked into another theory.

"It is the galactic equator, Barry. We will be in the middle of our galaxy. The spiritual and physical vibrations will be harmonic and they will set loose the new creation. The sun will rise at 7:06 a.m. on the 21st but the event will have occurred almost two hours earlier at 5:11 a.m."

"Harmonics?" I queried.

Paul raised his hands above him and twisted to encompass the room. "Everything breathes, Barry. There are harmonics in all things. Mother Earth exists with these vibrations and when they become harmonic, you, as K'ul'ulkan, vibrate your tail and cause the earth to move."

He stared at me and I shrugged my shoulders.

"An earthquake?" he said. "As the harmonics crest and trough in their vibrations, certain actions occur. Since all things vibrate..." he pointed above him, "then so does the universe. All these harmonics blending together will pull on earth."

"You said the sun will rise on the 21st," I smiled. "Are you sure? And are you preaching doomsday? Does not the Mayan calendar predict the end of time?"

"Ah, Barry, you of little faith," Paul said. "A young maiden will save us and bring us to the new world. The sun will continue to rise and set and man will be happy. It has been foretold many times a new age is dawning. In two days, it truly will. We will have memories of this era and its demise."

I cocked my head and narrowed my brows in thought. "Memories?"

"Have you not heard of Atlantis? Mu? Eden? Shangri La? They are memories, Barry. All of them. Memories of times passed. What do you think we'll remember? Only she who will command time knows."

"This girl you mention. Is her name Yax Ek' K'ahk' by any chance?"

"Yes. She exists. I have felt her presence at the ruins, the city and even in this village but she remains hidden from my sights. I will find her; Chac Tun B'alam has demanded that I, Chimalpopoca, to do so."

I sat there with the cup to my lips, slowly slurping the drink, analyzing what this great shaman was saying. Finally I had a break to ask my earlier question once more.

"What is the Conscience of Pacal? How do these items of K'inich Janahb' Pacal work?"

"The Eyes of Pacal? I am told the baton is held in a fist before your eyes, your longest finger pressed between the eyes at the bridge of the nose." He shrugged his shoulders. "I haven't seen it performed with the Eyes of Pacal but a mockup, a similar item called the Eyes of the Jaguar has been used before and I think that is why the chief's eyes are slightly cross-eyed." He grabbed a pencil from the table. "Here, try it yourself. We Mayans, for the most part, have given up the crossed-eyes as a sign of beauty."

I took the offered pencil and held it in my fist then put my hand to my head as Paul had described. My eyes crossed trying to focus.

"In the other hand, held aloft, is the Conscience of Pacal. The reason for holding it up high was to allow K'inich Janahb' Pacal to collect and concentrate the light of K'inich Ahau into a beam of energy or light on the eyes. I have never seen this performed, not even as a mock."

I placed my empty cup on the table. "You've never seen the Conscience of Pacal? You have no idea of what it looks like?"

He shook his head. "All I know is it is an item to collect or gather."

My mind raced to figure out what it could be when I suddenly realized what Montoya had gone in search of. I was sure he had went back to the museum to get the bag, the small beaded satchel the baton had been found in. What better item to be used to collect.

"I can tell by the light in your eyes you know what the Conscience of Pacal is." Paul watched me. "Will you share your enlightenment with me?"

I rubbed my hands together. It was nice; I was finally one

step ahead of somebody in this strange game I had gotten sucked into. Everyone else seemed to have the answers and enjoyed keeping me in the dark. Montoya had taken off in the middle of the night on some plan but hadn't shared his thoughts. Lucia learned things and kept them to herself and Diego knew things I didn't. Even Juan had taken advantage of me to some extent, yet, he had finally came forward and told me the secret he had kept hidden.

"Dr. Montoya went back to the museum to steal the beaded pouch which held the Eyes of Pacal."

"Pouch?" Paul jumped up in a shout. "Do you truly believe a simple beaded pouch would be the mighty Conscience of Pacal?"

"Why not?" I asked. "Would it not be something to collect in? Where better to store the Eyes of Pacal when not being used? It seems to be the only logical explanation."

I sat there watching Paul mull over my words and theories.

"Would you like more to drink?" he asked getting up and moving to the stove.

"No, thank you." I watched as he carefully poured himself another cup of the tasty liquid. "Do you agree with me or not, Paul?"

"You might be right, Barry. You may have discovered it."

I stood up and headed for the door.

"Where are you going?" Paul asked. "I am not finished."

"I am," I said and pushed the door open. "Which building did Diego take Lucia to show?"

"Would you be interested in learning what is needed for K'ul'ulkan to perform at the time of no time?"

I froze. He definitely had piqued my interest. Had he accepted me as K'ul'ulkan? My feet slowly turned forcing me to look at him.

"Perform?"

"Trust me, Barry. You are here for a reason. All the

prophecies are coming true. K'ul'ulkan, Yax Ek' K'ahk', Ah Pukuh and K'inich Ahau will join together to bring time to an end. The period of no time is under the control of Yax Ek' K'ahk' and only she can decide what K'inich Ahau will smile upon us."

I paused to consider my options.

Chapter 25:
The Reveal

Mayan Date: 1 Caban 0 Kankin ~ 12.19.19.17.17

*Chac Tun B'alam watches the night sky and beholds
the stars as they move about the heavens. A new
star brightens, the cosmos align themselves.*

*Views of Chac Tun B'alam
Ruler of L'akam Ha*

Palenque: 10:42p.m., Tuesday, December 18, 2012

Paul continued to stand at the stove, watching, analyzing
me, waiting to see if he had tipped the balance to his favor.

"You win," I said. "Pour me another cup and I'll let you
tell me about this."

Paul picked up the pot and poured dark liquid into my cup.
I walked over and sat back down on the beat up couch. Paul
handed me the cup and I couldn't wait to sip the drink.

"So, what is this ceremony?"

Paul smiled sheepishly. "I only know some of the secret,"
he said. "I know that Yax will be an integral part of the

167

ceremony. Actually, she will be the pivotal point. You, as K'ul'ulkan, will help to guide her."

I frowned since I had no idea where I would guide this person.

"Don't worry, Barry," Paul added. "I can see you are confused. You will know when you need to do what is necessary to be done."

"So what you're telling me is you have absolutely no idea what is going to happen." I eased back into the couch, wiggling to make myself comfortable. "So it's just going to be a lot of mumbo-jumbo hocus-pocus crap."

"Not crap." Paul sipped his drink. "The most crucial decision for the future is shared between Yax and you. Don't take it lightly. Even now your actions are guiding her to the final decision."

I stared at the floor and gave some serious thought to what Paul was telling me. At some point in the near future I was going to assist an unknown female to culminate time for mankind. I was going to be one of those who would be instrumental in the end of the world. It hit me. *"Holy shit,"* I thought. *"I am crucial in the end of the world!"* The words surfaced; the words he had said.

Even now your actions guide her

"Wait a minute." I set my cup down so I wouldn't spill it in the excitement. "You say I am guiding her now?"

"Yes." Paul smiled and nodded his head. "Remember, Barry. You are a god. You are K'ul'ulkan. You will know by divine intervention what you need to know. Don't start to fret, at least, not yet. Accept yourself and you will see what I have said. She watches you."

I gazed up at Paul and smiled. He was correct. I was K'ul'ulkan, if I could believe that. My hand shook a little as I picked up the cup; it vibrated lightly causing the dark liquid to ripple the surface. I stared at the moving ripples as they converged in the center. I frowned. The circles should have been expanding outward, not inward. I looked up at Paul.

"Laws are changing," he whispered and nodded at my cup.

I absently nodded my head in agreement but not fully understanding what was happening. As I prepared to open my mouth, Lucia charged in.

"You have got to come see this," she said and dodged back out the door.

Paul and I jumped to our feet and followed her.

"Behold the cosmos," she said and held her hands in the air, all the while twirling like a ballerina. "Look at the stars! You can almost touch them." She continued to dance about like a small girl. "Like sparkling jewels of white."

The campfire that had roared tall and strong just a short time before was now again a low, glowing of embers with a few flickering flames. Paul stirred them with a stick and soon there was again a roaring fire as the embers soared into flames. The myriad of stars, the cosmos, diminished and once again held their rule in the heavens above.

"Time is running out, K'ul'ulkan," Paul said. "It is time for us to become who we are destined to be." He turned to Lucia. "You are Sak Ek' Janahb, hand maiden to Yax Ek' K'ahk' who is the Mayan princess to whom time will come. You will be a corner post, a vessel of her thoughts to carry them to K'inich Ahau."

Lucia scowled at Paul. "Vessel? There are ominous tones in that word. They sound like an honor and position of prestige but beneath it all I feel there lurks something bad. I'm seeing a one way trip and I don't like that."

"I am Chimalpopoca," he said. "Go with honor, my daughter."

He turned to Diego. "Go back to the town and at the

designated time, bring those who are necessary."

Diego bowed. "As you wish, Chimalpopoca." He turned to me. "You are K'ul'ulkan, do you have any wishes of your servant, Diego?"

"Yes, I do," I said. "Take me back to town. I need to see Dr. Montoya."

Lucia jumped into the vehicle. "I think I want to go back to town, also." She glanced about the area. "I don't like it here."

I glared at Paul. "I'm not so sure I like it here, either." I scanned the area one last time. "It is time for K'ul'ulkan to awake from his memory sleep and find Yax Ek' Kahk' so I can assist her."

"K'inich Ahau will awake shortly and you will see more clearly in the daylight," Paul said. "I am Chimalpopoca, high priest to Chac Tun B'alam. Join me to greet K'inich Ahau." He smiled. "Bring Yax Ek' K'ahk' with you."

Diego started up the vehicle and proceeded back the way we'd come. We crested a small knoll. In the distance I could see the city glow of Palenque. Suddenly we were in the dark of the jungle and only an occasional flash of the heavens peeked through the overhead canopy of tropical growth. The top of the convertible was down and the warm night air was filled with heady scents of the jungle's night blooming flowers.

My mind raced to ascertain whom Yax Ek' K'ahk' could be. All the clues were there; he'd felt her presence at the ruins once; she was young, probably a child.

Suddenly it was clear: Lupe! Guadalupe! Juan's playmate.

* * * * *

I remembered the day we all went to the ruins for a picnic and Lupe's mom had made sandwiches. It was the same day Juan and I were transported to another time and place. It had to be Lupe who would become Yax Ek' K'ahk' and give us our new future.

A few more ruts and I could see we would finally be out of the jungle and on the fringe of Palenque. Diego drove to the hotel.

"If you don't mind, Barry," Lucia said. "I'd love to crash at your place tonight because I'm just too damned tired to go home."

Diego smiled.

"You're welcome to stay," I said and helped her out of the car. "A hot shower and you'll be ready to party all night."

She brushed back her long hair and cocked an eye at me. "A hot shower and I'll crash on the floor."

Being the gallant knight I am, I counter-offered. "You get the bed; this time I'll sleep on the couch. Nobody has to be on the floor."

Lucia stabbed an index at my nose and pushed the end of it. "You win," she said and winked.

Chapter 26:
Breakfast

Mayan Date: 2 Eznab 1 Kankin ~ 12.19.19.17.18

*Chac Tun B'alam scans the heavens to watch
the alignment. The sun hasn't risen in the East
yet a lightening of sky occurs.
Below him Chimalpopoca prepares
the sacrifice; a warrior.*

*Views of Chac Tun B'alam
Ruler of L'akam Ha*

Palenque: 8:03 a.m., Wednesday, December 19, 2012

Lucia sat opposite me, sipping coffee and watching me intently. I was trying to figure out exactly what her game was. One minute I seem to be the lover, the next I'm a stranger and we have separate agendas. Last night I was once again the lover, this morning, in the light of day, I was now the gringo from the big northern city.

"Señor Barry!"

I heard the familiar voice of Juan as he came racing into the restaurant. He stopped abruptly when he noticed Lucia. Following behind him was Lupe and her mother, Benita.

"I no come," Benita said and looked down at Juan. "I come." She frowned at Juan. "Tell you truth."

I held up my index finger to stop her.

"First," I said. "First we get breakfast and then we will attend to business." I eased down to Juan and Lupe. "Still like those breakfast fajitas? Yes?" They shook their heads vigorously in agreement. "Fine. Get into the chairs and Manuel will take your orders." I quickly motioned for Manuel to come over. It was then I noticed Benita still stood and I could tell she was slightly distressed.

"Please, señor Hargrove," she started. "I tell you truth. I lie to you, señor."

"Well, it can't be that bad, Benita," I said. "Sit down, have breakfast, then we will discuss it."

Benita pursed her lips, knitted her brows together in a small frown and glared at Juan. "Como quiera," she said and sat down between Lucia and I, directly opposite Juan and Lupe.

I looked to Lucia and she ever so slightly nodded her head to show that Benita was fine.

"Fajitas around?" I asked.

"Not for me, Barry," Lucia said. "I'm still not feeling all that well from last night. You say it was the water?"

"No fajitas," Benita said.

"Three orders of breakfast fajitas with extra eggs, Manuel. Three coffees and two orange juice, please."

Juan and Lupe giggled about something and kept looking over the ledge into the atrium of the hotel. I was suddenly reminded of what Paul had said last night about spying on me. I glanced over in the direction they were looking and noticed a slightly rotund gentleman sleeping with a glass of some sort resting on his heaving stomach.

"Lupe?" I called and placed my hand over hers to grab her attention. "Do you have an imagination? A dream world?"

"¿Qué?"

Juan immediately translated and beamed a smile at me. Lupe thought for a minute, miming the issue as strenuous deep

173

thought and finally by placing a finger to one cheek and tapping. Then she spoke. I looked to Juan for an answer.

He shrugged his shoulders before he started. "She wants see pink ponies, big orange birds Lupe can fly on the back, and rivers of chocolate." He frowned. "A place her dollies can play and tables of food."

"Interesting," I whispered.

"I wish white unicorns, señor Barry." Juan's eyes were wide with excitement. "And blue lakes and happy places. No cities. Only small little villages."

"That's nice," I replied. "Ask her if she could have any wishes–"

"Juan tell truth," Benita demanded.

I turned my attention to Benita and made eye contact with Lucia to let her know to help me if I got in too deep.

"Benita," I said. "In two days your calendar ends." She shrugged her shoulders. "You know who Diego thinks I am?" It was more statement than question. She nodded her head. "I think your daughter is Yax Ek' K'ahk' and will be the little girl who will guide us when that moment comes."

"Lupe?" Benita questioned in a whisper. "My Lupe?"

"Señor Barry?" Juan called to me.

"Ahora no," Benita said waving her hand. "You talk señor Barry another time. My Lupe?"

"I don't know for sure, Benita," I said. "I spoke with the village shaman last night and all we know is there will a young maiden who will be pivotal in the ceremony when time is ended. He said a small girl. I think it might be Lupe."

"But señor Barry," Juan whined. "I need to tell you–"

"Hush," Benita scolded. "Ahora no es el momento. Silencio."

I looked to Lucia since I knew Juan wouldn't probably translate whatever had transpired between the two of them. She lowered her eyes and shook her head slightly. I'd have to wait.

So I turned my attention once more to the children at the table. "Tell me how you would make a perfect world," I asked.

Lupe and Juan told me their ideas for a world according to them. I wasn't always sure who had the idea but found many things I felt were Lupe's and others I was sure was Juan's. The one thing I did notice, there was no war, no darkness. I knew in a world there are always two things and they are called 'the opposites' and apply to everything. Without darkness there couldn't be light and without war there could be no peace. This was the ying and the yang of life. I was sure Lupe was only wanting girls and such while I was sure Juan was holding out for a young boy's world. I knew neither could exist in the long run without the other. I listened and I realized why K'ul'ulkan was needed. I was the glue, the mixture to put it all together. Lupe would create, I would stabilize.

Manuel startled me when he came up to notify me of a phone call at the front desk.

* * * * *

"This is Barry Hargrove," I said into the phone.

"I have the item."

There was no doubt in my mind who I was talking to; it was Dr. Adam Montoya.

"Where are you?" I asked in a hushed tone.

"On my way back. I couldn't use your cell for fear they would be tapping it. I'm pretty sure they know who I am."

"Whatever are you blabbering about? Who knows?" I attempted to maintain a semblance of normality, while also trying to display a certain nonchalant calm of disinterest.

"I grabbed the bag last night while working with the cleaning crew," Montoya said. "Anyway, I'm working my way back down and should be in Palenque before sundown. Do you think Miss Camal could pick me up?"

175

"I can pick you up."

"No!" Montoya shouted. "They'll be watching you."

"Then they will be watching her, too," I replied. "Whatever you've gotten us into will now involve her. But I do know somebody who can get you. I'll have Diego take care of things. Just go with the man."

"Who's Diego?"

"Just listen to me," I raised my voice and then noticed people staring at me. I smiled politely and buried my head into my chest. "Don't worry about who Diego is; I'm not sending him. For once, you listen to me and I'll get you safely back to your house. We have a lot to discuss. I think I've found our missing maiden and you won't believe–"

"I have to go now," Montoya interrupted me. "My next flight is leaving. Later."

I stood there listening to dial tone then quietly hung up the phone and thanked the young lady at the front hotel desk.

My fajitas were cold, while Juan and Lupe had finished theirs. Benita and Lucia were in an idle conversation; I had no idea what they were discussing, since it wasn't English. Lucia looked up.

"May I ask who that was?" Lucia queried.

"Our partner in crime." I rolled my eyes. "He has located and procured the lost item and is currently making his way back. Is everyone finished here? I need to check out a couple of things and want to go to the ruins. Everyone find that acceptable?" I watched them nod in agreement.

I herded everyone out to the main lobby and Diego had my car brought to us. I sauntered over to Diego while the group waited.

"May I ask a favor of you?"

The man nodded. "Si, señor Hargrove. Anything K'ul'ulkan wishes."

I nervously glanced about the area. It wasn't busy but I

still got a sinking feeling in my stomach when somebody called me that name. "Please, call me Hargrove. Tell your shaman to find Ah Pukuh at the airport near sunset and take him home." Diego frowned at the request. I gave him ten dollars. "He should understand my wishes; if not, have him call me."

Diego stared at me momentarily then repeated my wishes. "Ah Pukuh. Airport. Sunset." He nodded his head. "Si, señor. As you wish."

I glanced out the door when I heard the car horn blat three times and could see everyone was now in my car and waiting for me. I shook hands with Diego and thanked him. I climbed into the car.

"We're on our way to L'akam Ha and our futures," I said, stepped on the gas pedal and sped toward the ruins.

Chapter 27:
The Sacrifice

Mayan Date: 2 Eznab 1 Kankin ~ 12.19.19.17.18

*"Mighty K'inich Ahau, let the blood of this
warrior bring you happiness with your servant.
The time of No Time is close at hand. Ah Pukuh
and K'ul'ulkan plot against me and the Time Maiden
has yet to be revealed to me.
Guide Chimalpopoca in his search."*

*Prayer of Chac Tun B'alam
Ruler of L'akam Ha*

Palenque Ruins: 9:26 a.m., Wednesday, December 19, 2012

I pulled the car into the parking spot and felt a shudder course through me. Something wasn't right, yet I couldn't put my finger on what it was. It wasn't like the earlier incidences when I passed through time. This was totally different. There was a silence. No birds. No howlers. The lush jungle in absolute quiet was eerie.

"You feel it, don't you, Barry," Lucia whispered gazing

about the trees and shadows.

I nodded my head.

"Señor Barry," Juan called and grabbed my hand between his and held tight.

I look back at Benita; she held Lupe close to her as we slowly made our way up the hidden path to the ruins. Lupe said something and again I glanced back. Lucia reached out and touched my shoulder bringing my attention to her.

"She's just scared, Barry."

My hand pushed the branch out of the way and I instantly saw the excitement at the foot of the Temple of Inscriptions. A cacophony of sounds assaulted me. A group of people were hurriedly milling about and there were flashing lights. A siren screamed in the distance; the howler monkeys shrieked their ire at the mechanical noise, birds cried and called to each other, taking flight in the melee before me. My mind raced to figure out what was going on. I was reminded of when I first saw the ruins and Lucia, with Montoya performing his sacrifice and the gunshot. That moment seemed so long ago – yet it had been only mere days before when I was in the freezing snow and starting on this escapade.

Escapade! A perfect term. What had started out as an assignment was now a great adventure, an escapade. I'd gone in search of an ancient baton and now was involved with bringing the end of the world to a conclusion.

"Lucia! Where the hell have you been?"

I turned to see Emil running toward the temple with Maribel close behind. Lucia rushed toward him, as did I with Juan in tow.

"What's going on?" Lucia asked immediately falling into newscaster mode.

"Either we have a murder or a sacrifice," Emil huffed. "Maybe both. I've been trying to get you all morning. I finally convinced the chief you were probably already here and he allowed me to head out with Maribel."

"Why didn't you call me?" Lucia asked.

"Like I haven't tried? Check your phone messages."

Lucia grabbed her phone and looked at it. "Dead," she said.

"You didn't think to call me?" I asked.

Emil stopped and grimaced at me. "Hell, I've been calling everyone I could think of. I've left messages with Lucia, you, Montoya, the hotel... half of Palenque knows I was looking for Lucia."

I snatched my phone out of its case. I'd discovered earlier that at the ruins I didn't have service, and as expected, it was dead.

"You ready to do this, Lucia?" Emil asked.

Maribel smoothed the last of the makeup and fluffed a few strands of hair. "You look good," she said.

Emil plowed into the group, pushing them aside to move forward to the scene. Lucia and I followed close behind. I'd left Juan to wait for Benita and Lupe since I didn't know exactly what was ahead but felt he didn't need to be subjected. Benita put a comforting arm about him as the small tide of people closed in behind me and I lost view of them.

Emil entered the open area before the temple and stopped, Lucia stepped to the side, followed by Maribel and me. There was the body.

Lucia was a professional. She immediately scanned the area and located a lone officer doing nothing and approached him, all the while tugging Emil behind her.

"Hi, Lucia Camal live at the scene. Can you tell me what has happened here?"

She shoved the microphone in the officer's face for an answer. She'd learned early on if she hesitated the official usually tried to get away. Catching them off-guard was the best way to get answers. He glanced at the camera and eased back. I could see him quickly searching the area for a superior to pass her to, or perhaps a possible escape route. The realization he would be on television became apparent. She noted his name on the small metal badge.

"Officer Sanchez," Lucia began again. "We were notified early this morning–"

"Law enforcement–" Sanchez smiled nervously and cleared his throat. "We were notified of a possible homicide here at the ruins. It was–" He reached down and pulled out a pad and flipped pages. "Yes, it was called in by the park police. At first they considered it a prank by the feathered idiot, the one they call Ah Pukuh, but he hasn't been seen here the last few days – plus, he uses goats. This is a human. It appears the victim was sacrificed at dawn this morning."

"What do you mean 'sacrificed'?" Lucia asked to stop the man's rambling.

"Beheaded, heart removed, lacerations. The typical–" Officer Sanchez's demeanor changed and was no longer casual. "Uh, there's Detective Olney. I'm sure he would have more and better information." He nodded to Lucia's left.

"Sanchez, go help them," Olney barked, snapped an arm up and pointed over his shoulder, all the time eyeing Lucia. "Miss Camal. Always nice of the press to show up."

I had no idea of what was being said but could see the demeanor changes of the people around me. Lucia pulled out her charms and wiles.

"Ah, Detective Olney." She turned to face him. "So good to see you again. It would seem you have a sacrifice on your hands, is that correct?"

Olney knitted his eyebrows in a small facial frown. "I would prefer to call this a homicide, if you don't mind. It appears to me something got a little out of hand last night and a young man was killed."

"Well, that certainly appeared to be native garb and holy

sacrificial blue paint I saw on the body when I passed it a few minutes ago. Are you saying there was a costume party going on here at the Palenque ruins last night?"

"Please, Miss Camal," Olney pleaded while putting a hand over the lens of Emil's camera. "Let's keep this one quiet for a couple of days." He leaned in. "We don't need a lot of pandemonium right now, if you get my drift." He cocked an eye and nodded back at the growing group.

I caught the nod and turned to see the tourists. There were more than usual. It quickly became apparent to me that the news of what had been going on here was being spread. I turned back to Olney and Lucia, leaned in to hear better and felt the shift, the change. People disappeared.

Chac Tun B'alam leered down at me from atop the temple.

"K'ul'ulkan!" He beckoned me up to him. "Chimalpopoca! Bring me the heart so I may offer it up to K'inich Ahau."

I watched, stunned, as Paul cut into the chest, following the rib cage of the victim who reclined on the small stone altar at the foot of the temple. There were no ropes of bondage; the man, very much alive, quietly and willingly offered his body to the gods. Chimalpopoca reached with both hands, one still holding the bloody obsidian knife, into the wound and pulled out the heart of the man. He placed the offering in a jade encrusted bowl then handed it to a young boy who stood nearby. The lad raced up the stairs, all the while being ever so careful not to trip or spill the prize. He knelt before the chief and lifted up the bowl as an offering.

"Mighty K'inich Ahau," Chac Tun B'alam intoned and lifted the bloody mass with both hands high into the sky. "I offer this pure heart of a warrior. Show me the maiden."

He slowly lowered his hands then pressed the heart to lips in a kiss before tossing it onto a small flaming brazier nearby. Blood ran down Chac Tun B'alam's arms and his lower face was smeared in red. He grinned, white teeth glaring through the blood.

"Barry?" Lucia whispered and I turned to her.

She stood there in a white tunic embroidered with conch shells and jade beads. Beside her stood Juan in a similar tunic. My mind was muddled; how did he get up here with Lucia? I couldn't see Lupe or Benita. There were the shadow people who Chac Tun B'alam cursed and I realized they were those we'd left in our travel through time. A horn sounded and I jerked to look back to the priest.

"She has come!" Chimalpopoca bellowed while lowering a shell horn. "I can feel her presence now."

I again looked behind me and could see Benita and Lupe walking through a fog toward us. Benita had a cloth wrapped around her waist and tied in a knot at the hip. Her long, dark hair flowed naturally down over her naked torso. She strutted with calm, regal motion. At her side walked Lupe in a simple tunic of white.

Chac Tun B'alam raised his hand at Benita indicating she should stop. He then looked down at Chimalpopoca. "Does K'inich Ahau demand another sacrifice?"

I looked up. The sky was clear with a couple of clouds; a light breeze fluttered the ceremonial feathers.

Paul moved from behind the altar and stared up at the sun, shading his eyes. Then he strutted about the area in front of the temple gazing at the trees, the clouds and listening to the birds. "There is no omen, Lord Chac Tun B'alam. Mighty K'inich Ahau is pleased."

"K'ul'ulkan! Bring me the maiden."

Juan grabbed my hand. "Don't go, señor Barry. Not good. I lied." He tugged at me. "Please. I tell you truth now."

"Not now, Juan," I whispered and let go his hand, pushing him to stay with Lucia. My strides were deliberate and solid as I walked toward the temple altar alone.

"Mighty Chac Tun B'alam," I shouted. "I am Lord K'ul'ulkan. I do no bidding for a man. Today is not the day."

I stared at Paul and he grinned. "You realize your time is short," he whispered. "He's not going to be satisfied with you putting him off like that. Remember, he is a Mayan lord and not accustomed to being told 'no' by anyone."

"Lord Chac Tun B'alam," I started. "When the time is at hand I will bring you the maiden and time will continue."

I watched the great Mayan leader standing at the top. He nodded a final approval.

"So be it, Lord K'ul'ulkan."

It was over and I turned. The impact of the shift hit me and I felt my eyes flutter before rolling out of focus. I blacked out.

"What the hell was all that about?" Olney screamed. "Who are you? Lucia? I want answers and I want them now."

I felt the warm earth beneath me and I sat up. "Lucia? You okay?"

"She's fine," Olney said in perfect English. "You Americano? Right now you are all coming with me. Somebody has a lot of explaining to do. I don't know exactly how you pulled off this trick, but you're going to tell me how it was done."

"It's not a trick," I mumbled.

"I don't give a shit," Olney snapped. "Who was the dead guy? Do you know how it was done? Who did it? Where is the body now?"

I rubbed my forehead in an attempt to rid myself of the major headache throbbing inside my head. Olney's voice blasted loudly in my ears and even though he was talking English, none of it made any sense.

Lucia knelt down beside me. "You okay, Barry?"

"Fine," I replied. "Just a thumper of a headache. Is everyone else okay?"

"That's right," Olney screamed. "Ignore me. Sanchez?

Take him into custody." He looked at Lucia. "Her, too." He pointed at Benita. "And that one, and grab the kids." He stomped away.

"Where do you want me to take them, detective?"

Olney turned back to face Sanchez. "Let's all go to Mexico City for vacation! Where did you think, officer? I'll be at my desk!" He turned back on his original path. "I'll be waiting! You'd best hurry. Nobody steals a body from under my nose. Nobody."

I gazed about. Olney was right. There was no sacrificed body, Chimalpopoca, Chac Tun B'alam, no temple boy. Just a bunch of people milling about wondering what had happened.

"Confiscate that camera, too," Olney bellowed back. "I want that tape!"

Emil smiled and handed Sanchez the equipment. "Be careful and call me when you're done with it. Here's my card." Emil flicked a card out of his shirt pocket. "He ain't going to like what he doesn't see." He wrinkled his nose at Sanchez. "Been there, done that."

Emil patted me on the shoulder. "You make one damned good show, Barry." He turned to Lucia. "And you looked good, too, but this time, the hottie was her." He nodded toward Benita. "Sorry."

Chapter 28:
Lockup

Mayan Date: 2 Eznab 1 Kankin ~ 12.19.19.17.18

*"Mighty K'inich Ahau, you have shown me the maiden.
Although K'ul'ulkan defies me, I thank
you and offer my blood."*

*Prayer of Chac Tun B'alam
Ruler of L'akam Ha*

Palenque: 2:42p.m., Wednesday, December 19, 2012

We sat huddled in a small room with a single locked, barred and frosted window; a cheap overhead fan circulating at almost ten revolutions a minute which barely caused a breeze; rudimentary furniture, at best; white washed walls and a wooden floor with unknown and questionable stains. The air was stagnant, the room reeked, and I was sweating profusely. I wondered which level of Mayan hell on their ceiba tree this was. I watched as Lucia pulled back sweat-laden strands of hair from her forehead.

Benita nervously eased beside Lucia. "What happened?"

Benita asked in native tongue. "Why did the people disappear? And me?" She motioned to her upper body. "My clothes?" She grabbed Lupe and clutched her close, holding her by the shoulders. "And my Lupe? Why?"

Juan gave me a quick translation. I looked to Lucia who nodded and proceeded to explain what had happened in her native tongue so she would better understand. My headache was subsiding but the excessive heat wasn't really helping it go away very fast.

Then I noticed the mirror. It was small, almost unobtrusive. Not huge like on the cop shows where you discover four or five people watching through it from the other side. This was just a small mirror approximately eighteen inches by maybe two foot. Actually, there were two of them, one each on opposing walls.

"Well, Olney knows what we know," I whispered to Lucia and nodded at the mirror to bring her attention to them. "They probably listened to you tell Benita what happened."

"Do you think they'll believe it?" she asked.

"Well, we've been here over two hours, that much I'm sure of. We got here a little before noon and they fed us. I don't know what's taking so long." I slid my palm up my forehead, pushing the sweat to my hairline.

"Probably going over Emil's tapes," Lucia giggled. "If it was like last time, nothing but static and Olney won't like that."

I winked at her. "We didn't like it either."

There was a click of a key in the lock. The door opened and Olney stepped in. He slowly strutted about the room watching us as our eyes followed him.

"Tell me, Miss Camal," Olney said, pulling the toothpick from his mouth. "Do you really think I'd believe that crap you told her? Time warp? Mayan king? Sun god?" He paused, leaned against the wall and folded his arms in front of him.

"Do I look like that kind of a fool?"

"What did the tape show you?" Lucia asked.

"Exactly what you wanted me to see. Are you going to let me in on the secret of how your man could erase the tape?"

"What did you see?" I asked. "You keep acting like we did something wrong, yet I don't know what that action is. You're accusing us of trickery but you haven't said what the supposed slight of hand is."

"Ah, Detective Hargrove. Exactly why are you here? What is your part in this game?"

I cocked an eye at Olney. "My part? I was hired by a museum to retrieve a stolen artifact. I was able to trace it down here and if all goes well, I will have it in my possession in the next two days."

"The Eyes of Pacal, right?" he sneered. "I've done a lot of research in the last couple of hours. Dr. Martinez was most helpful when I called him. Seems your partner, Dr. Montoya, has also stolen the beaded satchel. Pity he isn't home right now. Do you happen to know his whereabouts?"

I shrugged my shoulders. "Not really," I said. "His housekeeper told me he would be back in a couple of days so he should be back before the end of the week, I'd say."

Olney wagged his index finger in the air. "So, I guess I'm one up on you. Dr. Montoya skipped town immediately after the theft and was last seen at the Cincinnati, Ohio airport getting on a flight to Detroit, Michigan. He alluded security in Detroit and we don't know exactly where he is, but now we know he is headed this way."

"When was he in Detroit?" I asked innocently.

"Is it critical? His flight left Cincinnati at 6:47 a.m. this morning. He should have arrived in Detroit at about 7:30 a.m."

I made quick calculations in my head; 7:30 in Detroit would be 6:30 in Palenque. That was almost two hours before he called me. He knew they were on to him but he was already someplace else. Maybe Chicago? St. Louis?

"So when do we get out of here?" I demanded. "You really have no reason to hold us."

"You're not in the United States, Detective Hargrove. I'll hold you for as long as I want."

"Do you really think you can hold K'ul'ulkan?" I stood up for impact.

Olney walked over to me and thumped an index into my chest pushing me down. "You are not K'ul'ulkan. That much I am damned sure of so don't try pulling any more stupid mind tricks."

I sat back down. "It's not nice to treat a god with disrespect."

"You should be nice to señor Barry," Juan said and kicked Olney in the shin.

Olney reared back to strike but quickly lowered his arm and stepped away from Juan.

"What is it with these mopheads?" He pointed at Juan and Lupe. "Why?"

The door opened again and an officer stuck his head in.

"Detective Olney? They've been released at the request of a judge."

"They what?" Olney screamed. "What judge? How?"

The officer walked over and whispered into Olney's ear. The detective stood there fuming as the officer spoke.

"Fine," he yelled. "You can go." He walked over to the wall and pounded on it a couple of times with his fist before kicking a chair with his foot. "Go on! Get out of here!"

I stood up and motioned for the others to come with me. We'd been freed and I wasn't about to stick around to see if Olney would figure out a way to cancel the order.

Ix'iloom and Emil stood by the front door as we exited. Lucia and Emil hugged. I smiled at Ix'iloom.

"Is Dr. Montoya home?" I asked.

She smiled her ever-pleasant grin and shook her head no. I turned to Emil for answers. He stood there grinning proudly.

"Seems your amigo named Paul approached me after you got arrested. He said for me to go to Dr. Montoya's home and tell Ix'iloom to inform the judge. I did as I was told and here we are."

I shook Emil's hand and hugged Ix'iloom although she wasn't really sure why or what had happened. At least, I don't think she understood.

"Oh, Barry? Paul said something about hidden room at nine tomorrow with Pookie?"

I laughed. The shaman wanted to see the inside of the hidden room and I was to bring Ah Pukuh with me.

"Who's Pookie?" Lucia asked. "Should I be getting jealous?"

I wrapped my arm around her casually. "I don't think so, he's not my type."

Juan again came up to me and pulled on my hand.

"Señor Barry?"

"What is it Juan," I asked and got down on a knee to look him in the eye.

"I tell you truth. Now." There was a determination in his eyes; I was amazed at his resolve.

"Yes, Juan. What is this truth you must tell me?"

"Juan? Juan!" Benita snapped and ran up to him while grabbing his shoulders. "You. Lupe." She waved her hand in exasperation and pushed him toward Lupe.

Juan said something and Benita whispered back. They discussed fervently back and forth in hushed tones, finally Benita won. Juan hung his head and slumped his way to Lupe.

"Do you know what it is?" I asked of Benita.

"Nada," Benita replied. "Nothing, señor Barry." She turned to Lucia and spoke.

Lucia turned then informed me of Benita's wishes. "Benita

is going to get a cab and take the children home. She said she would be sure to have Juan and Lupe at the hotel by eight tomorrow if that is what I wanted."

It sounded fine to me. I nodded my head and then watched the three of them leave in a cab. I waved. Juan was not happy.

It was time to let Ix'iloom return home. I again thanked her for getting us out of detention. We weren't really ever in jail. I told her Dr. Montoya would be home tonight sometime. I wasn't going to be specific since he himself had been somewhat ambiguous.

Lucia's lips tightened and I could see her nibbling on the lower one; I knew something was on her mind. I asked.

"Juan has been attempting to tell you something all day. This morning Benita was on him to tell you the truth. Then suddenly she did a turn-around and didn't want him bothering you with the information. Something isn't right."

"What do you mean?" I asked.

"Not only her," Emil added. "You've pushed him aside when he's tried to talk to you about the truth he needs to tell." He giggled. "Imagine. Little Juan, a secret."

"Exactly," Lucia said. "Juan has a secret and he's been trying to tell you it for some time now. I think the next time he brings it up, you'd best listen to him. It might be important."

"Right now I want to get back to the room and get some rest." I hoped Lucia would join me. "I know Montoya will call me later and have me up all night. Do you need a lift?"

"I think I'll go to my apartment and get some rest, too," Lucia said and yawned.

Emil raised an eyebrow.

"It's not what you think," Lucia said catching the look. "I drank some bad water, got looped and crashed at his hotel last night."

Emil leered at us and stood there waving a pointing finger between us. "You mean to tell me with all the tension you two

191

have had these last few days... nothing? I'm not buying it. But..." He hesitated. "If that's the story you want us to believe, well, Lucia, you're going to have to sell it a lot better than that."

"Speaking of story, did you get the tape back?" Lucia was all business.

"Got it along with the camera and some dandy police documentation of today's little incident at the ruins. It should make for a good newscast... *if* you can get it together in time."

Lucia turned to me, leaned in and gave me a kiss. "Sorry, Barry, but work calls. Later?"

I absently nodded my head. "No problem. See you on the screen."

Palenque: 6:12p.m., Wednesday, December 19, 2012

I sat there in my room and stared at the television. The news was blasting but I wasn't giving it my full attention. My mind was drifting in different directions as to what Paul wanted tomorrow morning and what Montoya was really up to. I would occasionally glance up at the scrolling English text on the screen.

...has been a major rush. With only two more days left until the great event of 2012, much of the world's population is now looking to us for guidance. We are the descendants of the Maya; it is our calendar, our traditions, our world. But what of our world? Lucia Camal was at the ruins earlier today and has a report of a strange occurrence there. Lucia?

I'd heard Lucia's name and immediately stared at the television. A camera panned to another section of the station and Lucia stood there with microphone in hand and a background picture of the ruins of Palenque. The Temple of

Inscriptions was center stage. She started to speak and the English moved across the bottom of the screen. I read as fast as I could.

Thank you, Roberto. Today I went to the ruins and found at the base of the Temple of Inscriptions a grisly sacrifice. It was a human; a young man, prepared for sacrifice with both paint and apparel. It was obvious he was a warrior of the ancient Maya. He'd been decapitated but first his heart had been removed while he still breathed. At least, that is the method of a true Mayan human sacrifice. We don't know who did it or why. The incident remains under investigation by Detective Olney. There is a twist to this bizarre item. While I was there, for a short length of time, I, along with a few others, spoke in the ancient tongue of the Mayans. Those that didn't participate say we were suddenly dressed in ancient apparel and moved about as if we were participating in a ritual. This was all being taped by my cameraman, Emil Santiago. None of the action filmed. It is just a recording of noise and static. And, to add insult to injury, when I came to, the sacrificed body was missing. Detective Olney is investigating this phenomenon further but most leads are coming up short. If anyone who happened to be there today has any pictures of the incident, please contact this station. Back to you, Roberto.

Roberto smiled into the camera and nodded at Lucia who was off-screen.

Thank you, Lucia. In further news, a rocket exploded in an underground...

I flicked off the television. More disasters around the world but nothing overly-dramatic that hadn't been seen before. The mighty and the rich had made plans for this catastrophe. Back home I was sure the President and Congress were getting their families together and heading for the secured areas with their provisions. I smiled. Lucia had revealed the truth of what had happened. I sat there wondering if she had cleared it with Olney but decided I really didn't care. The clock chimed and I noted the time. 6:30 p.m. Lucia should be here in about an hour, maybe a little longer. Montoya? My mind filled with images of Lucia. He would just have to wait.

Chapter 29:
The Gathering

Mayan Date: 3 Cauac 2 Kankin ~ 12.19.19.17.19

"Mighty K'inich Ahau, your night sky vibrates to the harmony. To the center of birth, the maiden will offer you her dreams of creation. I am honored to see this."

> *Prayer of Chac Tun B'alam*
> *Ruler of L'akam Ha*

Palenque: 1:42 a.m., Thursday, December 20, 2012

The phone rang. I wanted to ignore it, but Lucia kept prodding at me. I finally relented and answered the ringing menace while noting the time.

"If somebody hasn't died, this better be universally important," I mumbled.

"This affects the universe," Montoya said. "Get your ass out of bed, tell Lucia to either go back to sleep or go home. You get over here, now!"

"First, you tell me why." I flopped back down onto my pillow and held the phone close to my ear. I could already feel my eyes closing.

"We have just over twenty-four hours to figure this out," he screamed.

"Fine," I said. "Meet me at the Temple of Inscriptions a little before nine tomorrow morning. We'll figure it all out them."

I plopped the phone back into the cradle, rolled over and snuggled in against Lucia. She moaned and I went back to sleep.

The phone rang again. I rolled over, picked up the receiver, dropped it, counted to three, then removed the receiver from the cradle and lay it by the phone. I lay there momentarily looking up at the ceiling when Lucia rubbed her hand across my chest, eased onto my shoulder and nibbled on my ear. "Sleepy?" she whispered.

Palenque: 7:52 a.m., Thursday, December 20, 2012

Diego escorted Benita, Lupe and Juan into the restaurant. He was pleasant and greeted both Lucia and I before excusing himself. Juan glared at me then at Lucia.

"Why is she here?" Juan asked. He scooted into a chair beside me and let Lupe have the chair beside Lucia; Benita sat opposite them.

"She's here to cover the story," I replied, unsure why he was upset. "Do you want a breakfast fajita with extra scrambled eggs?"

"No," he quipped. "Fresh fruit and an empanada." He sat at the table and stared off into the distance.

"I want a breakfast fajita with eggs," Lupe said. "Is that okay, señor Barry?"

"Whatever you want," I said.

Benita said something to Juan and he folded his arms in front of him defiantly.

"Is there a problem?" Lucia asked Benita.

She nonchalantly smiled at Lucia and shook her head. Then she said something to Lucia.

"Ah," Lucia said. "It seems Juan is upset at Lupe's sudden position of importance."

"Why her?" Juan blurted. "Why not me? Because she is a girl?"

"Juan," Benita said. "Esto es su forma de hacerlo. Su estilo. Silencio."

Lucia frowned. "I'm not sure what is going on Barry. Benita and Juan are discussing something yet she says it is nothing." She quietly put her hand over mine on the table. "Maybe later you can talk with Juan. You know, alone. Man to man."

I nodded my head. "Sure." I placed the orders and then rushed to get everyone to eat quickly.

"What is going on?" Lucia asked.

"Why am I rushing everyone?" I pointed at my watch. "Because we need to be at the ruins by 9 a.m. Dr. Montoya is back and is waiting for us and I really think he is going to be just a tad bit upset with me."

Palenque Ruins: 9:16 a.m., Thursday, December 20, 2012

"Where the hell have you been?" Montoya screamed at me. "I was here at 8:30 this morning. You said you'd be here before nine!"

I watched Paul approach from the palace ruins.

"You remember Paul, don't you?" I asked and reached out to shake hands with the newcomer.

"Uh... yeah," Montoya said. "He picked me up last night."

"Well, believe it or not, Paul here is none other than Chimalpopoca, high priest to Chac Tun B'alam." I smiled. "You should have been here yesterday morning, Adam... or

197

should I call you Ah Pukuh? We had ourselves a real party. Paul here did a sacrifice for the chief."

Montoya stood there totally speechless, fumbling for something to say or do. He glared first at me, then to Paul.

"Oh! Did I mention it was a human sacrifice?" I added.

I wanted to make sure that Dr. Adam Montoya totally understood that in his absence I had not been sitting idly by just waiting for his return.

"A sacrif... a human sacrifice?" Montoya asked.

"If it is of any consequence," Paul said. "The warrior was from another tribe who Chac Tun B'alam had captured." He gazed about. "Definitely not one of the tourists."

"What did the police and park security have to say?" Montoya asked.

"Funny you should ask," I said. "I take it that Ix'iloom didn't fill you in. We spent most of the day in lock-up. But, the real interesting part is, Chac Tun B'alam was able to find our missing maiden. The girl to whom time of no time will come. Meet Lupe."

I tugged Lupe up and held her in front of me so she could face Montoya.

"Paul, or should I say, Chimalpopoca could feel her presence from time to time when she came with me to the ruins, but it took the sacrifice to... how did you say it? Align the vibrations so one could see the truth?"

"I take it you didn't see my newscast last night?" Lucia said.

"Let me nutshell," I added. "We have a body. Detective Olney wants answers. We do the time switch Mayan thing, come back and the body is gone. Olney is pissed and wants more answers. Lucia put it all on the line with the newscast. And here we are."

Lucia grabbed my hand and squeezed. "That pretty well puts it all together."

Paul nodded his head in agreement. "There is only one question for you, Dr. Montoya." He leaned in and whispered. "Do you have the Conscience of Pacal? And did you bring it?"

"Actually, that is two questions," Montoya said. "And the answers are yes, and yes." He reached into his pocket and pulled out the beaded bag. "This is the Conscience of Pacal." He opened the bag and pulled out the small baton. "And the Eyes of Pacal."

Paul stared in amazement momentarily then his hands greedily moved through the air toward the two items Adam held.

Montoya pulled them back from Paul's outstretched hands.

"As I see it..." He held up the baton to his the bridge of his nose. "This goes here and I hold the bag over my head." He lifted the small bag up and over his head and stared into the eyes of Paul as best he could, his eyes crossed by the baton. He stood them momentarily. "Nothing," he finally said. "Absolutely nothing. Not even a buzz."

"Perhaps if it was held by a priest it might work," Paul hesitantly offered then lifted his hand to take the items. "If I may?"

Montoya was leery but gave them to Paul.

"It might be worth a try," Montoya said. "I'm only Ah Pukuh, Lord of the Underworld."

"And I'm only K'ul'ulkan," I said. "But right now, we aren't. We're of our world."

Paul held the items and pranced about the area mumbling words that I figured to be some mystical terms he knew. Juan and Lupe were laughing; Benita smiled openly. I had to agree with them that Paul did appear somewhat demented and silly. I was sure any of the nearby tourists would avoid us at all costs.

"He looks funny," Juan said. "Why does he hold the bag over his head?"

"It is to collect the conscience in, Juan," I replied. "It is a ritual K'inich Janahb' Pacal performed many centuries ago."

Juan shook his head. "Not with a bag, señor Barry." He giggled again and held onto me by placing his arm around my waist.

Paul stopped his hopping about, joined us and held the items out to me.

I took the baton and bag from him. Howler monkeys started to scream and yell, their voices being joined by others beyond. It was deafening. The jungle reverberated with the noise. Then, on queue, a flock of birds lifted into the air, their iridescent wings gleaming in the bright morning sun, becoming a moving rainbow in the sky. Nearby songbirds broke into music then the sun shone down, a wide beam of light on the Temple of Inscriptions.

My eyes followed the sunbeam on its path up the temple. At the top stood Chac Tun B'alam. I felt the shift.

"You have returned," Chac Tun B'alam said. "Ah Pukuh, god of the dead, joins K'ul'ulkan in the test."

"Test?" I echoed. "What test?" I shook my head. "Why is he always testing me?"

"Bring me the Eyes and Conscience of Pacal," the chief demanded. "We will see if K'ul'ulkan can see my inner self." He stretched and placed both hands on his hips. "You have returned my maiden of time. Watch and behold."

Chimalpopoca led the way up the stairs with Ah Pukuh and K'ul'ulkan following.

Chac Tun B'alam stared me in the eye. "Prepare yourself for the test of K'inich Janahb' Pacal. Look inside your faithful follower." He spread out his arms. "I am Chac Tun B'alam, chief of L'akam Ha. Behold my pureness."

I held the baton in my hand as I had been taught and brought it up to the bridge of my nose. My eyes crossed, there was no way to stop it and I couldn't focus. It was nauseating. I raised my arm over my head, the bag I held in my palm.

"What is this?" Chac Tun B'alam asked. "Where is the Conscience of Pacal?" He reached up and snatched the bag from my palm. "Do the gods play with me?"

Chimalpopoca immediately fell to his knees before the chief.

"Mighty Chac Tun B'alam," he said. "If this is not the Conscience of Pacal, please reveal to me the truth so I may attain it for K'ul'ulkan. I have failed you."

"No, the gods have failed me," he replied and slowly walked around me. "Does not K'ul'ulkan remember?" He pulled out a small dagger. "Are you truly a god? Do you bleed?"

"Chac Tun B'alam!" Chimalpopoca yelled. "You dare to challenge a god? You have tested him over and over. Did not your blade go through him with no effect? Did he not escape the hidden room? Did he not call on mighty K'inich Ahau in the night and bring fire from his hands?"

The chief returned the dagger to its place but stopped and glared into my eyes, searching for anything that would indicate a perceived flaw. If I flinched now it was over. I stared back at him with icy eyes.

"Come!" he demanded and led the way toward the stairs which went to K'inich Janahb' Pacal's resting place.

"That was close," Montoya whispered. "Fire from the hands? You didn't tell me everything."

"Behold," Chac Tun B'alam said and opened the hidden chamber. He stepped in and pointed at an image I'd missed when I was locked inside. It was K'inich Janahb' Pacal with a baton and he was holding a skull over his head.

"Oh, shit," Montoya whispered. "We need to do a sacrifice first?"

"Well I do know how to perform them," Paul said. "I don't like doing it but if needed."

"Chimalpopoca! Show them out."

Paul motioned for us to follow. Montoya again quickly scoured the area for anything he felt might be of importance. We followed the priest up the stairs. The sun was already at its zenith. Again, time had slipped by.

"Before K'inich Ahau sleeps today you will bring me the Conscience of Pacal," Chac Tun B'alam said. His voice was not demanding but it held an ominous promise if we failed. "I send Chimalpopoca to watch and assist you. Go!"

Two gods and a priest were dismissed. As I walked down the steps of the Temple of Inscriptions I could feel the shift again. My headdress was gone. In the distance I could see Lucia, Juan, Benita and Lupe. They, too, were once more citizens of the modern world.

I looked at my watch. 12:02 p.m. The scorching mid-day sun beat down on us. I could feel the sweat starting to gather on me.

"Shall we join forces at my villa?" Montoya asked. "It is cool there and Ix'iloom can fix us all a refreshing drink."

We left the ruins. In the distance, Chac Tun B'alam's eyes followed the group as they crossed the area in front of the palace, turned for the jungle and headed out the employee's entrance. He smiled.

"Yax Ek' K'ahk' continues to hide but I have found her," he said.

Chapter 30:
New Plans

Mayan Date: 3 Cauac 2 Kankin ~ 12.19.19.17.19

*"Mighty K'inich Ahau, will you accept my offering
when the time of no time comes? I seek the
Conscience of Pacal. Guide my brothers
in their search and return them to me."*

*Prayer of Chac Tun B'alam
Ruler of L'akam Ha*

Palenque: 1:20p.m., Thursday, December 20, 2012

We sat there in the living room of Dr. Montoya; not one of us had an idea what the Conscience of Pacal could be. Benita had taken Lupe home and Juan had fought to stay with us even though he was still being a bit rude to Lucia. Paul was quiet to the extent that one quickly forgot he was even present.

Ix'iloom came into the room with tall glasses of a misty yellow drink. I took a glass and sipped. Lemonade. Not exactly what I'd expected, but then I saw her daughter come in with a tray of treats. My mouth started to water when I recognized them as the same delectables that I'd had on an earlier visit.

My cell phone rang and I couldn't help but smile when I saw the name.

"Detective Hargrove," I said flipping it open.

"I'm sure you're probably sitting with the thief at this very moment," Dr. Martinez said. "Do you have both items now?"

"Ah, so *now* you call. I thought you fired me. Tell me, am I on retainer or not?"

I could hear him at the other end as he fussed and fumed. "Do not mock me, Mr. Hargrove. Have you secured the items we hired you to find?"

"It is Detective Hargrove," I corrected. "And again I ask you, am I on retainer? I distinctly remember you firing me a mere few days back. So, in reality, I'm no longer working for you. Besides, it was only one item I was to retrieve."

There was a momentary silence.

"Do you have the items or not? Both of them?" There was no denying Dr. Martinez was totally pissed and didn't want me being a smart ass.

"If you mean a small baton encrusted with gems, pieces of jade and turquoise. The answer is yes. If you mean a small beaded bag that would hold it, the answer is also yes. In fact I have them in my personal possession right this minute. I'm even rolling the baton between my thumb and forefinger as we speak." I attempted to be as casual as I could. I now had the old fart over the proverbial barrel.

"MR. HARGROVE!" Martinez screamed.

Lucia rolled her eyes and Montoya began to snicker.

"Detective Hargrove," I again corrected.

"Those items are rare antiques and not play toys. They should be handled with gloves and given the proper care." Martinez breathed heavily and I was sure he was nearing a heart attack. "You need to return those items immediately to the proper authorities here at the museum."

"Actually," I said. "I'll return them to the original owners later today. Seems a certain Mayan chief by the name of Chac Tun B'alam wants them for a ceremony."

"You wouldn't," Martinez said. "They are the property of this museum."

"Are you willing to bargain?" I asked. A thought occurred to me and I decided to see if I could bluff my way through to an answer.

"A bargain? What type of bargain?"

I'd piqued Martinez's curiosity. He wanted the two items and I needed information. I remembered him bragging about his interpretive skills and decided to test his knowledge.

"You tell me what the Conscience of Pacal is, and I'll make sure these items get back to you."

"Oh my god," he exclaimed. "Don't tell me he stole that, too."

The phone went dead.

"Dr. Martinez," I said. "Are you still there?" I shrugged my shoulders, flipped the phone shut and grimaced at the group. "I have no idea what happened. He wondered if you'd stolen that item."

"What item?" Montoya asked eagerly.

I again shrugged my shoulders and threw open my hands. "I don't know. He hung up."

"Who will be sacrificed?" Juan asked.

He had been quiet for most of the day except when he was being mean to Lucia. His words jolted me.

"What do you mean, Juan? What sacrifice?"

"I saw the picture. It showed a man holding a head over his head. A sacrifice. Yes?"

"You needn't worry," I said and placed a comforting arm around him for a hug to give him some hope.

"It was a small head, señor Barry," Juan replied. "A very small head." He hesitated. "A child's head?"

"I'm not so sure it was a head," I said.

"What makes you think that?" Montoya asked. "It certainly looked like one to me."

I glared at the man and then rolled my eyes with a slight nod toward Juan. He quickly realized what I was attempting to accomplish, but unfortunately too late.

"Juan?" Lucia called. "Would you like to go with me to the kitchen and see if we can help Ix'iloom? I bet she has some really delicious sweets there."

He looked to me and I nodded approval. I could see Juan's internal conflict since he'd been so nasty to her and Lucia was being nice back. Lucia took his hand and led him to the kitchen, away from us and our talk of sacrifices.

"I don't see any way around it," Montoya said. "Paul? You said you could do a sacrifice? Would it have to be somebody we knew?"

Paul grinned. "I have no idea who the sacrifice was yesterday. Chac Tun B'alam had him brought forward. I figured he was from a nearby village, a captive, so to speak."

"Hold on," I said.

"What you frowning about, Barry?" Montoya asked. He eased back into his chair and puffed on a cigar that he'd just lighted.

"That wall mural the chief showed us," I started. "There are others, and they are very detailed, including dripping blood."

"So?" Paul said.

"There was no dripping blood," I said excitedly. "K'inich Janahb' Pacal held up the skull or something that looked like a skull."

Montoya leaned forward. "Now that you mention it, there was absolutely no detail on the skull. Just an outline. Maybe we *thought* it was a skull, but it isn't that at all."

Again, my cell phone rang. It was Martinez.

"This is Detective Hargrove," I said. "And before we continue, you haven't stated whether or not I am in service to you. Am I on a retainer?"

"At least he didn't get the Conscience of Pacal," he said. "Return the two items and we will discuss your fees further."

I sat there stunned. The phone fell out of my hand and went skittering across the tiled floor to rest near a rug. Montoya reached over and picked up the phone.

"He has it," I mumbled. "He has the Conscience."

"What?" Montoya asked. He stared at the phone momentarily, and then brought it up to his ear. "You have the Conscience of Pacal?"

"Dr. Montoya, I assume," Martinez said snidely. "You are a thief and I want the museum pieces returned immediately. Do you hear me?"

Again the phone went silent.

"The bastard hung up," Montoya said. "He wants me to return these items."

"He said he had the Conscience of Pacal," I repeated. "*He* has it, not us."

"I really don't think the chief is going to like this," Paul said. "How will the ceremony be performed without all the proper pieces in play?"

My mind shifted into overdrive. If Martinez had the item and knew what it was, we could probably figure out what it was, too. Trying to attain the item in a timely fashion might prove more difficult. But before we could attain it, we needed to know what it was.

"I don't think we will be doing a sacrifice," Paul said.

I wasn't sure if he was happy or sad at the prospect but I nodded my head in agreement.

"You mentioned the mural," Montoya said. "In it I noticed K'inich Janahb' Pacal was painted, the sky was painted, the other natives were painted. Hell, even the baskets were painted

207

in a variety of colors. But the skull, the skull was just an outline. Why wasn't it painted? Why wasn't there blood if it was indeed a sacrifice?"

"No blood, no sacrifice," I said. Paul nodded. "No color. Was it white?"

"That doesn't make sense," Paul said. "K'inich Janahb' Pacal's eyes were white. Natives had on white. So the skull would have been painted white. Like we said earlier, maybe it isn't a skull."

"Maybe it is invisible," Juan said as he came back into the room with Lucia.

"Oh my god!" I exclaimed. "I was thinking it might be a mask but it isn't that. It is the crystal skull. Martinez still has the crystal skull. I remember seeing it at the museum when I first started this investigation!"

Montoya started to laugh.

"What is so funny?" Paul asked.

"He never had the skull," Montoya said. "He has a crystal skull but not the one from K'inich Janahb' Pacal's death chamber. Follow me."

Montoya got up and headed back to his office. I couldn't believe he was going to reveal his secret laboratory to everyone.

"This," he said and held up a crystal skull. "This is the skull from K'inich Janahb' Pacal's funerary. I had a duplicate commissioned and the museum displays it."

"You stole this?" I asked.

Lucia glared at him. "How many other items have you stolen from the ruins?" She shook her head. "I was starting to like you, but I'm starting to suspect that I was right about you from the start."

The skull glistened in the light and I was mesmerized by it. Suddenly I felt a tug in my fingers. The baton I still held was demanding attention.

"Would you mind?" I asked and reached for the skull. I raised my other hand with the Eyes of Pacal in it.

Montoya gently eased the crystal skull into my palm and I carefully lifted it over my head as the mural had indicated. I held the baton up to my eyes.

Although my eyes were crossed, I gazed into Paul's eyes. The connecting force was staggering. It was if the crystal skull was collecting the light and projecting it through my eyes, which was then concentrated by the baton. Not only could I see into Paul's mind, I could feel his emotions and his thoughts as if they were my own. My hand holding the baton dropped, and I blinked my eyes to straighten them. The baton continued to vibrate in my hand.

"My god! It was everything. I saw, felt, and heard everything Paul did."

"I felt nothing," Paul said, and then hesitated. "Well, I did feel like I wanted to escape. May I try?"

Montoya grabbed the baton and skull. "I have held the baton and skull before," he said. "Do you think I wouldn't have felt some inkling of power?"

Paul reached for the baton. "Again – may I try?"

Montoya held the baton to his eyes and lifted the glistening skull above his head. He looked into my eyes. I felt nothing and could see frustration in Montoya's face. He squinted his eyes then widened them. He lowered his hand and placed the skull and baton on the table.

"Why you?" he asked. "What makes you so special?"

Ix'iloom had been silently standing at the doorway with a tray. "You are Ah Pukuh, god of the underworld. You see death and in death there is nothing." She set the tray on the table. "I brought the refreshments here since you were no longer in the main room."

Paul had the baton and skull and was looking into Lucia's eyes.

209

"You are a lowly priest, Chimalpopoca," Ix'iloom said and smiled at Paul. "K'inich Janahb' Pacal was as a god. Only a god can command the toys of a god."

Paul put the items back down. "So only a limited few may use these?" he asked.

Ix'iloom nodded her head.

"How is it you know these items?" Montoya asked. "You know what the Eyes of Pacal and the Conscience of Pacal were and yet you said nothing?"

"My grandfather told me the stories of our people," Ix'iloom said. "His grandfather told him and his grandfather's grandfather told him. I know the legends and traditions. I am a Mayan."

"Do you know who Yax Ek' K'ahk' is?" I asked.

"She is hidden," the old woman said, a sly curl at the edge of her mouth. "At the time of need, she will come forward and all secrets will be known."

I grabbed a tasty morsel from the tray as Montoya strutted over to Ix'iloom.

"You are learned in the ancient Mayan legends," Montoya said as he circled Ix'iloom like a vulture over its carrion. "Have you passed your knowledge to another? To your daughter?"

"There is no need." She spoke with a monotone voice and cast a condescending glance in his direction. "Tomorrow ends time. It will be the time of new time and the old ways will be gone." She smiled, bowed her head then turned and headed for the door.

"Sort of ominous," Lucia said. "But at least she didn't say it was the end of the world."

On queue, the house shook as an earth tremor coursed its path through the planet.

Ix'iloom stood in the doorway and smiled, again it was that smile to shame the Mona Lisa. "This is not of your doing,

K'ul'ulkan. You have not wiggled your tail. This is the harmonic vibrations which have started. Time is coming to an end." She glanced over to Paul. "Is that not right, oh, mighty Chimalpopoca?"

I watched Ix'iloom; we had a new player in the game.

Chapter 31:
A Plot Thickens

Mayan Date: 3 Cauac 2 Kankin ~ 12.19.19.17.19

"Mighty K'inich Ahau, your journey will soon end.
Time is ending. Tomorrow you will smile
on a new day; a day of Yax Ek' K'ahk's making.
May the gods guide her."

Prayer of Chac Tun B'alam
Ruler of L'akam Ha

Palenque: 6:27p.m., Thursday, December 20, 2012

"K'ul'ulkan," Ix'iloom said and wagged a finger at me. "Since you no longer shake your tail and these tremors are not of your doing, rest for the battle that approaches. Mighty K'inich Ahau moves to sleep the night and the Bolontiku will do the bidding of Yax Ek' K'ahk' as she commands. You must be strong for her and await her call."

"Wait a minute," Montoya yelled. "This is my house. I will say what happens here."

Ix'iloom raised her hand to silence the doctor. Everyone in

the room stared at the old Mayan woman who suddenly now was in command of the situation.

"Chac Tun B'alam awaits you now at the Temple of Inscriptions. My son is patient but as ruler, he needs to be obeyed."

"Your son is Chac Tun B'alam?" Paul asked. "How is it all these years I have served him and never once knew this?"

Ix'iloom turned a casual glance to the little man. "Chimalpopoca, you have been trained in our ways, yet you have learned nothing. I saw in you the potential to be a great priest, but you have played local shaman. Your time at the school was a waste. Now at the time of no time, you will be thrust into the position for which you were groomed. You may succeed, you may fail. It is of your power and knowledge to decide the outcome." She glanced out the window. "The time has come, my son awaits your return. We must gather the others."

"The others?" I asked. I had been standing there with a morsel melting in my mouth. I was in shock of what was happening. "Who are the others?"

"Those needed to fulfill the destiny," Ix'iloom said and removed her apron. "Diego, Lupe, and Benita. I shall get my daughter."

Juan ran to me and tugged so he could whisper in my ear. "Will they sacrifice Lupe?" Juan asked. "She is my friend." A tear slowly rolled down his cheek.

"I don't think so," I whispered back and gently wiped his cheek with my thumb. "I think she is Yax Ek' K'ahk', so I don't think they'd sacrifice her."

"Oh," he said. With an unusual sober and solemn expression. "It will be another's fate for sacrifice. If that is what is to happen..." He didn't finish his sentence.

Ix'iloom kneeled down to Juan and spoke quickly in the local dialect.

"What'd she say?" I asked.

"She said this sacrifice is an honor reserved for one of the royal family." Montoya frowned at his words. "Like Yax Ek' K'ahk', the chosen will come forward when needed."

"They are here," Ix'iloom said.

"Who's here?" I asked. I was totally perplexed.

"This is my damned house!" Montoya shouted. "Who is here?"

"You don't get it?" Lucia said. She stood there with her arms folded in front of her and shaking her head. "You two aren't in command any more." She turned to Emil. "Are you getting all this? It will look great on tomorrow's broadcast."

"If there is one," I quipped. "You suddenly seem quite at ease with all that is going on."

"There is one thing I have learned as a reporter and newscaster," Lucia said. "Roll with the punches." She wrinkled her nose at me before pinching and wiggling the end of my nose in her fingers. "Besides, this is too good not to just go with the flow."

Ix'iloom's daughter entered the room followed by Diego, Benita and Lupe.

"I brought them as instructed," Diego said and nodded to Ix'iloom.

Again, the tremors rocked the house and I steadied myself with the table while keeping the scepter and skull from falling onto the floor. I could only start to wonder what was happening elsewhere in the world.

"What is this?" Paul asked. "You worked with me, Diego. Why are you doing her bidding now?"

"I have always done her bidding," Diego said. "You only thought I worked with you. That was the way it was to be." He held his head up with a certain authority. "I am sorry to have deceived you."

Distant drums started beating; the tempo was hypnotic,

demanding and calling.

"K'ul'ulkan," Ix'iloom called. "If you will carry the items of the ceremony, we should all now gather in the two vehicles outside and go to my son." She smiled. "As you have learned, it is not wise to keep him waiting."

"What if I don't want to go?" I asked. "What if I have decided this is just a bunch of crap and–" I folded my arms in front of me defiantly. "What if I refuse to go? I'm tired of being told to do this or go there."

"You are K'ul'ulkan. You will do as needed." Ix'iloom looked about the room for anyone else to refuse. "You all will do as I tell you."

"My family has always been good to you," Montoya started. He walked to her with outstretched arms. "Have I not been fair with you? Was not my father? My grandfather? Why do you do this?"

"It is not you to us but us to you," she replied. "We have been very good to you, Ah Pukuh. We have made sure your family was provided for, given a good life, wealth, prestige and honor. In doing so, it helped us, the royal Mayan family. It was known Ah Pukuh would be of this family and it was destined you would arouse K'ul'ulkan to bring him back to our land. All that has occurred was written before K'inich Janahb' Pacal ruled. As time ends so do the prophecies. Now the kindness to your family is to be repaid. The prophecy must be complete." She nodded to the kitchen door. I could see six or seven strong Mayan warriors waiting in the kitchen. "I do not want to use force. Shall we go to L'akam Ha?"

As I stepped out of the cool, air conditioned room of Montoya's domicile, my mind wrapped around Ix'iloom's words. Montoya had been sent, even though he thought he went of his own volition, to steal the baton. It was necessary to bring me, the white war god, K'ul'ulkan, to L'akam Ha. I was startled to see my car sitting there. It was parked right next to

Montoya's car, which is what had brought us from the jailhouse here. My mind raced to put it all together; Diego had taken my car to pick up Benita and Lupe. I could see the keys in the ignition. It only took me a couple of seconds to open the driver's door and sit down; I had my seat.

"I'm riding with you," Lucia said and hopped into the front passenger seat.

"Actually, Miss Camal," Ix'iloom said. "You will ride with Dr. Montoya."

Lucia cocked an eye at the old Mayan woman but there was something in Ix'iloom's voice that forced Lucia to decide she wanted to ride with Montoya.

"Sure, no problem," Lucia finally said, and got out.

"Lupe, Juan, please," Ix'iloom said and waved the two children over to my convertible.

Benita started to walk with Lupe to the car.

"No!" Ix'iloom said and glared at Benita. The old Mayan woman quickly jerked her head at the other car and Benita let go of Lupe's hand. She slowly slunk her way to Montoya's vehicle.

"My daughter and I will also go in this car. The rest of you will go in that car."

I glanced over at Ix'iloom. She had taken control of the group and we were children doing exactly as we were told. It was time to be the bratty child. "I want Lucia to ride with us," I demanded.

Ix'iloom glared at me. "You are a god and as such, your demands should be acknowledged and obeyed." She slowly turned to Lucia and I couldn't see Ix'iloom's face. "Do you wish to ride with this man?" she asked.

Lucia slowly pushed back her long, dark hair over her left ear, looked at the old woman and froze. Lucia's eyes told it all. They reflected a fear. "No," she muttered and lowered her eyes. "I wish to ride there." Lucia pointed at Montoya's vehicle and slowly sauntered toward it.

Ix'iloom turned back to me. There was no denying the small smile or smug glint in her eyes; she was a Mayan Mona Lisa. She had controlled Lucia just as she was controlling the rest of us.

There was a niggling at the back of my mind. If I was a god and must be obeyed, why was it acceptable for Lucia to refuse my demand? Did she command special treatment? Who was Lucia? What was her part in this game we were playing?

The old Mayan woman opened the door to the convertible and allowed Juan, Lupe and her daughter to get into the back seat. Juan gave me a furtive look and I could only make a small grimace and hope he would understand. Ix'iloom then plopped her body in the front passenger seat.

I'd been holding the two items, the baton in its beaded bag and the crystal skull. I placed them carefully between Ix'iloom and me. She watched and nodded approval.

"My son, Lord Chac Tun B'alam awaits us. We go." Ix'iloom voice left no questions to be asked.

I eased the convertible out of Montoya's compound and I was soon headed on the road to the ruins. A quick glance in the rear view mirror let me know Montoya hadn't dallied and was following right behind me on our path to our future or to our end.

The jungle welcomed us. Howler monkeys raised a cacophony of grunts and howls. Birds flitted in front of us; quick darts of color. L'akam Ha called.

Chapter 32:
The Death of Venus

Mayan Date: 3 Cauac 2 Kankin ~ 12.19.19.17.19

"Mighty K'inich Ahau, your last journey ends. The Conscience of Pacal calls and soon I shall see that which only the gods know. Yax Ek' K'ahk' comes."

> *Prayer of Chac Tun B'alam*
> *Ruler of L'akam Ha*

Palenque Ruins: 8:42p.m., Thursday, December 20, 2012

I worked my way through the fence, pushing it open to make it easier for the others to follow me. The workers had secured it for the evening. The sun had yet to fully set, but still the shadows deepened in the forest. In the distance the howler monkeys crooned to one another; the jungle was quietly making the preparations for another night. There was strangeness in the sounds... or possibly the lack of sounds. It was as if the world beyond the realm of man knew what was happening. A stone gave way beneath my shoe.

"Be careful, señor Barry," Juan said.

My little companion had been silent for the most part and I knew he was thinking about the possibility of a sacrifice. Ix'iloom had been very blunt that only a member of the royal family would be acceptable. Still, I believed Juan wasn't fully satisfied with the answer.

I moved from the dense jungle growth into the open area of the ruins. Lucia hustled up to join me and snuggled close with an arm intertwined in mine.

"We go," Ix'iloom stated. "My son waits."

I hesitated and took a look at our small group. The park was closed. I was surprised that no park security was walking about, but figured they probably only did rounds from time to time.

The group. I shook my head at the motley makeup of such an eclectic group. Lucia Camal, newscaster. Emil Santiago, news cameraman. Dr. Adam Montoya, thief and archeologist, also known as Ah Pukuh, god of the underworld. Paul, the local Mayan shaman mystic who was also Chimalpopoca, priest to Chac Tun B'alam. Ix'iloom, an elderly Mayan and her daughter. Benita, another younger Mayan woman. Diego, a Mayan man. I glanced down at Juan who held tightly onto Lupe's hand. Two children, and one of them was going to make the decision of the new world. I had wanted to talk to Lupe more so I had a better understanding of what she liked and what she could possibly create, but time had not allowed me that luxury. And then there was me, a two-bit private detective that couldn't even do a job right, who had stumbled into this mess without even trying. I was also K'ul'ulkan, a god, right-hand man to K'inich Ahau.

We strolled across the open pavilion of grass in front of the royal palace toward the Temple of Inscriptions. The sun hid behind the trees but the dusky light allowed us to easily see our way.

Suddenly, the top of the Temple of Inscriptions

illuminated as a large beam of sunlight broke through the jungle growth to light the building. The winter equinox was close at hand.

My vision blurred and head shifted as I felt the weight of the headdress on me. I could feel the leather straps across the chest, the heavy gold necklace. My legs chafed a little with the loincloth but still the weight of the harness with its embellishments was obvious. I strode forward as K'ul'ulkan, the Feathered Serpent. Beside me, Lucia now wore a white cotton skirt with a minimum of embellishments. Around her neck were necklaces of beads and shells and her dark raven hair flowed softly down her back. There were white markings on her face. She was Sak Ek' Janahb. Montoya was in his dark skeletal garb and appeared quite garish and frightening; he was Ah Pukuh, the Lord of the Underworld.

A small hand grabbed hold of me and I looked down to see Juan. He was in a white, cotton tunic; his hair, now long, was pulled back in what appeared almost a ponytail. Beside him was Lupe in a matching tunic with her hair pulled back to duplicate Juan's. They appeared like twins and again, something niggled at me; they looked so much alike.

"Is this what you guys saw?" Emil whispered. "I wish I had my camera now. This is unbelievable."

I turned to look at him as he followed me. He was bare-chested, long hair pulled back from the sides and held by a shell broach while the rest hung down his back. It was very unlike Juan's. He wore a simple white loincloth with a few decorations. Emil had black lines curling across his face. Diego was beside him and he, too, wore a similar outfit to match Emil's. The markings on Diego's face were red. Close to Diego was Benita. She again was dressed in a white skirt with a slit on the side; a belt of silver cinched her waist. She also had necklaces of beads and bells around her neck. Her long hair barely covered her breasts. The markings on her face were yellow and zigzagged down her cheeks like miniature lightning bolts.

Where were Ix'iloom and her daughter? I turned and looked the other way, beyond Lucia, and saw them. Ix'iloom was regal appearing. She wore a multi-colored skirt decorated with pearls and small metal beads. Around her neck was a necklace of jade and turquoise that lay atop the small cape she wore for modesty purposes. Ix'iloom's hair was held atop her head with a comb of jade and silver. In her hands she carried the Conscience of Pacal and the Eyes of Pacal. Her daughter walked beside her in a skirt of pure white cotton. She wore a cape of iridescent blue green, which I soon realized was made of thousands of small feathers.

The compound was alive. Torches flickered. The ruins of Palenque were no more. I was walking in the reality of L'akam Ha. This was the city of flowing waters. A jewel in the jungle.

Before me stood Chac Tun B'alam resplendent with his bare chest and blue-green cape. His headdress of gold and iridescent feathers glistened in the firelight. There was another beside him. It was Paul. No, it was Chimalpopoca. He wore a plain loincloth and a large cape of blue-colored feathers. His headdress was a mix of serpent and skull with more feathers. I wondered how he had gotten to Chac Tun B'alam before me, but I decided that was how shaman's worked.

"K'ul'ulkan! Ah Pukuh!" Chac Tun B'alam called. "You return. Do you bring me the Eyes of Pacal? Have you located the Conscience of Pacal?"

"My son," Ix'iloom said. "I bring to you that which you seek." She moved forward lifting her arms to show the items she held in her hands. She walked proudly toward her son the chief.

Chac Tun B'alam turned his head slowly to her and cast a downward glance. The displeasure was obvious on his face.

"You have spent too much time as a servant, my mother,"

he said with disdain. "You forget your position; you are of the royal family. Allow a servant to bring them to me."

Ix'iloom stumbled, upset; she stopped and let her hands collapse to her sides. Juan immediately ran up to her and started to take the items.

"No!" Chac Tun B'alam yelled. His eyes were wide and the whites quite visible in the waning twilight.

A native slowly approached Ix'iloom but the chief raised his hand and waved the young man to stop. He then pointed at Lupe.

"You. Bring me the Eyes and Conscience of Pacal."

Lupe had grabbed hold of my hand when Juan had run to Ix'iloom. I realized it seemed proper that the girl who would bring in the new world should be the one to take the items to the current ruler. It took a little encouragement but I got Lupe to go to Ix'iloom.

The small girl, obviously intimidated by the hoopla around her, carefully took the items from Ix'iloom then slowly walked toward Chac Tun B'alam. She raised her arms with the items as she had seen the old Mayan woman do. She stood quietly facing the chief.

"Do you not kneel before your ruler?" Chac Tun B'alam asked. He gave her a snarly look then snatched the items from her and placed them on the small altar at the foot of the temple. Like the strike of a snake, he grabbed Lupe's wrist and pulled her to Chimalpopoca. "Our first offering to the gods," he said. "Puny, but young."

"*Offering? A sacrifice?*" I thought. "*He couldn't be doing that... not to Lupe, she was Yax Ek' K'ahk'.*"

"Do you not kneel before your gods?" I demanded and stepped forward. "Do you also plan to offer yourself as sacrifice?" A movement to my side caught my attention and I saw Juan starting to race toward Lupe. "No!" I yelled, and raised my hand to stop him. I looked back to the three at the base of the temple. "Lupe, come here," I said.

She struggled with the grip Chimalpopoca had on her but couldn't find a way free.

"Let her go," I said to the priest. To my left I saw Montoya come forward. "Chimalpopoca, I–"

Lupe kicked the little priest in the shin. He yelped and released her. She ran toward me and both Lupe and Juan hugged me at the same time.

"So the War Serpent, the great Feathered Serpent is now the defender of children?" Chac Tun B'alam's words were snide and meant to sting me.

"Mock not the gods," Ix'iloom said. "Tonight you stand in the presence of K'ul'ulkan and Ah Pukuh. One can raise you up to the sun, the other can take you to the lowest depths of the underworld. Remember, my son, you may be a ruler but you are still mortal, only a man."

Chac Tun B'alam jerked about to face his mother. His eyes narrowed with anger and his nose flared as he breathed. "Again, my mother, you have forgotten your place," he snarled.

"My lord," Chimalpopoca said. "Behold the star." He pointed at a bright star on the western horizon. "It begins, the death of Venus."

I felt a tug at my heart and my knees weakened.

Chac Tun B'alam leered at me. "So it is, mighty K'ul'ulkan. Your star–" He pointed to the bright star on the horizon barely above the treetops. "Tonight it dies and with it, the reign of the Plumed Serpent ends." His eyes twinkled with delight. "Yes. Tonight you die, K'ul'ulkan."

Chapter 33:
The Conscience of Pacal

Mayan Date: 3 Cauac 2 Kankin ~ 12.19.19.17.19

"Mighty K'ul'ulkan, Lady Yax Ek' K'ahk'
Lead us to our destiny."

Prayer of Pacal Tun B'alam
Son of Chac Tun B'alam

L'akam Ha: 9:37p.m., Thursday, December 20, 2012

Juan grabbed me by my waist and hugged me tightly.

"No, señor Barry. No," he cried. "You cannot die."

I reached down and turned his pouty face up to me. Tears rolled down the cheeks from puffy red eyes. In so few days this kid had reached in and wrapped himself around my heart, and now he tugged at its strings.

"I'm not going to die," I said in the most convincing voice I could muster. If what Chac Tun B'alam had said was right, perhaps my time was coming to an end. I glanced over at Lucia and could tell there was a welling of tears in her eyes as well.

"If somebody must die, let it be me," Juan said and pulled

away. "I have been lying. I am just an orphan and nobody will miss me. Bad people should die, not good ones. I deserve to die."

"Now wait a minute." I kneeled down to him. "Exactly where do you get the idea you're a bad person? Juan, you've been the best interpreter anyone could ever want. You've helped me out more times than I can count." I attempted to ruffle his hair but with it pulled back so tightly, I just rubbed the top of his head. "You've been the best amigo I could ever hope for."

Again Juan pulled away from me.

"I have lied," he said defiantly. His eyes searched my face, my eyes, for anything to show him I was upset or annoyed, maybe even compassion. "That makes me bad."

"Come, Juan," Benita said and placed a comforting arm about him. See looked at me then to the chief. "You have important business. This is not the time for a child's hysterics." She reached for Lupe's hand and the three of them backed into the shadows behind us. Diego joined her.

"Behold!" Chimalpopoca said and pointed to the east. "They shall continue to lift into the sky until the time of the new world. The center of birth and renewal has risen. To the west is the death of Venus, to the east is birth."

I could the Pleiades on the horizon. There was a flash on memory; an article I'd read about the Pleiades. It was something about the scientists finding a cloud or whatever near there where the actual birth of the universe appeared to be happening. My mind raced with the knowledge. How had these Mayans known that? And so long ago?

Chac Tun B'alam again leered at me. "Watch your demise, mighty K'ul'ulkan. You have Ah Pukuh to lead you to your final resting." He laughed and picked up the Eyes and Conscience of Pacal. "Come to me, oh mighty K'ul'ulkan. Show me the glories of a god."

225

"You mock the gods," Ix'iloom said.

Chac Tun B'alam glared at his mother. "Be still, old woman. Learn your place." He turned again to me. "Come, Lord K'ul'ulkan."

Not to be intimidated, I strode calmly forward and faced the Mayan chief. He lifted the baton to his eyes and they crossed. Then he lifted the skull above him and stared up into my eyes.

"You wish to see the glories of a god?" I asked. "Look closely, little man, and you shall see your demise."

I had never noticed the height difference until that moment; he was much shorter. I saw him edge back ever so slightly. I'd succeeded in making him doubt, yet he stared into my eyes. Inside me was turmoil, anger and I seethed in hatred. Still he looked.

"No! This cannot be!" Chac Tun B'alam screamed.

He dropped his hands and I grabbed the crystal skull before the chief dropped it. Chimalpopoca reached for the baton and took it from Chac Tun B'alam.

"I am the chief." He reached up and raked his hands down his face leaving bloody tracks in his cheeks. "I am he who will lead forth my people into the new time." There was a blood-curdling scream and Chac Tun B'alam crumbled to the ground. He writhed momentarily, convulsing and fighting an unseen opponent within his mind. Then Chac Tun B'alam was still, his face frozen in a bizarre mask of horror, eyes wide in pure fear.

I thought perhaps someone would come to the chief's aid but none moved except for a young man who stood in the shadows nearby. He solemnly approached, knelt down and placed a hand on Chac Tun B'alam's chest.

"He is gone," the young man said. "I am Pacal Tun B'alam, son of Chac Tun. I am the new ruler of L'akam Ha." The young man, actually more boy than man then removed a necklace from his father and placed it over his head. He stood to face me. "I have seen the vision and knew my father would not see the time of no time. I have quietly waited."

Ix'iloom approached with her daughter and another woman approached from where Pacal Tun B'alam had come. The other woman reached down to Chac Tun B'alam, but Pacal Tun B'alam brought a foot down on the old chief's chest. He held his hand out to stop her.

"He mocked the gods, my mother. There is no time for a proper funeral and he deserves none." The young chief turned to the priest. "Chimalpopoca, take this husk away." He then turned to look at Montoya. "Ah Pukuh, be gentle with him. My father was a proud man who tried to deal with the shadow people. I should pray for him to be lifted up the Holy Ceiba Tree but his fear of K'ul'ulkan was great." He bowed to Montoya then turned to gaze directly at me. "K'ul'ulkan, I ask for your guidance. My father feared you, even though he thought you to be a false god."

I studied the young man before me. "Do you think I am a god? Do you truly believe I am K'ul'ulkan? Do you wish to use the Eyes and Conscience of Pacal to see inside me?"

Pacal Tun B'alam fingered the two items that now once again rested on the small altar at the base of the temple. He cocked his head and eyed me suspiciously.

"Tell me, mighty K'ul'ulkan. Do you know of the Chamber of Twelve Doors?"

"It exists?" Montoya asked. "You know where it is?"

Pacal Tun B'alam's face knitted into a frown and his eyes darted downward in thought at Montoya's words.

I shook my head. "Never heard of it," I said and nodded down at the items. "Use them to read my mind, see what I know. I assure you, I cannot kill you."

"But you killed my father," Pacal Tun B'alam said.

"He killed himself," I replied. "He wanted to see inside the mind of a god. He did not find what he was looking for."

Pacal Tun B'alam cautiously picked up the baton and skull. He brought the baton to his eyes and I could see them cross. The skull he lifted in his hand, almost tipping it out of his palm. Chimalpopoca grabbed it and helped him adjust it above his head. He stared into my eyes.

I could feel him, he searched through my mind and memories flooded me, some that I'd almost forgotten. Then it happened. I saw a room with a long curving stone staircase leading down to a large open area. The room was circular and there were twelve doors – or shutters – that covered small alcoves. A lone chair was located in the center of the room. Four long, colored poles created a pyramid over the chair. Then it was gone and I, a plumed serpent, flew through the air to finally land and wander through a jungle of lush growth. I stumbled upon two ears of maize on the ground and smiled at the find. One ear of corn became a man, the other a woman. They, the maize people, praised me. In the distance I could hear the howler monkeys and other jungle creatures in a raucous round of useless chatter. Those creatures had been given their chance to worship me and had failed. These two people danced and sang about the gods. I was pleased and when I found a river of cool and refreshing blue, I swam in its waters.

"You are K'ul'ulkan," Pacal Tun B'alam said. "You are a god. You remember the Chamber of Twelve Doors. Behold your servant." He handed me the Eyes and Conscience.

I lifted the skull over my head and placed the baton in front of my eyes. I could feel the muscles in my eyes as they crossed and I gazed into the young chief's eyes.

My mind was assaulted with visions of buildings being constructed and the city of L'akam Ha coming into existence. I saw K'inich Janahb' Pacal and the Temple of Inscriptions. The whole Mayan history flashed before me. I reeled at the knowledge imparted.

I awoke in Lucia's lap with Montoya and Pacal Tun B'alam staring down at me. It was dark and the stars glistened with an unseen before beauty.

"Did I die?" I asked groggily.

"No, you live, K'ul'ulkan," Lucia said. She softly touched my forehead with her hand and let it trail to my cheek and chin. The tips of her fingers gently caressed my lips.

"What time is it?" Suddenly there was an urgency within me.

"You have returned to us K'ul'ulkan," Pacal Tun B'alam said. "Your vision will help us to weave time as time ends." He stood up. "Come. The room awaits us."

Chapter 34:
The Room of Twelve Doors

Mayan Date: 4 Ahau 3 Kankin ~ 13.0.0.0.0

*"The gateway to tomorrow is through
the doorway of the past. Light must have
dark and good must have evil."*

*Thoughts of Yak Ek' K'ahk'
Creator of L'akam Ha*

L'akam Ha: 3:46 a.m., Friday, December 21, 2012

"Come," Pacal Tun B'alam said and waved for us to follow him. He placed the skull and baton in a bag then turned to his mother and whispered. She nodded her head and followed him with her head down.

"Do we all go?" I asked.

"Yes," Pacal Tun B'alam replied. "We need thirteen." He grabbed a torch and motioned that we should also do the same.

Slowly we made our way up the stairs of the Temple of Inscriptions. When he got to the top, he hesitated and looked to the sky. I looked up. Ribbons of color - reds, blues, greens and yellows - rippled in sheets and waves above us, iridescent and beautiful with the Milky Way for a backdrop. I heard Juan gasp and a few others. For the Aurora Borealis to be visible this far south, in the lush equatorial jungles, I realized it had to be one huge solar flare. I nodded my head; I now knew this was all very real. Pacal Tun B'alam motioned for us to follow then proceeded to the entrance to K'inich Janahb' Pacal's funerary. We carefully made our way down the steps. I was intrigued. He didn't lead us into the room of his great grandfather but instead pushed on the wall to open the secret chamber door.

"The secret chamber?" Montoya asked.

Pacal Tun B'alam turned to him. "It is the path to where we need to go. My grandmother, Ix'iloom, taught me these things so I would know them when I needed."

Montoya looked over at Ix'iloom. "You knew about this secret chamber? You never told me?"

"It was not a secret to me," she said nonchalantly. "But it is of no matter now. Go." She motioned him forward.

Pacal Tun B'alam pushed on a glyph and another door slid open. The scent of stale air permeated the room.

"My great grandfather built this temple to hide the Room of Twelve Doors from those who would use it unwisely." He hesitated. "Who would look for a hidden room within a hidden room?"

"I always thought the Room of Twelve Doors was a passage between worlds," Montoya asked. "Isn't that the legend?"

"Patience, Ah Pukuh. All will be revealed." Pacal Tun B'alam held up a finger to stop any more conversation on the topic. "We go."

He stepped into the dark hole of a doorway and then disappeared from sight as he moved to the right. As I stepped into the opening I felt a small hand grab hold of mine. It was Juan.

231

"Please, señor Barry, let me go with you."

I was tempted to pick him up and carry but not being familiar with the terrain I thought it better to let him follow me while I held his hand. My other hand carried the torch before us.

The steps weren't steep but nonetheless they were difficult to maneuver. They had been chiseled flat but over the centuries, moisture and debris had taken its toll. Suddenly the tunnel around me was gone. There was only the one wall to my right; darkness loomed beyond the glow of the torch. I could see the steps below and the wall. I leaned back against the wall since my torch reflected on it and I could see if it ended before I got to it. In the distance before and below me I could see Pacal Tun B'alam's torch. I knew the wall curved by that view. Dark, dismal, stale air. I wanted to toss my torch out into the unknown to watch it flicker on its path down like they do in the movies but I didn't. This was my light, my only light.

"I don't like this," Juan whispered.

"Just stay close to the wall," I replied. "I don't like it, either."

Juan giggled. I felt better.

My foot hit loose, flat dirt. Was it a platform? I stepped carefully forward. Ahead of me I could see Pacal Tun B'alam. He was lighting torches along a wall. The room came into focus. It was the one from my memories. I started to count the shuttered doors. There were twelve. In the center of the room was a small throne like chair under the four poles of the pyramid. Each of the poles was a different color: black, white, red and yellow.

What I hadn't seen in my memory dream was the nine wooden doors on the floor within the pseudo pyramid. I was perplexed.

"We must hurry," Pacal Tun B'alam said. "Time is closing upon us."

"What do we do?" I asked.

"First, Yax Ek' K'ahk' must sit in the Throne of Knowledge and Learning."

Benita pushed Lupe forward and the small girl cautiously walked toward the chief.

"You are not her!" he said. "Go back to your mother, little girl. I need Yax Ek' K'ahk' now. You!" He pointed at Juan. "You are the hidden one my father sought. You are Yax Ek' K'ahk' and it is you who must sit upon the Throne of Knowledge and Learning."

"Juan?" I said and looked over at him standing there in his white tunic and long pulled back hair.

"Juanita," Juan said. "My true name is Juanita." He hung his head. "I am a girl."

She, Juanita, lifted her head slowly and looked at me with pain in her eyes.

"I am sorry, señor Barry. I have lied to you." Tears started to flow.

It made sense. I could see it now. I remembered back to when we'd first met and the man was looking for Juanita.

"Was that man your uncle?" I demanded.

"I have told you the truth," Juanita cried. "Except about being a girl. I knew you wouldn't help me if I was a girl."

Suddenly I was irked. "Fine," I said. "Get up on the chair. You are Yax Ek' K'ahk' and you are the one to give us a new world."

Just as quickly I regretted my sudden actions. This little girl who had been playing a boy for who knew how many years; she was going to create the new world. What type of world would it be?

Juanita hesitated and looked at the group. Her expression tugged at my heart.

"Come," I said softly. "Now is the time." I took her hand. "It matters not to me if you are Juan or Juanita. You will always be my little buddy." I helped her into the chair.

"Now, Yak Ek' K'ahk'," Pacal Tun B'alam said. "Relax and learn what our ancestors knew. See the knowledge of the twelve solar civilizations preceding ours; they will aid you in your endeavor."

He took the crystal skull out of the satchel and carefully placed it at the peak of the four-armed pyramid. Pacal Tun B'alam turned and faced us.

"Each of you take a doorway. Stand to the side and open it. Do not stand in front of the doors after opening them."

I stepped to the closest doorway and thought it strange. Sidestepping, I pulled the wooden door open.

A skull was inside. It was a crystal skull, similar, yet different than the one above Juanita. I shook my head at calling her that. My skull was green, almost like a huge emerald. I looked about the room. Each doorway held a skull, each different, yet similar. All of them were of different colors.

There was a hum. A vibration. A harmonic. I could see Juanita grabbing her temples yet she didn't seem to be in pain. A light, a rainbow of lights emanated from each of the twelve skulls toward the crystal skull over her head. A pure white light emanated down from the crystal skull to her.

My dream memory came to me again. I saw strangers. They gave the skulls to the maize people. There was knowledge in each skull. All the skulls communicated with the crystal skull. I realized then I was seeing the knowledge of the twelve solar civilizations being shared.

I was startled when the doors of my alcove slammed shut. The others also closed. The silence of the chamber had almost been deafening and this sudden sound crashed on my eardrums.

"It is time," Yax Ek' K'ahk' said. Her voice was deep, mature. "I have seen the past, I can make the future." Gone was the childlike quality I'd enjoyed in Juan, her eyes were dark pools of knowledge. "Time comes to me. We must go to time."

The walls disappeared. We stood in an open expanse with the nine doors on the ground still inside the pyramid. The stars of the Milky Way coalesced above us. The harmonic vibrations could be felt. We were in the center or quickly approaching it.

"Come," Yax Ek' K'ahk' said, motioning to Lucia. "Stand here." She pointed to far end of the white pole of the pyramid. She then motioned Emil forward and told him to stand at the black pole's end. She repeated it two more times, Diego to the red pole and Benita to the yellow one.

"You are my Bacab, my four ordinals who hold the world up." She pointed at each one and named them: (white) Can Tzienal, (black) Zac Cimi, (yellow) Hozanek and (red) Hobnil. It was then I noticed the painted markings on each person's face matched their pole of the pyramid.

"There are nine doors on the ground. The rest of you choose and stand on a door. These represent the Bolontiku, the Nine Gods of Night in the Underworld. By standing on the door you hold the demons of that level at bay and they can not join the new world."

"But there are only eight of us left," I said. "Who will stand on the ninth door?"

"You deny me a little pleasure?" Montoya asked. He was Ah Pukuh, Lord of the Underworld and its nine levels of darkness.

"One door will remain unguarded so it may open, if so desired, by the demon below it," Yax Ek' K'ahk' said. "Without evil there can be no good. Without darkness there can be no light. The single door left unattended will only allow the demon from that level to escape." She turned to look at Ah Pukuh. "You, Ah Pukuh, will stand on the door of your own level. It is the deepest and darkest and I will not allow it in my new world." She watched him with narrowed eyes. "You know which door is yours. Choose now."

235

Ah Pukuh glared at her but strode to a door and stood upon it. "I shall contain my worst demons," he said.

I stared at my little friend. Juan was Juanita and now Juanita was Yax Ek' K'ahk' and very mature in her thinking. She was now in control of the situation. I stepped on a doorway and immediately felt a pounding beneath me. I had trapped the demon and it wanted out. The others stepped on doors of their choice within the within the pyramid bounded by the four Bacab. Lupe had chosen the one directly beside me and she jumped when the demon below the door bellowed and howled.

Ah Pukuh laughed and the chamber echoed the maniacal sound. "She has chosen the door to level eight." He leered at her. "Be strong little girl."

I glared at him. This was not the man I remembered earlier. Ix'iloom stood to my other side. "It was my duty to watch Ah Pukuh," she said. I frowned at her words. "The gods always walk among us. Sometimes they know they are a god, sometimes they have forgotten. You forgot who you were. Ah Pukuh has remembered. Be wary."

Pacal Tun B'alam stretched out his hand and gave Yax Ek' K'ahk' an item. It was the baton. He quickly stepped on a doorway. The only unguarded door was the one next to Lupe, beyond me. Something niggled at me that this was not a good thing.

Yax Ek' K'ahk' lifted the baton to her eyes. "I see my world," she whispered.

The ground disappeared and we stood on the doors suspended in space with the stars as our companions. Sheets and ribbons of the Aurora Borealis danced around us. The doors started to spin in a circle around the chair where Yax Ek' K'ahk' sat. I fought to maintain my balance. I saw Lucia and she was struggling to stand up. The corner where she stood was attempting to lift and fold in on itself, joining with the other three like a fried wonton wrapper. Actually, all four of those who Yax Ek' K'ahk' had called her Bacab were fighting to remain standing.

The wind whirled about us in a fury. The noise was deafening and worse than any day of walking under the howler monkeys in full fury. The Aurora Borealis faded away. The stars, a dizzying blur of white was blinding as they brightened in the encroaching blackness of space.

Suddenly the door left unguarded, one next to Lupe snapped opened.

A creature of pure darkness crawled out. Long muscular arms with hands ending in claws scratched and snagged at the wooden door for a grip. The body was a mixture of armored scales and rolling flesh. Wings of deepest black leather flexed open then folded back against the body. There was no doubt in my mind it was a demon; I didn't know which level I stood on but now feared what might be under me. I only hoped this was not something from within the mind of Yax Ek' K'ahk'. The creature snarled at Lupe who stood on the door next to me; she was frightened. The creature had a bulbous head and its long, yellowish, pointed teeth drooled a foam. The forked tongue stretched out and flickered about like a snake's tongue, tasting the air. The eyes were fiery slits of red. It sat there, muscles tensed and poised to leap. Lupe started to back away toward me and I could see her door lifting beneath her; a flaming claw curled around the edge. The demon she contained could easily toss her and be released.

"Stay in the middle of the door!" I screamed at her hoping she could hear me above the howl of the wind. "Be brave!"

The demon from the unguarded door lunged and Lupe fell flat to the door. A hideous snarling cry vibrated the air and the door she fell on shut. She lay sprawled out, crying but had kept the door under guard. The loose creature had leapt toward Lupe but used her door only to reach Yax Ek' K'ahk'. It now padded upright on two back feet. It snarled and circled around her as we all hovered in the sparkling nothingness of space.

The door dropped from beneath me; my gut wrenched and my mind twisted. Suddenly I was tipped up and sucked into a vortex of fury. I saw the others coming with me. Then, there was nothing and I floated in a space of blackness. I could see the others. I counted. Twelve humans and one demon; the thirteen. Yax Ek' K'ahk' popped into existence in the center. Then I saw the cluster of stars. They were familiar; I'd seen them before: the Pleiades!

"Holy Tzab-ek," Yax Ek' K'ahk' chanted. "I have seen my world. I give it to you to create."

The Milky Way emerged from the darkness within the cluster of stars known as the Pleiades, the center of birth. Below me I saw Earth come into existence. It seemed the same yet there were some differences. The blues were clearer, the white clouds seemed purer and a green covered much of the planet.

"Juan... Juanita," I called. "What have you done?"

She dropped the baton and ran to me. We were now in a jungle clearing. I could see Lucia and all the rest. I didn't see the Montoya or the demon.

"Do not worry, señor Barry," Juanita said. "I am no longer Yax Ek' K'ahk', I am Juanita. Ah Pukuh and the demon have gone to their new home I created for them. They will be happy in our world. We will be happy in our world."

I looked around.

"What do we do?" I asked her.

"We will ride a unicorn," she said then turned to Guadalupe. "There is a pink one for you, too, Lupe."

"What of the world we knew?" I was totally perplexed and lost as to what had happened.

"This is the new world," Juanita said. "I made some of it like the last one with a few changes. There are no cities. There is L'akam Ha; I thought it too beautiful to destroy."

"And the people?" I asked.

"There were many with darkness in their hearts and others who could not understand the vibrations or live in the harmony I created. They no longer exist. I learned from the crystal skulls and I saw so many places in different worlds. I could choose any of those places for my new world I could create but I liked what I had. Do you not feel it, señor Barry? The harmony?"

I did feel it. There was a sense of being with the jungle. A simpler life. I felt an arm slide around me. It was Lucia. We were like the maize people of my memory. We were happy.